Beyond the Sun

A novel

By Durwood White

Dedication

For Dexter Nilsson who gave me the idea for this novel. Thanks Dex.

Acknowledgement

I acknowledge the assistance of an aerospace engineer who by request will remain anonymous. He agreed to read the manuscript but neither approved nor disapproved the storyline. He simply pointed out the sections that are not exactly scientific, even with literary license. There are aerospace terms in the text like "radiative" and "plasmoid" which he introduced.

I should like also to acknowledge a friend, Dan Kish, who is a young wizard with computer software; without gurus like him, there would be no encouragement for computer idiots like me.

Oblivion

A ROARING FIRE snapped and popped, glowing embers leaped out on the hearth like fiery little demons, as dancing flames lit the expansive foyer in a château near the outskirts of Paris. German soldiers frantically tossed papers by the fistful into the stony fireplace, and choking smoke filled the giant room. The odor of charring French white oak permeated the air masking the pungent smell of perspiring technicians scurrying from room to room. The noise of stomping boots in the long hallway rattled the chandeliers that hung from the vaulted ceiling in the front foyer.

The Commanding General sat in his office on the second floor, a converted bedroom, screaming into the telephone and waving his hands as if he were an energized preacher. He slammed the receiver into its cradle and placed his elbows on the desk with his head supported in his hands. Orders were explicit—destroy incrementing documents. The allied forces had punched through the defensive lines just ten miles from the French border, and Panzer tanks were not allocated as promised by the high command in Berlin.

The General suddenly called out to Shultz who ran past the door, his arms laden with documents. Shultz abruptly stopped, dropped the papers into a drum, and clicked his heels together with a proper salute.

"Ja, mein General."

The exhausted commander rustled in his chair, and gestured for his longtime aide to come into his office. The sound of his respectful reply attenuated the confusion on the first floor to a tolerable level of bedlam. His tired mind digressed.

Weary nights of allocating meager supplies and depleting ordnance had aged the General, the war-torn effects of the Paris occupation. A slight movement cracked his dry lips, and the pain seemed to vanish into the warm ashes of his cigarette extended on a 4-inch silver holder. He watched the smoke curling to the ceiling, his red eyes blinked twice and he screwed his knuckles in his dark eye sockets. He slumped into his chair and the uncommon stillness relaxed his nagging sore throat as he quietly stared into the expectant eyes of his aide. He finally spoke in a deep hollow gloomy voice.

"What of the crates, Shultz?"

The aide respectfully leaned forward and whispered. "The crates are stacked neatly in the cavern beneath this chateau, mein General. Engineers completed the bedroom entrance only this morning, sir."

He sighed deeply, rolled his blurred eyes to the armoire that stood against the back wall behind his desk, as the leathery wrinkles around his bloodshot eyes relaxed. "You have done well, my ole friend," he smiled, inhaling a deep breath. "The SS will arrive soon to remove the crates—I want you to inform me at the earliest possible moment of their arrival."

"As you command, mein General," he replied and quickly stood to attention. Shultz cared not for the politics or glory of war, only the respect for his General who had used his influence that kept his two sons in Berlin, and off the front lines.

As the faithful aide left his office, the General removed his cap and ran his slender fingers through the graying hair of his temples, grimacing as he mused of the afternoon the crates had arrived. They came by naval courier from a submarine, which had docked near the coast at Le Havre port, and by boat up the Seine River to Paris. When the crates arrived at the chateau the General had received orders to safely store them, no mention of its contents. Yet he authorized Shultz to open a crate: gold bars, twelve heavy crates; an immense sum that he had not counted, nor was he aware of the intended purpose for the gold, only suspicions. The sound of running boots in the hallway outside the General's office raised his head. The Captain banged his fist on the door and burst inside, his tactless entrance interrupted the General's musing. The Commander's face registered anger yet the Captain was obviously terrified.

"Sir, I must tell you that your SS group will not be coming. Submarine S187 has been sunk with all hands aboard," he screeched.

The General's eyes opened widely, not even the irritation of the cigarette disturbed his mental calculations. All hands aboard, he curiously thought, then the gold was his, he deviously smiled.

And then the front foyer buzzed with whispering voices, feet scrambling in every direction. Shultz rushed into the office with a note, and quickly handed it to the Captain. The telephone lines had been cut and the message had just arrived by motorcycle courier. The message required evacuation; no time to burn other documents, or time to check out the passageway to the gold. Suddenly, they heard the familiar grinding of tanks in the distant forests.

A sudden explosion of 75-mm projectiles erupted in the courtyard, smoke billowing into the gray sky, debris scattering over the landscape, rock walls crumbling. The General raced to the window and saw the silhouette of M4 Sherman tanks on the far hillside. The gold must be abandoned, but he knew it was concealed safely in the caverns; Shultz was trustworthy.

As the General ran from the occupied chateau behind his escaping men, his mind rapidly formed questions: Would he ever return, could he ever return for the gold? All around him explosions filled the air with deadly shrapnel. Before the General placed his foot on the running board of his open-seated Mercedes-Benz, he grabbed his chest, and crumpled on the ground, mortally wounded. Shultz stumbled toward him, a jagged metal stake thrust into his back as he fell dead upon the General's motionless body.

Chapter 1

INDUSTRIALIST MAGNATE, Dr. Jacque Chevet, ripped a page from his calendar as he picked up an official document left on his desk. His eyes suddenly swelled open as he read the document, and his weak heart fluttered erratically. And the words sent shockwaves through his mind, and he burst into rage as profanity echoed through the outer rooms of his Paris office building.

The familiar outburst brought his personal valet, Jean-Pierre to the door but his hands steeled before he twisted the doorknob. He knew the master wanted no interruptions, and he was well aware that storage drums of radioactive waste had piled up on the company power plants scattered over Europe with no approved disposal sites on the continent. The international Atomic Energy officials had relentlessly hounded Chevet to remove the waste, and they had filed a report that Jean-Pierre had placed on the master's desk that very night.

Jean-Pierre had been the valet for the old master since the early days when this chemical genius had established Chevet Energy, Ltd., and amassed a king's fortune. The master was rarely home, and so Jean-Pierre had cared for Mme.

Chevet when she became ill. Her death weighed heavily on the masters mind, and he was never the same since her funeral.

After Madam's death, Jean-Pierre had managed the enormous estate and the affairs of the historic château, also issued the payroll of the household staff. Though now, much of his time centered on rearing the master's adolescent granddaughter whom he had fostered after an airline crash had left her as the only remaining heir.

Chevet crushed the document in his fist and threw it at the trashcan. The wad missed the mark and slid across the waxed tile; the resident cat batted the wad of paper under his desk.

The old master made a necessarily quick decision, and the thought produced a grunt—dyspepsia. All of his decisions of late were rushed. His vice-president was having an affair, and a new granddaughter lived in the château, his only living relative . . . how old was she, anyway? He had forgotten.

The distraction produced an intimate memory that surfaced from his scarred heart. His darling wife had convalesced for some ten years before her death. He had always discussed matters with her and arrived at a sensible decision. And oh, how he missed her calming voice. Old age was so cruel.

The revelry somehow soothed his mind, but nagging reality seized his awareness as he reread the last sentence in the cover letter:

Should the waste NOT be disposed of within ninety days, procedures will commence to shut down six of Chevet Energy, Ltd. nuclear plants.

His head dropped; the weight of fatigue, he had already faced financial setbacks by massive fines, and now this threat of shutdowns had spread rumors among the board of directors. The European Stock

Market galvanized the bad news: the active stock dropped ten points just before the market closed that afternoon with rumblings of hostile takeover. He was a desperate man in need of a miracle. Alas, not of religious persuasion, he had to produce the miracle himself.

Chevet grudgingly placed a half-empty glass of Cognac on the desk. Trembling hands slowly released the glass as he finalized his thoughts. Deeply sighing, he opened the bottom draw of his desk and took out his old Underwood portable typewriter. He had not used the antique for years, although he carried it through college and graduate school, it had no hard drives that concealed evidence. His upper lip stiffened as he exercised his fingers and positioned his shaky hands on the keys. His tormented mind transferred agonizing words through nervous fingers, and a proposal slowly formed on the page, one excruciating word after another.

The paranoid executive finally rocked back in his chair, and sipped the Cognac as he quietly reread the message. It said what had to be said. Incriminating? Yes. He gripped the platen's knurled knob and rolled out the page, and quickly faxed it through his recently purchased machine. The original copy of his letter appeared in the bottom tray.

It was done, finished.

Chevet tore the original letter into tiny squares. He flipped open the typewriter cover, removed the nylon ribbon, and placed the spool and the paper squares in a glass ashtray that sat on his desk. Chevet sighed as he took a can of lighter fluid from a drawer, and soaked the ribbon. A flick of his cigarette lighter ignited the ribbon and paper in a puff of fire. The despondent man stared at the curling smoke until the black mass crinkled into charred residue.

Finally, he opened a window, and the breeze fanned the perspiration on his face, the only pleasant experience resulting from his decision. Stoically he held the ashtray in the whipping winds as the charred mass separated into countless pieces of black specks, reminding him of the cremated ashes of his wife's body.

A tear rolled down his wrinkled cheek.

He stepped out of the direct turbulence of the window into the darkness of his office, literally shivering, not from the wind but how his decision affected his company, his estate, Jean-Pierre, and the legacy of his granddaughter. Chevet sighed ruefully, and rubbed the back of his neck. Drained of energy, he closed the window and stood in the darkness for a brief moment, while he reviewed his actions once more. His numb mind fuzzily validated the decision: It was the only option; he had considered the implications, but his mind reeled at such a connotation. His brain relentlessly accused his conscience, and created an emotional battle against his self-preservation. Irrepressible neurosis denied the conflict, and he rationalized other alternatives.

The ultimate answer surfaced: He would forever regret this decision—a restless, empty life, abandoned of comfort, and dulled by alcoholism.

The bewildered, wizened corporate executive quietly entered his private elevator, and descended to the first floor. Dr. Jacque Chevet entered the bar off the lobby, a place he frequented too often, but now it was a habit, and he even enjoyed the addiction. He always sat at the bar in the shadows of the far end, and drowned his troubles in countless glasses of Calvados.

Hours of constant drinking placed his elbows on the counter. He aimlessly circled his arms and dropped his weighty head on his hands. The bartender had kept his eyes on the old man. The Chevet Corporation owned the building, and the truth of it, this old man was a good tipper. It became commonplace; when he dozed off like this, the bartender called his valet.

Finally the bartender finished polishing the glasses, and tossed his towel on the counter. He walked toward the opposite end to the telephone, raised the receiver to his ear, and punched a memorized code.

Chapter 2

THE RAINS POURED from a gray and bleak sky, drenching the little graveyard behind St. Bernadette's Catholic Church. Umbrellas bunched together on each side of a casket like huddling penguins on a wintry beach. Mourners stood around the burial site trembling in the chill, clutching their collars to shield the cold morning air. The summer storm suddenly increased to black churning clouds, thundering and lightning as if the Devil himself waited to claim the departed soul.

A small boy held an umbrella over a Spanish priest straining against a gust of wind. The priest loudly spoke to be heard above the whipping gusts. Tiny trickles of rain rolled down the stitched binding of an open Testament and dripped off the spine. Whistling winds curled the thin pages, noisily flapping the umbrella like a poltergeist had been unleashed from the open grave. The priest undauntedly delivered the last rights to Dr. Jacque Chevet, prominent European industrial magnate.

Mourners were few; corporate VPs were present, the private valet, and a pretty young granddaughter, destined to be an heiress. The priest announced the last amen, and the small gathering dispersed to the dry warmth of waiting limousines.

The tired old industrialist died with his secret, his demise not from cancer, but cirrhosis of the liver because of his addiction to alcohol. Jean-Pierre, his private valet knew about his master's addiction, and a secret diary he always kept in his possession. The contents of the diary had worried the valet immensely for twenty years. This faithful family servant had suffered through many sleepless nights while the master had abused his drinking habit.

Monique, the granddaughter, was uppermost in the valet's mind. Through the years, Jean-Pierre had concealed the master's secret from the child, and now, the old master was dead and decisions must be made. The granddaughter was an overnight heiress of the Chevet fortune.

Monique Chevet returned from the ghastly solitude of her grandfather's funeral into the more peaceful surroundings of her château, and went directly to her bedroom. The twenty-four year old damsel stretched out on her bed, and gazed up at the crystal chandelier hanging from an ornately sculptured ceiling. Her mind wandered to the graveside and musingly drifted back into her childhood years.

Her grandfather had graciously allowed her to live in the château when her parents were killed, because she had no other living relatives. Monique had barely reached three years-of-age at the time. She recalled only one rare appearance of her grandfather, and that on her twelfth birthday. As far back as she could remember, Jean-Pierre had taken the place of her deceased parents, and she loved him dearly; the only father she had ever known.

The curtains of an open window rustled from a sudden cooling breeze and disturbed her thoughts. Monique rose and sat on the bedside. The fanning pages of her grandfather's diary caught her attention lying open on the end of her bed. Jean-Pierre had given it at graveside and insisted that she kept it. Out of kindness for her faithful tutor, she took the tattered book. Strangely, she now remembered how Jean-Pierre had always seemed as if he guarded some deep, dark secret. He was never too talkative, but extremely efficient in his duties. As the caretaker of the Chevet estate, he directed the duties of sixty-five staff to maintain the historic château and the vast, two hundred acre estate. Now it was all hers, the estate, the château, and CEO of Chevet Energy, Ltd. The thought of such responsibility unnerved her vanity, not her ability.

She propped on her elbows face down in the middle of her bed, slender legs bent at the knee, and cursorily thumbed the tattered pages. The dog-eared leaflets were filled mostly with business notes and corporate details. It seemed as if her grandfather had trusted no one, and considered his diary as a silent partner of sorts. He had recorded most of his thoughts on the corporation vice-presidents; their leadership strengths and weaknesses, bonuses and promotions.

Her doe eyes casually wandered over a passage that starkly registered on the projection screen of her retina. She reread the passage for clarity, yet disbelieved her conclusions. The frightful words streaked across the macular area in blinding flashes of red. She unnervingly bounced from the bed, stared in disbelief at the pages.

"Omigod!"

Monique quickly closed the diary, expecting disappearance of the pages in her mind. But the pages were still there; her glazed eyes gazed into space like a zombie. She stepped from the bedside, and idly moved to the other side of the room stirred by confusion, anxiety, and fear. The young damsel knew not the science, only the horror it implied, but that was enough incentive.

She left the bedside and sat down at her personal computer. The mouse browsed the Internet for a tense moment, but found not the site in her mind; instead, she typed a keyword: *solar.* Tabulations flashed on screen and her eyes seized on Wilcox Solar Observatory at Stanford University in California, U.S.A. *"That's it,"* her mind exclaimed! She clicked on 'print' and a copy rolled out of a laser printer. *Oh! What to do?*

Acting on a whim, she stuffed the folded printout in her purse, grabbed the diary, dashed downstairs, and burst opened the door. She raced outside and slid into the driver's seat of her red Ferrari. The sports car rounded a curved driveway, tires screaming; the 570 horsepower engine purred like a cat, its claws gripped the pavement. Her mind raced faster than the Ferrari and wondered who she could trust with this horrible secret. Monique set her course for the university campus. Many questions flashed through her mind as the Ferrari zipped along the highway, swerving around slower cars.

When her fuzzy thoughts had cleared, she found herself on the university campus and barely remembered the trip. Monique drove toward the student recreation hall, all the while she restrained the urge to cry. Finally, she parked and glanced up-and-down the parking lot looking for a familiar car. Good! Marquee is here, she thought. She checked her lipstick in the rearview mirror, licked an index finger and caressed each eyebrow, and then bounced out of the sports car like a gazelle on the northern deserts of Africa.

She gracefully strode across the parking lot and entered the building, her mind confused by a myriad of dismal questions. Finally, she took a seat in the quietest corner. Quickly Monique spotted Marquee his tall frame stood head and shoulders above most everyone else. She waved and finally caught his attention. He briskly weaved through the crowd of college coeds and bent his lanky body around the marble support columns. His long legs glided through a row of tables, face glowing with a deep tan.

Marquee was a senior graduate student, majored in astrophysics. Monique had known him only casually, although she remembered his reputation as a romantic Frenchman. His objective was obvious; nonetheless, she knew he had the answers to her puzzling questions.

"Monique!" Marquee yelled above the noisy crowd of students as he twisted toward her table. "Sorry to hear about your grandfather—"

"Sit down, Marquee!" she interrupted in a casual voice that obviously was a command. Idle chitchat was not her style, and there was more demanding information that she needed.

He pulled up a chair and sat with his long arms folded in his lap. "Okay. Now what's on your mind, Monique?" he chuckled.

Without hesitation Monique grilled the trapped man. "What is radioactive waste?"

He seemed unimpressed by her question, but answered warily. "It's the spent material from a nuclear reactor, usually in the form of isotopes. Why do you ask?" he hedged.

She evaded his query. "Just answer my questions please, Marquee," announced another command.

"All right," he smiled, and casually repositioned his lengthy forearm on the textbooks.

"Why does this waste have to be taken out of the reactor?" she asked as she flagged a waitress. "Red wine, please—want one, Marquee?"

He frowned apologetically. "No alcohol, please, got an exam next hour."

"Bring him a cola," she told the waitress. "Now, why must you take waste out of a reactor?"

The questions piqued his curiosity. "It's spent material, used up by reaction. If not removed, it could cause the reactor to overheat," the doctoral candidate answered.

Greek! But she wanted all the information he had. It was extremely important to her, and perhaps to the world, too. "So, what usually happens to this waste?"

Now, where is she going with these questions, he wondered? "It's radioactive and harmful if released into the atmosphere. They usually store it in special drums, underground at present."

"I see," she replied, the logic not the science, as she stirred in her purse for payment. Her scratching fingers unloosed the printout and it fell open on the table. "How are these drums eliminated?" she asked annoyingly, a mental stimulus spurred remembrance at the university when she had not found her credit card.

He rocked back in his chair not even sure he should answer the question, yet he decided he must; she seemed so distant and needy.

"That's a question to which the world would like an answer," he replied as he glimpsed the bold title on the printout.

"Don't be coy, Marquee," she barked and lifted her hands above the sliding tray of beverages. "Put it on my tab, dear," she told the waitress.

Marquee's tanned countenance shifted through mixed emotions, much like a chameleon changed its colors.   Somehow he hoped he had the answers although the reason for the questions was unknown. "Monique, these are serious questions.   Can't you tell me why you need this information?"

"Not now, Marquee," she insisted.   "Tell me what would happen if a lot of this stuff hit the sun?"

A wrinkled eyebrow quizzically arched, but now her questions seemed somewhat clearer.   He had heard rumors about Dr. Chevet's folly; could they be true?

"Don't know precisely," he slowly whispered, "it would take a great amount to affect a mass like the sun.   But why—"

"What about a thousand drums?" she persisted.

His face twisted like a corkscrew as if his cola were a lemon.   Perhaps the rumors were true, he thought: the old man had launched his hazardous waste into outer space!

"That's a tremendous mass of waste, Monique, but I just can't give you a good answer.   You must talk with someone conducting serious solar study," he replied and pointed to the printout.   "Dr. Bruce Randall directs the sun observatory at Stanford University in California USA.   He would have the answers to your questions.   I strongly suggest you to go to America immediately," he advised with a nod at the paper on the table.

Monique sipped her wine as she assimilated the information.   Long fingers took her arm, an impulse Marquee had resisted without opportunity.   For two years he'd used his considerable cunning and charm without even a date or a chance to be alone with this wealthy heiress.

Monique stood with one hand on her hip, his grimy hand on her arm as she looked into his puzzled face.   Suddenly she gripped his sleeve with thumb and index finger as if it were diseased, stared in his face for a fleeting moment, and whispered. "Thanks Marquee—Take a cold shower, good bye."

Marquee slumped deflated as she walked out of his life; a deep feeling of revenge swelled his ego.

Monique rushed back to her château a million questions stirring in her mind. She pushed the Ferrari at top speed with thoughts of what must be done. An umpteen million questions frazzled her mind. What of Jean-Pierre, the company, the stock? There were no answers, none at least in her thoughts. She finally pulled into the driveway of the château and ran up the stairs.

Monique threw back the doors to her closet and jerked out several items for packing. It took only an hour before she was at the vanity fussing with her hair. She gathered toiletries, cosmetics, plus a sundry of items, and threw them into a handbag. Sudden tension seized her muscles and thrust her against the chair. She exhaled a deep sigh, straightened her back, and stretched her arms skyward. Monique stared relentlessly at the image in the mirror.

"What am I doing?" she asked the person in the mirror.

"What you must do, my child," Jean-Pierre replied as he cracked open her bedroom door.

She whirled from the stool and plunged into his arms. "Oh, Jean-Pierre, this is madness!"

"I know, my dear. I've known for twenty years," the valet responded.

She gazed into his aging face, her eyes flooded with tears of respect and gratitude. "Dear, dear Jean-Pierre, what would I ever do without you?"

He smiled, embraced her as he had often done. Somehow he knew that he was about to lose the child he had reared. "You'll manage, my child. I've always known that, too."

She slid from his embrace now confident in her decision. Monique picked up the gold encased European-style telephone and keyed a number. "I want passage to America, Stanford University in California."

A voice in the receiver responded. "One moment please . . . I can get you a direct flight to New York, departing this afternoon. There's a one-hour layover in New York for your connecting flight to Palo Alto, California."

"I'll take it," she said, and recited a credit card number; the same card she had not found while at the university. Humph. It was still on the vanity where she had left it, tangible proof that too much on her mind.

Again the voice responded: "You're scheduled on Flight 479, departing Airbus Airline at four thirty this afternoon. Your connecting flight in New York is Western Airlines Flight 726. Be at the Charles De Gaulle Airport three hours early. Security is very tight these days."

"Thank you."

Monique sat the ornate phone receiver in its cradle, and tuned to the stalwart valet, but he had already left. She caught his shadow as it moved down the staircase with her luggage. She rushed through the bedroom door and followed him down the winding staircase. Monique clutched the diary against her wildly thumping heart as she wondered what could be said to the only father she had ever known.

Jean-Pierre waited in the foyer, secretly brushing the moisture from his eyes. "Will you be away for long, mademoiselle?" he asked, a futile reclamation attempt of his composure, as he opened the four-foot château door. He secretly wiped a tear from his eye.

"Perhaps a month, Jean-Pierre, I'll be in touch," she said, but words had not expressed her emotions. This château had been her home for twenty years; it held many secrets, not all known to her, although she had searched every nook and cranny. Jean-Pierre had told her many stories related to this historic mansion, and he could be reached, any day or night at any time. "Take care, my old friend," she sniffed as tears welled in her doe eyes.

The aging valet grievously understood and somehow managed to smile, a rare expression for him, yet the heartache brought a glitter of tears in his tired eyes. Monique slithered into the bucket seats of her Ferrari, while Jean-Pierre packed the luggage in the trunk. As the Ferrari moved, their hand's stretched out and almost touched like Michelangelo's scene on the ceiling of the Sistine Chapel.

She drove away.

Monique's mannerisms told Jean-Pierre that the secret in the old master's diary would somehow be dealt with. In her adolescent years, she had impressed him with her youthful spirit, a spirit he once saw in the old master. Monique had inherited the old man's tenacity, yet she was impulsively stubborn and arrogantly young. And now she was alone, soon to be in America. Who would watch over her now, he thought? He pondered the nagging question in his heart as he lowered his head and whispered a prayer: *Merciful God, I give her to you. Bring her back to me when you can. I love her as my own daughter.*

An immature young man sat at a table with an older monsieur in a café near the Eiffel Tower. The monsieur sipped his coffee and surveyed the young man's wimpy face as he wondered if he could be trusted with such an important task. And yet, he had the mental qualifications, and his melancholy personality would protect his secret—he'd ascertain it himself.

The devious monsieur had often met the young man, not casually but purposely, even had studied his arrest profile after he was charged with vagrancy. He shadowed his every move from his low-rent apartment to the pawnshops where the man traded personal articles for money. The monsieur finally approached him in the park where he often flew his model airplanes. Low esteem made him the perfect candidate, and his mechanical aptitude was essential to the task in the monsieur's plans.

Misty steam rose from the hot cup and the vapors entered the monsieur's nostrils. The caffeine saturated his mind and it seemed that his body floated to a faraway place, a memorable time of his youth . . . when he was just a teenager, how long ago was that? It was the day his mother died, the day he set his mind and raised himself above the poverty, the day he was certain poverty conditions had killed his mother. And he kept that promise to himself, and for the last ten years he had made plans to purchase a château in the historic district of Paris, a place of power and high society. But the owner, Dr. Chevet, had denied him the purchase on several occasions before he died . . .

A noise!

His mind snapped to reality. It was the voice of the young man. "What exactly is it you want me to do, sir?" he asked curiously.

The young man was intelligent yet lacked the necessary ambition to better his lifestyle, but his hobby would be the spark that would ignite a fire in his heart when directed by the monsieur. His favorite pastime was building model airplanes, and the desire to understand the electronic remotes and the mechanics of the tiny engines had prompted him to take a few engineering courses at the urging of the monsieur.

Finally, he had received a degree, and even a license to fly private jet airplanes, all the while influenced by his patron. He realized that this monsieur had carefully guided his future, paid for his education, and had gotten him a job in the aircraft industry. Yes, he owed this man.

The renewed confidence of the young man reminded him how he once harbored reservations after he first met this monsieur. But his trust had grown immensely when the gentleman had paid his fine for vagrancy at a local Commissariat de Police. This monsieur had been good to him and he would do whatever he asked.

The monsieur answered his question vaguely. "We shall see when the time is right."

Chapter 3

DR. BRUCE RANDALL of Stanford University, prominent astronomer and professor of solar science at Wilcox Solar Observatory, peered through his spectacles at a star chart of the Milky Way galaxy. He flipped his spectacles from the bridge of his nose to the top of his head. Agile fingers punched a code into the keyboard controlling the attitude of the Hubble Space Telescope (HST). The marvel of telescopic engineering orbited at three hundred seventy-three miles above the earth, far beyond atmospheric aberrations. He pointed the powerful astronomical mirror toward a distant double star in his comparative study of variable stars, using the earth's sun as a standard for comparison.

These studies were compiled into a paper for presentation to the International Solar Terrestrial Physics (ISTP) group at its annual meeting in Brussels in just three days. But more data were required to confirm Randall's hypothesis, and his schedule time for using the Hubble ended with this weekend session.

Randall carefully adjusted the grating of an infrared spectrometer that recorded electromagnetic spectra at the sun's umbra margin. Down a flight of stairs in the instrument room, his assistant busily collimated the Ceolestat, alignment of the solar mirror with its optics. He watched the digital monitor above his head, and carefully adjusted the resolution of the solar image that slowly focused on the monitor screen.

Most of the observatory's solar telescope was buried beneath the complex with the objective tube rested on the surface. A series of prisms bent the light rays through a geometric pattern to accommodate the cumbersome focal length.

The hundred-foot focal length finally focused on the Ceolestat in the instrument room. Spencer Jenson, doctoral candidate and the professor's assistant, stirred in the instrument room and carefully watched the image on the Ceolestat, the same image Randall saw in the viewing monitor on the main floor.

"That's perfect alignment of the Ceolestat, Dr. Randall," Spencer reported through headphones. "Hold it right there . . . Mark! Collimation is complete," he remarked excitedly.

"Resolution is astounding today, Spence," Randall replied as he flipped a switch on the intercom. "Maybe we can finalize our report today."

The professor shifted his pipe stem from under a raw tongue. The sting caused a grimace. Hmm, new tobacco, he thought while he gripped the rosewood bowl for inspection.

Spencer tore the Z-folded papers from the printer and studied the long column of numbers while Dr. Randall relit his pipe. The professor and his assistant gathered their many papers and moved to the conference room where they waited for the photos from the Hubble to printout from Goddard Space Flight Center.

Randall leaned back in his chair, spectacles perched on the end his nose. "Not much change in the figures from last week," he surmised as he puzzled over the computations.

Spencer only grunted; his ears were perked for Goddard's cue at the printer. Then he heard activation of the laser printer and rushed to the computer room, and left the professor's study of the columns of spectral computations. When he reached the room, three glossy prints lay in the printer tray. He grabbed the photos, curiously read the cover letter as he strolled back to the conference room.

"There' is a significant increase in sunspots, sir. I think the solar flares are going to be critical this season."

Randall tapped the rosewood bowl of his pipe on the ashtray while he examined the photos, and saw a need to correct his student. "Only speculation, Spence," he replied. "Although we are now recording significantly more solar radiation than the Solar Max databank, we cannot confirm my theory."

Spencer rebutted. "But sir, if your theory is correct about mounting radioactive waste accumulating inside the core of the sun, wouldn't we expect more residual radiation escaping with these flare-ups?"

He thumped the stem of his pipe on a photo admiring the student's keen analytical mind, an intelligence that he had seen in this student when he had applied for the appointment under his tutorship. "These new measurements only support the theory, Spence, they don't prove it. At this moment we can only postulate."

Spencer persisted with more rebuttals. "But if you're right about an unusual breakup of solar mass flying off into space during this solar maximum, we should be working on a time-frame for the event. We need some idea of when it's likely to occur."

Randall stabbed the stem of his pipe at Spencer, the warm bowl gripped in the palm of his hand. "Yes Spencer, but are you prepared to tell the world that the earth's magnetosphere is about to be bombarded with surges of solar protons more radioactive than the shockwaves of Hiroshima. Maybe even destruction of the ozone layer?"

The sudden ring of the telephone disturbed Spencer's thoughts while he attempted to assimilate Randall's piercing statements. He wagged his head and answered the ringing nuisance, his eyes still pensively glued on the professor's face.

A frightened young woman sat in a booth at the Stanford University Student Center, a cup of hot chocolate cuddled in her hands, her elbows resting on a diary. She had crossed an ocean alone and brought extremely important information worthy of presidential attention. Yet, there she sat in a most curious place among university students who chatted about midterm exams and the homecoming football game. In her heart pounded not the cheerleader's pomp, but the dismal reality of world chaos.

A handsome young man with curly blonde hair, blue eyes, and ruddy complexion entered the foyer to the student center. His tall six-two frame stood in the doorway and panned the room in search of a young French girl to whom he had described his appearance. A waving hand caught his attention. He walked over and crammed his lanky body into the booth opposite a beautiful young lady who looked much like her voice had expressed her in his mind. Their eyes met in a silent stare, not pryingly but purposely. Neither said a word. Spencer Jenson sat flabbergasted and the Monique Chevet seemed mesmerized. Her eyes fluttered, she cleared her throat, and barely spoke audible words.

"You're Spencer?" she whispered, from the depths of her loneliness rising to the heights of reality.

"Uh-huh."

"Thank you for coming," she said in broken English.

"I didn't even get your name when you called," he said as his eyes studied the trimness of her shape.

"Monique. Monique Chevet."

"Uh . . . what's this about a diary containing solar data, Monique?"

She bowed her pixy face into the steamy mist of hot chocolate, harboring a desperately hope that this young man understood her desire.

"I heard of Dr. Randall's lecture on solar activity at the University of Paris," she probed."

Spencer's face wrinkled with curiosity. "Are you a student of astronomy?"

"No, nothing like that, it's what I read in my grandfather's diary that worries me," she remorsefully uttered, and pushed the dog-eared diary toward him.

As the young man read, his eyes drifted from the tattered pages, distracted by the pleasant beauty of this Cinderella from a faraway place who had suddenly drifted into his mundane life. The sound of her name rang in his ears like a tinkling harp, but the information recorded on the diary pages demanded his attention.

He reluctantly refocused on the pages, the ghastly contents slowly seeped into his mind, and the Cherub music dissipated.

"Omigod!"

Spencer could hardly believe what he read almost as if he had finished a horror story—perhaps he had. His head slowly rose from the pages, and his mind blurted out a question.

"Did your grandfather come with you to America?"

Her eyes glazed; he had expressed the same reaction as she, when the words on the tattered pages seeped into her mind. "Oh, uh, I'm afraid he died last week," she replied as she released her thoughts.

His head sheepishly lowered embarrassed by his stupidity. "I'm sorry Monique, didn't mean to pry. Suppose I could get you an audience with Dr. Randall. Would you be interested?"

"Oh yes, Spencer—that's why I came!" she replied with glazed eyes, and yet an unrecognized peace suddenly swelled in her heart.

"How about this afternoon, I'm due back at the observatory to help Dr. Randall with his report?"

Her hand uncontrollably touched his. "Oh, I'd like that very much."

Her youthful face blossomed like a flower, and displayed the signs of inward peace, not evident after the rainy funeral of her grandfather. Yet, here she sat in faraway America seated beside a stranger that she sensed was different than Marque, always on the prowl for a conquest.

Two young strangers blended into the student surroundings like so many other coeds seated in the soda shop, although their booth seemed separated from the rest of the world concealed in a cloud of rhapsody. Between questions, mostly from Monique, Spencer examined the diary in more detail in his taciturn way. Monique watched every expression of this charming young man with hopeful expectancy, relieved now that someone in this distant country also knew about the hazardous rocket orbiting in outer space.

Time marched toward the noon hour without their notice. Monique came to realize that just being with Spencer somehow eased the punishing guilt that festered in her heart. Although a physical attraction had drawn the young couple emotionally, the hellish information recorded in the diary would weld them together in the coming solar calamity.

Chapter 4

COLLEGE STUDENTS suddenly flooded the Stanford campus with a sea of coeds that rushed to their next classes. Monique and Spencer strolled hand-in-hand through the milling students headed for the solar observatory. They were total strangers just a few hours before, now drawn together by harrowing circumstances: Radioactive waste launched into space. Two lonely, young hearts had secretly found a mutual hiding place. Neither realized beforehand the joy of youthful companionship. Precious moments together kindled a spark of romance known only to the very young at heart. Neither dared reveal their thoughts, nor even ventured to broach their inward feelings.

"That's the observatory right up there," Spencer announced, tugging at Monique's slender arm.

A weird sort of wedge-shaped structure sat on a hill adjacent to a domed building, glistening in the sun like an abstract art object. Solar telescope designs departed from the classic tubular shape, mainly because of the long focal length required to focus the distant sun. They often presented an unusual shape sitting on the surface, but not as unusual as the complex section buried beneath the facility.

"You work up there?" she asked, screening her eyes from the blinding sun with her hand, forgetting the sunglasses perched on her head.

"Spend most of my waking hours with Dr. Randall. He's working on an important theory," Spencer responded.

"Theory, thought you scientists only worked with facts."

Spencer intended only a smile, but displayed a bashful cough. "Every hypothesis begins with some basis of fact, yet unproved."

His boyish expression and kindly mannerism urged Monique to speak from her heart. "Could our meeting be some sort of factual reality or just a fantasy?"

He raked his long fingers through kinky hair, gathered confidence in response to the beautiful lady, still unsure of his reply. "You're certainly the most exciting experiment I've ever conducted, Monique."

Her expectant heart kindled a sudden spark reflected in her disarming smile, even added a spirited bounce to her step.

The young couple leaped up several concrete steps to the observatory landing. Spencer grabbed the handles on two large, glass doors that slowly opened into the lobby of a huge planetarium. "Here's where we study the movement of stars, and one particular star, our sun," Spencer explained.

They walked through another set of doors that sealed the planetarium in blackness. Monique tilted her head and looked up at a simulated constellation in the curved dome. Her face grimly soured with sudden awareness. Somehow her mind's eye visualized a rocket loaded with radioactive waste superimposed over the millions of stars. Hidden emotions crumbled uncontrollably, the momentary peace evaporated. She slowly lifted the diary, tears rolled down her rosy cheeks. "I still can't believe the words on these pages," she sniffed.

"Let's show the diary to Dr. Randall," Spencer whispered and dared to console her in his arms for a pleasant moment. Monique's heart melted in his gentle embrace, peace returned with even more sympathy than before. This kind young man possessed a magical touch and she loved his sweet manner.

Dr. Bruce Randall sat immersed in thought hidden behind piles of data pages and books. A puffy cloud of aromatic smoke hovered over the several stacks of documents like an active volcano about to erupt. He had directed the sun telescope for ten years and was now in an important study of the solar flares. Randall had received his doctoral degree from UCLA, graduating *cum a sum lade*.

As a kid from the Kansas wheat fields, the wide-open skies had given him many nights of joy and enthusiasm as he whiled away the late hours lying on his back in the wheat There in solitude he watched the stars and meteors flash through the broad expanse of atmosphere. His wheat-farming family had scraped tirelessly to pay for his college undergraduate studies, but thankfully Randall's grades merited him a scholarship to UCLA.

"Dr. Randall?" Spencer called, as he and Monique walked into the director's office.

"Yes," the professor's subconscious voice replied, but his conscious mind stayed glued to the pages of his book.

"Sir, we have a guest."

"We have a—what?"

He lifted his spectacles, whirled around, and slumped embarrassingly into his chair. "My!

Camelot does exist—who is this charming young lady, Spence?" he exclaimed, suddenly standing.

Spencer's face beamed. "I'd like you to meet Monique Chevet," he said like a kid with a new toy. "She's come all the way from Paris to see you, sir."

"Well! Please sit down, Monique," he replied, her youthful smile somehow wrestling the professor's concentration from his books.

"Sir, you remember the telephone ringing this morning?" Spencer injected.

"Oh, yes, that telephone call. And Monique was on the other end."

"Yes, sir," his excited voice agreed.

Nudging the spectacles to the end of his nose, he stared over the rims. "My goodness, you must bear important news to come all this far."

Monique blushed. "Sir, I implore you to look at my grandfather's diary."

"Diary?" he puzzled aloud, swapping glances with Spencer as he took the tattered document from her outstretched hands. He sat down in his chair with the diary laid open on his desk and inquiringly thumbed the splotched pages. Suddenly his countenance changed from indifference to vivacity. "Omigod, one thousand drums of uranium radioactive waste launched into space!" he barked, as he chewed down on the stem of his pipe.

"All this happened twenty years ago, sir," Monique ashamedly responded as a tear trickled down her rosy cheek.

"Look at page 22, sir," Spencer suggested.

Randall fanned the pages, speed-reading as the musty leaflets flipped by like a kaleidoscope. "These smudges here look like coordinates."

He hurriedly laid the diary on the desk and mounted a gantry to the 60-inch reflector telescope.

The eager professor set the declination axes on the equatorial mount and powered up the synchronous drive. Randall punched a series of digital codes into a computer that calculated the current position of the coordinates in the diary.

Screens flashed on the monitor, each successive screen recreated a simulation based on estimated weights verses time in space; celestial positions estimated by planetary positions and gravitational forces in 1982 compared to the present time. The telescope motor hummed, helical gears rotated. Finally Randall moved his spectacles to the top of his head, and gazed at the eyepiece reflection projected on a white surface with hopeful anticipation. His anticipation was rewarded.

"There's something just beyond the corona!" he gasped and flipped the eyepiece turret to a Barlow lens that enlarged the image. "It's just a speck, but there it is—power up the orbital computer, Spence. Compute these numbers coming down."

Spencer slid into a seat and rapidly punched certain keys. "She's computing the orbit now, sir," the doctoral student said, captivated by digital data plotting a graph on the monitor that steadily trended toward a celestial body. Suddenly his mouth gaped wide opened. "Dr. Randall!" he soberly exclaimed. "It's . . . it's on a collision course with the sun!" he whispered in disbelief.

Monique clasped her hands over her mouth. "Oh no, what has my grandfather done?"

Randall chewed on his pipe stem, his mind wandering somewhere in outer space focused on a rocket loaded with hazardous waste. He gently tapped the stem of his pipe against his cheek, reasoned it was all a dream, but his scientific mind drew him down from the clouds of doubt. Unspoken thoughts finally released from his mind and pierced the silence.

`"A uranium bomb with the sun as detonation source; this changes our conclusions, Spence."

"Sir," Spencer quizzed?

"We're talking equilibrium. That much uranium mass suddenly poured into the core could set off a chain reaction. The sun's internal pressure would automatically seek to balance equilibrium by blowing off core mass."

Spencer got the picture. "We'd better get busy revising those equations—when does your flight depart to Brussels?"

"Tomorrow afternoon," Randall replied, his eyes still locked on the numbers as equations computed in his mind.

Monique's heart thumped wildly. At last she had found someone who had the knowledge to deal with the ghastly secret in the diary. "Oh God, thank you," she whispered.

Randall gazed at the distraught young woman and found her presence surprisingly stimulating. "Put on a pot of coffee, Monique. We may be here awhile," he said, with a smiling wink at the French beauty.

Monique's responsive smile announced the release of her anxiety, but not the burden of guilt that heavily weighted in her chest. And her face beamed with a glimmer of hope, confirmed by her inner thoughts. As she walked out of the telescope room and wandered into the side office where she had seen a coffee pot, the past events rushed through her thoughts. Meeting Spencer was among the highlights but Dr. Randall was a real sweetheart. How she surprisingly loved them both? That, too, was easy. Dr. Randall reminded her of what a real father may have been. Spencer was her Prince

Charming that had ridden out of a dream. Was it a fairytale? Perhaps not, she silently pleaded. And these crazy Americans were such carefree 'work-a-holics.' Oh how she fervently whished the dream was real, although the prospect was a nightmare, yet she stood firm. There were so many questions still unanswered, so many hearts that would be broken because of the news she had brought to America. But the most critical question still stirred in her heart, and it dealt with this young man she had met, Spencer Jenkins. He was so different, so caring, and so kind. Jean-Pierre would be pleased, she thought.

Chapter 5

PROMINENT SCIENTISTS FROM around the world convened at the International Solar Terrestrial Physics annual meeting in Brussels. The gathering crowd buzzed with shoptalk, each had received copies of Randall's report, but skepticism soured the frowning faces of several scientists. Undergraduate students were released from their classes for this meeting, and jammed the gallery that overlooked the semicircular amphitheater. It was reminiscent of an ancient Roman arena where crowds watched gladiators kill their opponents.

The MC tapped his gavel several times. "Quiet, please, ladies and gentlemen. Without further delay, it's my pleasure to introduce our keynote speaker tonight, the director of Wilcox Solar Observatory, Dr. Bruce Randall."

Randall quickly rose from his seat, and walked to the lectern unguarded by the security of his pipe. He rustled his papers and finally located the remote to the slide projector. Facing his anxious colleagues of science, he took several swallows of water, calming his jittery nerves. He sat the glass of water on a shelf behind the lectern, and gazed for a silent moment around the crowd anxiously waiting his report.

"I am not here to predict the end of the world," Randall began.

A faint chuckle echoed over the crowd, easing the tension.

"Indeed," Randall said as the rumbles stilled. "This may be an opportunity for the world to unite without the catalyst of war."

He sensed the best he could hope for was to be tarred and feathered and exiled to the moon. The worst he didn't want to think about. He clicked the remote. Then, it occurred to him that he had not checked the sequence of the slides. A picture of the boiling sun appeared on the large overhead screen, giant flares lashing out into space. Randall breathed a sigh of relief—perhaps his last.

"What I am predicting is a massive eruption of the sun's gaseous core on an unprecedented scale, concurrent with the solar maximum. We can expect our communication satellites to fail. Many of North America's power grids will go off-line. And the ozone layer may be impaired by bombardment of massive solar wind that will dump its cosmic mass onto the earth's magnetosphere.

"We have never detected an isolated magnetic pole on the sun, since magnetic poles, unlike positive protons and negative electrons, cannot exist singly in nature. But an isolated magnetic pole would have enormous energy. My calculations do not support the formation of such a pole; neither do they exclude the possibility on this massive scale. But if the surging force of the newly energized solar wind reaches the earth in sufficient energy, there is a possibility that an isolated magnetic pole could be established with the earth's magnetic field.

Randall paused for a drink of bottled water stored beneath the lectern, and removed his spectacles. The quietness of the crowd was unnerving at best.

"In such an event, gentlemen, the earth's magnetic poles would reverse polarity."

The quietness vanished.

Noisy arguments moved through the group like a rumbling storm and flowed up into the gallery. Several students hung over the balcony rail and jeered at the speaker with clinched fists.

Cameras flashed, lenses zoomed.

Reporters fingered laptops as television networks beamed the picture of Dr. Bruce Randall over the satellites and out to the viewing world. The theatre literarily boiled in fiery debate, each scientist angrily matched his skills to debunk Randall's alarming theory. The MC called for quiet as he madly pounded the gavel like the parliamentarian of a political rally.

A robust astronomer from Russia stormed to his feet. The noisy crowd calmed. "I've heard crackpot theories before, my learned sir. But I never expected a man of your prominence to stoop to such idiotic sensationalism."

The crowd annoyingly jeered at Randall but he sternly stood at the podium. The MC pounded the gavel. The noise continued from the unruly crowd.

"Dr. Stravinsky," the MC acknowledged between the pounds of his gavel, and then wiped his face on his sleeve.

A distinguished and compact man with bushy hair stood and massaged his neatly trimmed mandrake beard. The noise slowly quieted in decrescendo as in a Mozart sonata.

"Dr. Randall, surely some outside force besides solar maximum activity must be required to trigger such an event."

Randall stabbed the pointer at the scientist as he bobbed his head. "Precisely, Dr. Stravinsky, and that trigger is in orbit as we speak. It will collide with the sun at the zenith of the solar maximum, setting off a chain reaction in the core."

Again, the crowd buzzed.

"Can you describe this trigger?" Stravinsky asked and held his hands aloft that calmed the impatient students in the gallery.

Randall clicked the remote again. A highly magnified photo taken by the Hubble telescope flashed on the wide screen. "This, gentlemen, is the trigger," he said and pointed at the screen. "This little elongation here is a rocket loaded with one thousand drums of radioactive waste. It was launched from earth in 1982. Apparently, it has been in a wide loop around the sun until recent years. Its backward orbit steadily degraded, pulling it closer to the sun. Until three days ago, it had been hiding behind the sun."

The atmosphere loomed electric.

The same people who had screamed in disrespect sat stunned in guarded silence. Not even a murmur broke the spell. But, then the eerie silence finally rustled with whispers that melted into a sea of sound.

A lone man stood and scolded the noisy balcony students until the silenced. "Why haven't our telescopes seen this thing before now, Dr. Randall?"

Randall seemed relieved with a sane question. "My guess is that it looked like space debris. The space-trash charts don't note its position because the launch was not reported."

"Dr. Thatcher," the MC acknowledged with a nod, surprised by the momentary silence.

"You said 1982. What idiot launched radioactive waste into outer space?" the English scientist rhetorically asked.

Rumbling murmurs echoed like the sound of flowing water just before it rushed over a waterfall.

"That question is still unclear," Randall said, not wanting to implicate Monique at this venture. "It's a miracle that we even know what's out there. The real question is: What will we do about it, gentlemen?"

Dr. Braun of Strasburg University stood and gripped the wooly lapels of his coat, his stomach protruded because of his robust size, hair unkempt like many other absent-minded professors. He cleared his throat, the crowd silenced expectantly.

"I have reviewed your calculations, Dr. Randall. What you're saying in the worst-case scenario is the reversal of earth's polarity, which I cannot support from your assumptions. As to the solar wind effect, neither do I see the magnitude of solar upheavals you describe."

Randall exhaled a deep sigh. "I cannot disagree with your assessment, Dr. Braun. Theories are often questioned. But my guess is we are dealing with isotopes of Uranium 233, and as you know, gentlemen, U-233 is a highly fissional material. When that rocket slams into the sun's gaseous surface, the resulting chain reaction will overheat the core, a sort of meltdown, if you will."

A storm of angry voices roared over the crowd like a twisting tornado. Boos and hisses echoed off the walls in an avalanche of sound. Fists shook. Faces jeered, tongues lashed out with vehemence. Energized with fear, agitated scientists rustled about in their seats and barked their arguments to anyone within earshot.

The MC could not quiet the storm of frightened students in the gallery nor the rude scientists below. The lions were unleashed upon a lone gladiator. Cameras zoomed in for the kill.

But Randall grabbed the mike and moved to center stage, eyes blazing, feet firmly planted.

"Gentlemen!"

Simmering silence seized the crowd.

"We have precisely twenty-six days to prevent this calamity. I am prepared to risk my reputation on the validity of my findings. Are *you* prepared to risk such a catastrophe on this planet by your inactions?"

A wave of frantic scientists bolted into the aisles like a herd of cattle, stampeded by Randall's stinging words. Remote cameras focused on the stormy audience. World-wide reporters rapidly delivered their summations by cellphones and laptops. The panicky crowds pushed into the jammed corridors as if there were a bomb scare.

And there was in outer space.

But Dr. Jason Maunder, English astronomy, remained in his seat and calmly watched the mob of angry scientists stomp from the auditorium in a rage. The nattily dressed and bespectacled scientist ambled to the dais where Dr. Randall stood.

"Well, Bruce you certainly know how to influence people."

Randall grinned at his colleague as he filled his lungs. "There's nothing like putting the fear of God in a group of atheists," he clarified to his old friend.

Maunder grinned. "Surely, that wasn't your mission."

"There is no time for pussyfooting around, Jason."

"It's that serious, huh?"

"Urgent is the word, Jason."

"Come Bruce. Let me buy you dinner. I'd like to look at those equations."

Chapter 6

NEWS OF THE explosive meeting in Brussels crossed the Atlantic and reached the U.S. Capitol. The White House staff reeled with the intoxicating news—a looming crisis, ready-made for the eager politician during re-election. Some congressmen whet their appetites and expected a mob in the streets for the character assassination of Dr. Bruce Randall. A few campaign directors even planned an effigy bonfire on the White House lawn. And others simply sat astir like 'Chicken Little' while they visualized a falling sky.

Andrew Evans, White House Chief of Staff, reluctantly left the emergency meeting for an appointment somewhere within the Beltway. Evans held an advanced degree in political science from Dartmouth. When the current President had served two terms as a congressman during the earlier days of his political career, Evans had directed his successful bid for the Senate. And when the Senator announced his candidacy for the Whitehouse, Evans was brought aboard to lead the national campaign. For his successful leadership in the election, he was appointed to chief of staff.

Evans was amiable but arrogant, cocky at times, willing to gamble, but incapable of compromising the President. Nobody got into the

Oval Office unless he approved entry, not a congressman, neither a senator, nor even a member of the cabinet. If they dared to cross him, they ended up on the Beltway blacklist.

As Evans left the elevator and took the first corridor to the parking lot, many political tangles stirred his thoughts. But whether or not Randall's theory was accurate, there apparently was a rocket in space loaded with radioactive waste. That fact alone was political dynamite, and that's why he had called the staff meeting. And now there was another political hole to plug, this Dr. Randall.

Evans finally reached his car and entered the Beltway traffic. He headed to a popular coffee shop where many politicians gathered for drinks and fellowship. The police had placed a barricade at Constitution Avenue, and he turned at the next block to avoid the Washington traffic. The coffee shop was on the corner two streets down, that is, if he remembered correctly.

Bill Watson, senior Congressman from Florida peered through the swirling smoke that rose from his Havana cigar seated in a corner coffee shop. He waved at Andrew Evans when he entered the door, slightly smiled at his disturbed demeanor. Evans strode toward the table beyond the long counter and wondered whether Watson was agreeable with the President's position or would he had abandoned the party at this crucial moment. Already the cigarette smoke competed with the steamy mist from the hot grills at this early hour. A waitress followed Evans with a menu.

"Who is this guy, Dr. Bruce Randall?" Evans asked as he slid his lanky body into a seat. "I'll take a glass of orange juice, please," he told the waitress.

Watson chewed on his cigar and watched Evans squirm. "Director of Wilcox Solar Observatory at Stanford University, a reputable solar scientist," the legislator replied, rolled the cigar to the opposite corner of his mouth.

"Well, he certainly dropped a bomb in Brussels. The President received a steaming letter yesterday through the Russian ambassador," Evans growled and straightened his necktie. He had not expected a humorous response from this congressman. Humor was not in his vocabulary.

Watson chuckled. "Just think of it, radioactive waste in outer space."

The waitress sat the glass of orange juice under Evans' nose.

"Thank you," he grinned, and immediately faced the congressman. "Damn it Watson, we could have a panic on our hands. This guy has scared the living hell out of the scientific community. Why just an hour ago, Dr. Stravinsky of Berlin's Astrophysics Laboratory called the director of the Science Foundation, who called the President," he snarled, and sipped his OJ.

Watson placed his hot cup of coffee on the table, licked his tongue across his bottom lip, and extinguished the irritating burn. "Getting a little hot for the President, Andrew? If Randall is right, things will really begin to heat up."

Evans leaned forward on the table, pushed aside the half-empty glass of OJ. "The President would like a little time to consult with his science advisors, Watson."

The Florida congressman puffed on his cigar already aware of where Evans was going with this conversation. "Wants a hearing, right?"

Evans nodded and drained the OJ glass.

Watson leaned back into the plastic seat, the cigar clinched between his teeth. "I've already called a hearing for tomorrow. I think we at least owe Dr. Randall a platform in America to defend his theory. If we don't, the press will twist his story out of focus and you'll have your panic, Andrew."

"Watson," Evan's burped. "Let's be damned sure this Randall is no crackpot."

The U.S. Congress met in open session to consider political fallout from the blockbuster announcement by Dr. Bruce Randall in Brussels. Dr. Jason Maunder represented the ISTP. Dr. Adrian Brown, the administrator of NASA, sat between Dr. Maunder and Dr. Randall. Monique and Spencer sat in the audience behind Randall's table.

Congressman Bill Watson, the chairman, moved a microphone near his chair, glancing at his notes.

"We are gathered today to hear the facts of a recent meeting in Brussels. The chair requests that you hold you questions until Dr. Randall has time to gather his notes." He faced the conference table directly in front of the committee, and waited for Randall to reach the microphone. "Dr. Randall, are you prepared to give testimony?"

Randall nodded affirmatively. It couldn't be worse than the mob in Brussels.

Watson rustled his papers. "Your rather astounding announcement has stirred up a storm in the scientific community. I assume there is a simple explanation for this theory of yours."

The other four panelists sat with stony faces, not amused by any stretch of imagination. Randall took a deep breath as he pulled over the mike, knowing he faced difficult odds. He had seen his share of what could happen when the media chewed up a professor. It wasn't pretty.

"Mr. Chairman and distinguished members of this committee," he began. "The origin of the sunspot cycle is not known. Why . . .

Watson's face blushed with sudden political fright thinking the professor expected him to answer the question, but Randall relieved his anxiety and answered the question.

". . . Because there is no reason that a star in radiative equilibrium should produce such turbulent magnetic fields, as does our sun.

"My solar studies indicate that radioactive waste is accumulating inside the sun's core, explaining why we've been unable to measure appreciative levels of radiation in the Sun-Earth system with our satellites. This accumulation increases fissionable mass that will further imbalance the core."

One panelist leaned into his mike. "Dr. Randall, aren't you describing a scenario for a supernova?"

"In time, perhaps," Randall answered with a nod. "Stars only have two fates: a nova burnout, or a supernova explosion. I tend to believe that massive quantities of radioactive plasma will spew out of the sun's umbra when the trigger impacts."

Obvious concern reflected from the face of a female panelist as she pulled the mike over closer to her position. "And the trigger is this rocket of radioactive waste?"

"Precisely, madam."

"Could you elaborate in terms that a layman can understand, Dr. Randall?" Watson advised.

"Certainly," he replied, taking a swallow of water. "The sun is the largest nuclear reactor in our solar system, a gigantic ball of superheated gas kept hot by atomic reaction in its core. The sun's atomic reaction is hydrogen fusion; that is, four hydrogen atoms combine to form one helium atom. Heat of reaction produces extreme temperatures at the sun's core, approaching twenty million degrees Celsius. The surface temperature averages six thousand degrees Centigrade, that's about eleven thousand degrees Fahrenheit. Like every reactor, it requires a certain minimum amount of fuel to sustain a chain reaction. This amount we call the critical mass; it varies according to the size of the reaction.

News networks focused their remote cameras, listening through headphones; reporters fingered the keys on laptops, radio jockeys whispered in their microphones. The committee sat intrigued, without comment, as Randall continued his opening remarks.

"The balance between effective mass and critical mass is precarious, to say the least. If the effective mass decreases, the reactor power decreases. Should effective mass increase above critical mass, the chain reaction becomes more rapid, progressing toward meltdown."

The room reeked with silence until a question came from the panel.

"Well, Dr. Randall. Doesn't this all sound just a little academic?" said a stone-faced congressmen.

Randall smiled within his mind. "Cataclysmic is the correct word, sir," he clarified. "The sudden insertion of twenty-thousand kilos of radioactive waste into the sun's core during a solar maximum will increase effective mass. The sun will attempt to cast off the buildup of mass to retain its equilibrium. Solar flares will erupt unlike any we've never seen," Randall concluded.

Watson stared at Dr. Randall. This guy's either a genius or a frigging loony, he thought as he alternately poled the panel surprised that only one senator had a question.

"Senator Greenwald," the chairman announced.

The female senator from Georgia leaned into the mike. "Dr. Randall, why do you suppose no other astronomer has discovered this rocket?"

"Good question, senator. I suppose it looked like space debris. That's a weak answer I know, but it's entirely plausible."

The New Jersey senator uncrossed her long legs and pulled over a mike. "Wouldn't the orbit of the rocket have been a tip off?"

"Again, it's possible. This rocket is in a backward orbit, launched in the opposite direction of the earth's rotation, requiring brut power with no midcourse correction."

A congressman rebutted. "Only a Russian moon rocket has that kind of brute force."

Randall stared at the senator's sneering face for a crucial moment. "I'm not going there, senator—speculation."

Watson fixed his eyes upon Dr. Randall, as did everyone else in the room. He cracked a slight smile thinking maybe he's smarter than Evans realized.

The chairman polled each panel member for comments until satisfied that no one had a question, and then addressed his questions to the scientists seated at a conference table beneath the dais.

"Dr. Maunder. Would you care to comment?"

The English astronomer from the ISTP cleared his throat. He had spent an evening pouring over Randall's equations in Brussels. And he had known Dr. Randall for some years, even had collaborated with him on several projects in the past. Maunder knew of Randall's professionalism firsthand, but even reputable scientists rarely agreed completely with a colleague's findings.

"While I don't totally agree with the entire scenario, I do agree with Dr. Randall's calculations on the magnitude of solar eruption. I think we should alert the agencies of the ISTP, and use the precious time available to gather as much information as possible. It's an unprecedented opportunity to gather data."

"Thank you, Dr. Maunder. Dr. Brown, how does NASA see this thing?"

The administrator of NASA pulled over the mike; his bald head glistened in the bright TV camera lights. An engineer by profession, Brown preferred science rather than politics. "Dr. Randall poses a phenomenal question and argues his point well. Rather than play the advocate, it's wiser to join in the search for a solution. Dr. Randall is a respected solar authority, not an alarmist. If he's right, and we must assume that he is, we should be talking about emergency matters not debating the validity of his theory. He predicts that rocket will impact the sun in about twenty-two days. I say it's time to get ready for a calamity here on earth."

The reporters and people on the perimeter of the conference room rustled and noisily prated. Some reporters quietly moved toward the exits even before the meeting had adjourned.

"Well gentlemen," Watson replied in closing. "I think the federal government must do its part by funding the NASA budget. Those rocket boys will have to find a way to protect this planet. This committee is recessed until three o'clock this afternoon."

Chapter 7

BACK CORRIDORS of the White House pressroom were packed with secret service agents reviewing their assignments while they whispered though headsets. Washington had gone on alert, preplanned policies were in effect. Andrew Evans had demanded that safety procedures be invoked to protect the President and the House Speaker. Agents were discussing the options in the adjoining room. Evans stood with his arms folded across his chest as he watched the well-practiced process unfold. He checked the time on his Rolex for the umpteenth time. From the corner of his eye, he saw the President walking up the hall.

The press secretary stepped to the end of the dais. "Ladies and gentlemen: the President of the United States."

Winston Darcy strode past the agents, winked at Evans, and entered the short corridor to the Briefing Room. He walked toward the lectern, scanning the crowd as he pulled a card from his inside coat pocket.

"I have today declared a state of national emergency," Winston Darcy announced. "We have confirmed Dr. Bruce Randall's report that a rocket loaded with radioactive waste is indeed presently hurtling through space. I am advised that it will plunge into the sun."

The gravity of the President's remarks seemed to grip the meeting in a tense moment of disbelief mingled with journalistic confusion. Although the media blitz featured Dr. Randall, every reporter in the room and across the world knew the news had no precedent. It was the story of the century, perhaps the millennium. And the remarks of the President of the United States added credibility to Randall's theory.

One reporter stood with the first question. "Mr. President, how much waste are we talking about?"

"One thousand drums, Jim. It will hit the sun, assuming it stays on its present course."

Several reporters in the crowd jumped from their seats. Hands went up, front to center. Chatter increased to yelling. A reporter pushed forward amid numerous waving hands, vying to be heard.

"What about radiation, sir. The ozone—

Darcy seized the floor as he sensed a panic. "That, too, is under investigation. Let's wait for some answers, gentlemen, before we run off half-cocked."

Mumblings randomly silenced over a sea of reporters.

A reporter raised his hand with an obvious question, the same question that had afflicted the minds of every reporter who had followed Dr. Randall's explosive report from Brussels to the floor of the Congress.

`"Who launched a rocket into outer space loaded with radioactive waste, Mr. President?"

Darcy responded quickly determined to hold back nothing. "Those details are being investigated by the CIA and the Atomic Energy Board and we should have a report by next week."

Another reporter shielded in the crowd directly in front of podium interrupted with a question. "Are we really sure when it will impact?"

"We can expect the rocket to hit the sun in about twenty days. I'm told some communication satellites are already experiencing the effects of the solar maximum. But I'm also advised that this timetable could change with any fluctuation in the solar wind."

Anxious reporters were still attempting to process the historical announcement of the President. They seemed perplexed and unsure of the right questions to ask. Journalistic behavior pushed them forward, nonetheless.

A seasoned reporter finally stood from a location near the front. "What is the administration doing to prepare the country for this ominous event?"

"Our task will include informing the nations of the world. Here in America, FEMA and the Red Cross will remain on highest alert. The National Guard will also stand on alert in the states. Our emergency organizations in the states are now directly tied to federal agencies, including the FBI and local law enforcement groups. We have alerted our foreign embassies and the United Nations."

"Mr. President," a voice shouted from the rear. "Is there anything NASA can do to prevent this calamity?"

Darcy swallowed a gulp of water, replacing the bottle beneath the podium. "I have formed a taskforce to include General LaCroix, chairman of the Joint Chiefs, Dr. Bruce Randall of Wilcox Solar Observatory, Colonel Griffin of NASA, and Bo Stringer, Program Manager of the Shuttle. Similar taskforce groups are working on this problem in London, Tokyo, and Paris."

"But sir, can NASA respond to this emergency with the administration's latest reduction in funds?"

Darcy loosened his collar. "I have already authorized emergency funds under the National Security Act. I'll ask Bo Stringer to answer for NASA."

He nodded at the shuttle manager.

Bo Stringer wormed his way to the mike forming his remarks as he zigzagged toward the stage. Bo was handed a mike and turned to the crowd. "We can't risk a launch at this time because we expect electrical glitches and power outages. We've got to put all our gas-generated power into the command facilities to service Solar I already in orbit."

"Surely America is in position to do something," a despondent reporter sputtered, angrily leaping from his seat wiping his neck with a tissue.

Bo stared at the reporter but held his mounting exasperation; it was his weakness as an engineer when novices placed irresponsible judgment on matters of their lack of skill.

"Sir, we are a world dependent on electricity. The sun's solar activity, if suddenly expanded, could terminate communication. Not just NASA's launch capability, but telephones and televisions, even point-of-sale machines and ATMs. The banking system could collapse, as well as the stock markets. All sorts of transportation would cease. Not just subways, but airports and planes. Even cars— imagine driving without stoplights or a city suddenly plunged into total darkness."

The reporter sat down, embarrassment flushed his face.

A hazel-eyed redhead sat in the rear, calmly listening to the discussion. She gripped her cellphone and stood, unafraid, trained at asking questions, skilled at rebuttals.

"Mr. President, Dr. Maunder told WOFF NEWS today that the ozone layer has been impaired by the increasing winds of the solar maximum. Can you comment?"

He peered toward the rear of the room, recognized the reporter. "Colonel Griffin, will handle that question, Kim," he said with a nod at the NASA spokesman.

While Griffin waited for the boom microphone, his mind reviewed this reporter's reputation: Kim Marshall, Pulitzer winner, and anchor of Washington Drumbeat on WOFF NEWS, an honest reporter.

"NASA is currently repositioning Solar I for a polar orbit in an attempt to take some ozone readings, Kim. We are also attempting to gather ozone data from three other satellites, without any response I might add."

The redhead's hazel eyes narrowed. "What does all that mean, Colonel?"

Griffin shuffled his stance mentally previewed the nature of his response and decided to give her the raw truth.

"It means our satellites are blind until we can make repairs. Right now our top priority is dealing with this coming catastrophe. The ozone layer will have to wait."

A confused reporter sat in the crowd flipping pages in his notepad, hurriedly thinking of the environmental angle to his story. But these facts pointed to an emergency of global proportions. The ozone layer could only be a byline. He finally found an opening and stood in the uncommon silence.

"Colonel Griffin, if we're already losing satellite communications, what can we expect when that rocket hits the sun?"

Griffin sensed the sincerity of the question.

"We would still have the transatlantic cable. And we are hopeful that the Hubble space telescope can still communicate through the radio antennas at Greenwich, if not at Greenbelt, giving us valuable pictures of the target."

Kim Marshall seized the floor again, her mind crammed with unanswered questions. "Mr. President. You said Dr. Randall is on this taskforce. Where is he, sir?"

Darcy's eyebrow arched as he remembered Kim's keen insight and contacts in the military.

"He's working on the taskforce agenda, Kim. It's vitally important for the taskforce to ask the right questions. Time is too precious to squander. If you've a question, perhaps Colonel Griffin can answer it."

Kim rotated her slender body and faced Griffin. "Colonel, what if the taskforce doesn't find a way to stop that rocket?"

The crowd steeled in anxious silence.

Griffin gazed at the redhead reporter for a brief moment, every eye in the room fixed upon his answer, indeed the world. The President had briefed the taskforce, and advised them to answer questions forthrightly and honestly, and they were going to get it. "One-half of North America's power grids would black out; many other communication satellites would fail. The surge of solar wind would impregnate the troposphere along the polar magnetic fields, causing torrential flooding in the eastern U.S. The aurora would be nothing less than spectacular, possibly spreading down as far as the equator. And God only knows if radioactive particles will be riding on that solar wind soaring toward earth."

A professor from Georgetown University stormed to his feet with the same implausible idea held by seventy percent of the planet. "Surely the sun is too far from earth to cause this kind of calamity," he wistfully replied, adjusting his horn rim glasses as if he held the answer.

Griffin rebutted. "Sir, make no mistake about it, this world will face total chaos. We could experience all the things we only imagined would happen from the Y2K event."

The professor's face smirked and he sat down.

There were no easy answers, but adequate problems for professionals to handle. Some reporters wagged their heads and attempted to grasp the gravity of the dismal events; others stared vacantly into space. But Kim Marshall pushed through the crowd toward an exit, her cellphone pressed to an ear.

The press secretary stepped on the dais. "That's all the time we have, ladies and gentlemen. You'll find a list of federal and state emergency activities on the table as you exit."

Chapter 8

"I'M KIM MARSHALL and you are watching WOFF NEWS. Tonight we have a special edition of Washington Drumbeat featuring a top story alert: A rocket loaded with one thousand drums of uranium waste is at this very moment soaring through outer space, and sources say it's on a collision course with the sun. Astronomers tell us that many of our communication satellites will be disarmed and several electrical power grids will shut down. We'll be right back in a moment with our special guest, Dr. Bruce Randall, of President Darcy's taskforce. Stay with us for all the breaking news."

Dr. Randall sat a chair in the news cubical as instructed and waited for the red light on the camera. He briefly chatted with Kim, anchor of Washington Drumbeat. She suddenly broke into a smile, hazel-eyes gleamed.

"No smoking on the set, Dr. Randall," Kim said with a smile and nodded at a technician who took his pipe.

The red light lit.

"Good evening. This is Kim Marshall. My special guest tonight is Dr. Bruce Randall, director of Wilcox Solar Observatory at Stanford University.

Thank you for taking the time away from your busy schedule, Dr. Randall."

"My pleasure, Kim," Randall said, a bit nervously.

"Dr. Randall. You first shocked the world with news of this coming calamity. Tells us exactly what will happen when that rocket hits the sun?"

"There is some scientific basis that says the rocket might not impact on the sun's surface."

"You're saying it won't hit the sun?"

"Let me clarify. Temperatures at the sun's surface can soar upward to fifty thousand degrees. That much heat could vaporize the rocket superstructure before it would impact the surface."

"Then how will that possibility affect earth?"

"First of all we must remember that we're in a solar maximum greater than any reported thus far. Therefore, the sun's equilibrium is tenuous and more sensitive to pressure changes. Should the rocket implode, the shockwave would aggravate the umbra."

"Umbra, isn't that the site of sunspot activity?"

"Exactly, it appears as a deep scar on the surface."

"Would you explain solar maximum for our viewing audience, Dr. Randall?"

"A solar maximum occurs on eleven year and sometimes twenty-one year cycles always at the height of sunspot activity. And likewise we have a solar minimum during years of nominal sunspot activity. These periods of maximum are referred to as hot earth days, and similarly cold earth days in a solar minimum."

"What about this solar wind?"

"The so-called solar wind is a type of plasma surging from the umbra that rushes toward earth's magnetosphere at over one million miles per hour with the energy of a billion megatons of TNT."

"Plasma, doctor?"

"The concentration of extreme heat over ten thousand degrees changes matter into a fourth stage, called plasma: gas, liquid, solid, plasma."

"I see. And what exactly causes these solar flares, Dr. Randall?"

"The mystery of solar flares is better understood today owing to increasing knowledge that pours in from NASA. Solar flares occur when magnetic fields of the sun's surface release massive amounts of energy, extending out about a hundred thousand miles into deep space. Scientists theorize that these magnetic fields, still anchored on the sun, arch backward forming new connections to the sun. These magnetic loops snap back into place like stretched rubber bands."

"Do you have an update of when impact will occur, Dr. Randall?"

"Our computers say impact with the sun will occur in about sixteen days, obviously sooner if the rocket does vaporize. In either case, the plasma surge will hit the earth; these impact estimates change daily, of course, because plasma moves slower than light. But I'm told our communication satellites are already experiencing anomalies from highly unusual flare ups in this solar maximum."

"I take it then, you don't expect loss of life during this solar event?"

"No Kim. I don't mean to infer that. Yet, there could be any number of casualties resulting from serious atmospheric storms, tornados, and floods. Nobody can accurately estimate the severity of causalities. Much depends on the earth's magnetosphere, the seismic shock, and atmospheric turbulence that could set off magnetic storms and torrential flooding.   Power grids would be at risk, and some orbiting satellites.   An event of this magnitude would increase public unrest resulting in riots and plundering.   I would caution the people of America to prepare for loss of utilities and drinking water.   And I would also urge them to stay close to emergency broadcast networks."

"Thank you, Dr. Randall.   We'll continue our fascinating   discussion   with   Dr.   Bruce   Randall, Director   of   the   Wilcox   Observatory,   after   these messages.   This   is   WOFF   NEWS,   Kim   Marshall reporting."

Chapter 9

THE SUN'S UMBRA unleashed rapid major flares one after the other in less than twelve days. The unusual event shocked astronomers around the globe, mainly because Dr. Randall had warned the world of this very outcome and they were negligent to seriously study his equations. It was a phenomenal occurrence never before witnessed at this magnitude and history would record the event. The catalogue of severe (X) solar spots had logged new entries: two monster flares as X10s, and two more that followed in rapid succession as X20 and X26 classifications. NOAA's Space Environmental Center recorded ten more X-class flares over a twelve-day period. These flares entered the record books as Sunspots 526 through 535. Astronomers became more troubled knowing they had disbelieved Dr. Randall's report. Now there was no doubt to their dismay that Dr. Randall had been correct.

The heavens seemed to ignite. Aurora lights swirled across the night sky like a gigantic purple amoeba. Unusual clouds swelled in the atmosphere like pregnant pillows building up electrons in a graying mixture of static energy. Lightning zigzagged across the heavens with violent discharges. Geomagnetic storms invaded the electronic airwaves disarming satellites and electrical switching networks. Torrential rains plummeted to the earth and created flash floods in diverse places. Rivers rose over the flood banks. Small communities and cities flooded downstream as levels broke. Tornados twisted across mid-America, even in places like San Diego, Phoenix, Canada, and Alaska. Power grids collapsed. Millions of people plunged into sudden darkness. The number of homeless and dead was incalculable amid the chaos.

A massive communications blackout isolated North America from the rest of the world. The ominous rocket still hurtled toward the sun and left a catastrophe in its gravitational wake. The solar maximum had released unprecedented solar flares; astronomical forces were unleashed upon a helpless world as its inhabitants fearfully waited for the collision.

The street urchins moved out of their hiding places armed with flashlights and firearms. They pilfered the streets and alleys and wrecked everything in sight. Bricks went through windows. Garbage cans rolled into the streets. Parked cars were set ablaze, Watts II, magnified tenfold.

The criminal element grabbed everything of pawning value: televisions, stereos, computers, watches, and jewelry. Policemen on motorcycles rushed up-and-down the darkened streets dressed in riot gear. Paddy wagons backed into cross streets. Hordes of rioting people were marched, dragged, or pushed into the wagons. The rioters fought back with clubs and guns. The melee began in a cloud of pepper spray.

As streetlights failed, autos piled up like stacks of dominos. Panic ruled the darkened highways. Cuts, bruises, and broken bones jammed the emergency medical facilities. Rape cases intensified the worst statistic of all. Darkness and panic had unleashed the scourge of society.

City police set up huge lights in the city parks powered by gasoline generators. They gathered people into these central areas, as charity groups, aided by the Red Cross, provided chairs, tables, and food provisions. The Army had set up tents lighted with gas lanterns supplied by FEMA. People from all over the city were stranded by the sudden power outage. Elevators lost power and stopped between floors. Firemen rescued hundreds of people from ceiling trapdoors and from high-rise apartments. When the city finally settled into the reality of emergency status, the mayor and civic leaders addressed the huddled thousands using battery-powered bullhorns. This scenario appeared in countless cities and towns across the nation, indeed across the globe: A world in chaos.

Monique Chevet carefully walked through the maze of hurting people that sat on cots and chairs in an emergency shelter located somewhere in southern California. The burden of guilt literally crushed her spirit, her heart a muddle of nerves. Nurses and volunteers were busy applying bandages and patching up bleeding wounds. Most non-traffic injuries were sustained by falls while people ran and pushed in mobs of panicky situations. In this one of many shelters, countless patients were displaced from their neighborhoods. People sat in shock, blurred eyes stared with strange, vacant stares. Spencer took Monique out of the shelter; the misery tortured her, and he abhorred it.

They drove away without plan or purpose until the road ended at the Pacific coast. A waning moon sat on the horizon and waited for morning. The blazing ball of cosmic energy sank deeper into the ocean. It was a peaceful contrast to the misery back in the shelter.

Monique sobbed with hands clasped over her pixy face. "This is my fault; I'm so ashamed and sorry."

"It's not your fault, Monique," Spencer insisted and placed his arm around her shoulders.

"But my grandfather put that horrible stuff in orbit," she hopelessly pleaded.

"That rocket has not even hit the sun, yet."

"But it will. There will be more misery than you see now."

"I'm sure your grandfather never visualized the danger. Even the U.S. Congress once debated the feasibility of launching nuclear waste into the sun. In a way, he has shown the world that such lunacy is neither practical nor sane."

Her heart felt relieved. "You're so kind and considerate, Spence," she softly whispered, took his hand and pressed it against her tear-wet cheek.

Spencer's ruddy cheeks suddenly blushed, not from embarrassment, but the uncommon joy that this woman had brought into his carefree life. "All of us make mistakes, Monique. I don't want to mistake this feeling I have for you as some kind of infatuation."

Her heart surged with hope, a feeling so rare in her life without John-Pierre, and now she had found someone who really cared for her in a way she desperately needed, someone who could be with her always. "Oh, Spence, darling, there is no mistake. It's real and I feel it, too."

Spencer helplessly answered the urge of his hormones as their faces met. He gently joined his lips to hers. She reciprocated. He embraced her with a soft kiss. She returned the kiss, wrapped her slender arms around his neck, and hugged with all her strength.

They hung somewhere in space suspended in a drifting cloud high above the placid Pacific. The couple stretched out on a beach blanket and watched the surf as it lapped upon the timeless shore and then rolled back into the eternal sea. Seagulls swooped down and plucked their dinners from the foaming surf that reminded their genes that nature was still alive. And the sea was very still once more as the gentle waves lapped upon the shoreline where the couple lay. Although they knew that this wonderful peace was temporary, they rested in the stillness of time for this one brief night alone. There beneath a beach blanket, two lonely hearts melted into one.

But the ominous rocket pushed silently onward toward the sun, caught in the grip of invisible gravity like a celestial traction beam.

Chapter 10

A TEENAGE COUPLE sat in a booth at Propst Drugstore and sipped on chocolate sodas with an occasional giggle into each other's face. Neither adolescent knew the time, nor were they aware of the report of power outages. Straws noisily gurgled from the bottom of empty glasses and broke the romantic silence. In sudden dismay, Samantha realized emergency power dimly lit the drugstore. She glanced at the clock on the wall. It had strangely stopped at 3:45 o'clock but it seemed much later to her. Wrinkles creased Samantha's pristine forehead. Her mother would be worried.

"You kids had better get on home before the streets become dangerous," the druggist warned.

"Dangerous?"

"Street gangs and perverts come out at night. Darkness is their cover."

The two teens rose slowly from their chairs. The lad assisted Samantha with her jacket. As they thanked the druggist, Samantha looked frightfully into his bespectacled eyes.

"Could I use your phone?"

"Sure," he replied, handed over the cellular. She punched the keypad and the circuits clicked through emergency relays.

"Hello, Mom!"

"Samantha, honey, where are you?"

"Jeff and I are at Propst Drugstore. We're coming home now."

"You stay there. Your dad will be there in about thirty minutes."

"Okay, mom, I love you."

Samantha gave the phone back to the druggist with a silent thank you from her speechless lips. The nervous teens walked back to the table and sat down. "Dad's coming," she whispered.

Jeff nodded. "Want another soda?"

A loud crash of breaking glass exploded behind their booth as Jeff and Samantha sat sipping on sodas. Two thugs rushed into the drugstore, each waving pistols.

"Okay, Pop! Open that register!"

The druggist moved behind the counter with his hands aloft, but hesitated. His foot stepped on a button on the floor.

"Open that register—NOW!" he screamed, and crashed the pistol on his head.

The wounded druggist opened the register, and picked up his broken spectacles from the floor. The thug rushed behind the counter and hurriedly shoved cash bills into his pockets.

The other thug guarded the nervous teens. Roving eyes suddenly seized on the young girl and the thug grabbed her arm, pulled her into his chest. "You're a cute little bird," he observed lustfully.

His dirty hands rubbed over the curves of her torso and hips. He ripped open her blouse. She screamed and jerked away. The maddened lad leaped from his chair like a leopard, and broke his soda glass on the thug's head. The surprised thug turned; blood streamed down his face. He pistol-whipped the helpless boy. The undaunted lad's muscles surged with adrenaline. Rage swelled in his throat. He recklessly plunged into the goon's stomach. The angry lad wrestled the startled goon to the floor, repeatedly pounded his fists into a bloody face.

The second thug grabbed the lad's collar and pulled him to his feet. Beady eyes stared into the lad's raging face. "You got spunk, kid. I like it." He released his collar and angrily kicked his partner. "Get up, stupid! Let's get out of here."

The cowering man received repeated kicks in the buttocks as they left. They drove off in the night just before shrilling sirens echoed over the neighborhood, the noise scattered dogs and cats into the alleys, eardrums numbed by the piecing sound.

A police car rounded the corner and screeched to the curb in front of Propst Drugstore. Two policemen bounded into store, broken glass crunched underfoot. One officer attended the wounded druggist, the other questioned Jeff.

"What happened here, sir?"

The druggist pressed a towel on his bleeding skull and addressed the officers. "Two thugs robbed the cash register, officer. That young man there saved my life and protected his girlfriend."

The officer smiled. "Good work, son. You two want a lift home?"

"I'll take them, officer," a man announced as he walked through the door. He had overheard every word. The man embraced his daughter, and put his other arm around the lad. "Jeff, I'm mighty grateful and extremely proud of you, son. Let's go home."

Chapter 11

THE URANIUM ROCKET finally imploded two days ahead of its predicted timetable somewhere near the solar surface. The gaseous ball of plasma seared and churned along its seething umbra. Fiery fingers from the sun's surface lashed out into dark space. Giant flares leaped tens-of-thousands of miles into blackness like ghastly tongues from Hades, and then snapped back to the sizzling surface. And somehow the boiling sun was no longer the familiar life-giver. A smoldering stranger hung in outer space with sinister motives.

The minds of despondent people dwelling on the wounded planet were terrorized by psychoses. Strange events transpired in the cities, towns, and communities around the globe, events of immense scale. Electrical power, still in the frantic process of restoration, suddenly shutdown again, stranded two-thirds of the planet in chilling darkness. A second nightmarish calamity gripped the earth at its axis. The physiological effect was devastating, much like the after-shock of an off-scale earthquake, immeasurable by technology. A dazed world went indoors and huddled around candles and hurricane lamps. Some, though not all, were connected to the outside world by battery radios and TV's with blank raster screens.

The moon finally reappeared from obscurity, suspended in its proper place, and warmly reflected the sun's light. Its lunar face seemed to be the only friendly reflection in the ominous sky. Yet the world surmised that a catastrophe of immense proportions lingered in space, its ominous fingers gripping the planet.

"This is Kim Marshall coming to you on emergency power from our WOFF NEWS studios in Washington, D.C. Power grids servicing the nation's capital has collapsed. Canada, too, is in darkness. This news coming from FEMA just half past the hour: All systems reporting are now on gas-generated power.

"Reports from the northeast are even more alarming. New York is partially blacked-out, only Queens and the Bronx sections still have power. The traffic lights are still operable in parts of the Bronx, but none in Queens and the authorities say they can't guarantee how long before all the power goes down. Thousands of cars are stranded on expressways and bridges.

"Cleveland, Boston, Buffalo, even Chicago, all the northeastern border states, and the eastern coastline of the U.S. are without electrical power tonight." She cupped her ear. "We have breaking news of a massive traffic pileup on the Washington Expressway at this moment. Reports are garbled and sketchy, but fifty-four people are confirmed dead. Rescue work is hampered by loss of power. The city is calling for extra emergency crews and larger gas generators.

"This is WOFF NEWS and I'm Kim Marshall. To recap: The northeastern sectors of the U.S. are without power. There is no news, as yet, from the west coast. FEMA reports are coming in describing massive traffic jams and pileups. Rescue workers are swamped with stuck elevators, missing people, and now looting is on the rise—and this just in: the Tennessee Valley Authority has lost its power link to the national grid. Atlanta, Birmingham, Tupelo, and all through the Mid-Atlantic States are without power.

"We'll break for just a moment. Our power level here at the station is dropping. Until we come back on the air, you can tune to our AM broadcast on 1420 kilohertz. This is Kim Marshall reporting."

The program director met Kim at her dressing table, his face somber. "It sure looks like we'll be off the air for a spell, Kim. We're trying now to kick-in larger gas generators. Question is how many people out there still have power to operate their TVs?"

Kim busily powdered her nose in the reflection of her studio mirror. "You just be sure we stay on the air, Brad. Our signal can be picked-up in places where power is unaffected." She turned on her dressing stool. "The world has to know, Brad. We must stay on the airwaves."

Brad's tired face smiled. "That's the grit I've learned to expect from you, Kim. Get back to your monitor. I'll get you power."

Chapter 12

THE HOUR NEARED closing time for Courtney Morgan, a single salesperson who worked in a high-rise apartment store somewhere in the Bronx. All day the news of power outages had given her great concern but the shoppers kept coming and bought everything on the shelves. Her roommate had called twice, but the boss just wouldn't close the doors.

Her department was on the fifth floor where people bought flashlights, batteries, bottled water, and camping gear. The overhead lights suddenly blinked once, then twice. Courtney felt surely the power was about to blackout, but it was her boss warning the customers of closing time.

Courtney hustled to clean her area and do all the other mundane chores before she left. As she finally donned her coat, the lights dimmed again. This time it was a brownout caused by the utility company. Fearing a power outage, she ran to the time clock and punched out.

The crowds moved generally fast. Many used the elevators, and some the stairs. But Courtney's tired feet and legs persuaded her to take the elevators.

Eight people crammed into one elevator that included Courtney. As the Otis descended, scary pictures rushed through her mind. Her roommate was adamantly against her decision to work today. Her paranoid friend had watched television all weekend. The alarming news had predicted the coming disaster with blackouts and loss of utilities, which had terrified her roommate. She knew all the horrifying details about the upheaval on the sun and the solar wind that rushed toward the earth, and she existed in a self-made trance. It was as if it were her destiny that harbored the problems of the world in her mind.

But the news was all a mystery to Courtney, foreign to her lifestyle. Courtney had suffered through a divorce at age twenty-four but fortunately had no children. Her roommate, a former high school classmate experienced the same domestic problems. They lived in a rental townhouse in the Bronx for the past four years.

A jerk of the elevator suddenly shook her thoughts to reality. The overhead light blinked out. The Otis stopped abruptly. Chilling darkness filled the tiny space. Startled eyes finally adjusted to a dim light. Pixel lights glowed with battery emergency power on the aging control panel. They had stopped on the second floor.

The anxious people inside the darkened elevator said nothing at first. Then nervous feminine screams shattered the spooky silence. A man raised his hand, yelling while waving a flashlight.

"Quiet, please! Settle down! It's only the second floor. We can get down."

Six desperate women stood huddled together like newborn chicks, while two courageous men planned their escape. They'd seen this situation too many times on the late-night TV movies. The obvious exit was through the ceiling; however, entering the elevator shaft through the ceiling was no easy task, maybe for Bruce Willis, not for them. Somehow they knew it was their only chance.

A burly man snapped his fingers at the smaller gentleman pointing to his knee. He assisted the smaller man from his knee onto his broad shoulders like an acrobatic team. The acrobat on the top steadied himself against the wall and pushed out the ceiling tile feeling more like a novice than he appeared. Someone handed over the flashlight and he thrust the beam into the darkened shaft. A myriad of cables and wheels painted a dim picture that concerned the ability of the women regarding the dirty, greasy cables? He waved the light and spotted handholds on the wall, evenly spaced like a ladder. "I see a way out!" he yelled. "Help me down."

The burly man on the bottom squatted, released the weight on his shoulders. He leaned against the wall and caught his breath. Courtney wiped the sweat from his forehead, keenly pleased by his gentle countenance. Their eyes met briefly and they exchanged smiles.

"There are handholds on this wall here," the smaller man said, his fists pounded the wall. "We can climb to the third floor and pry open the elevator doors. Then we'll take the stairway down to the street."

The report seemed encouraging. The prospect of freedom prompted a few guarded smiles but one obvious problem chilled their hopes. The doors were firmly held by air pressure.

The burly man had a suggestion. "I've got a pocket knife. Think we can cut that air line?"

"If it's not a metal line," replied an anxious response. "Let's do it."

Again, the novice acrobatic team took their positions. The smaller man climbed into the attic from the shoulders of the burly man; knife in his pocket, flashlight in his hand. But location of the airline was obscured by dangling lines and it took longer than suspected. He finally found a short, flexible section of tubing connected to a steel tube with a solenoid valve assembly mounted against the wall. That's got to be it, he thought. He sawed the flexible tubing with the knife blade and raggedly cut until a whooshing surge of air bathed his face. He instantly heard the solenoid plunger retract, and the doors on the third floor surprisingly opened into blackness.

"Hey down there; they opened, the darn doors opened!"

Sighs of relief rumbled from below augmented by the sound of clapping hands and stomping feet.

The burly man smiled. "Okay. You stay up there, buddy. I'll pass up the ladies." One-by-one the ladies stepped on the burly man's knee, and climbed onto his broad, manly shoulders. They were lifted into the shaft by their extended arms.

The flashlight was jammed between two cables that lit the pathway to the handholds. It was a precarious trip to the wall that required cautious steps on supports that held the suspended ceiling. The burly man had only his head and shoulders through the ceiling hole, when Courtney suddenly screamed! One of her legs had plunged through the ceiling tile. The burly man quickly lurched at her descending leg. "Gotcha, it's okay—easy now."

She nervously grabbed a cable and lifted herself onto the ceiling frame. Her trembling hand gripped the handhold. In emergency times, the body reacts with surging energy flowing in the bloodstream. This was the case with Courtney.

The last one out dropped from the shaft. "Here's your pocket knife, buddy. And thanks for the use of your shoulders, too."

They moved toward the stairway following the shaft of light from the flashlight. Comradeship had developed among the group, a common phenomenon of mutually shared traumatic experiences. Two jovial men descended the steps ahead of the six women walking shoulder-to-shoulder with the flashlight lighting the path. The girls chattered nervous trivia as if it were a spring day, with birds chirping and squirrels scampering about a freshly trimmed lawn.

Courtney had a mile to walk to her townhouse because her car was parked in a garage below the office complex. With power out, her coded card would not open the garage door.

She stood at the curb wondering how she could safely make the trip on foot down the darkened streets. Someone nudged her shoulder. "I've got my car right down here. Can I give you a lift?" the burly man asked.

His manly smile pleased her. "Yes, that would be wonderful."

They walked through the eerie darkness focused on an emergency squad of policemen busily setting up gas generators and huge spotlights. The burly man lit a cigarette as they walked and chatted. Courtney gazed through the flickering flame at the face of her knightly rescuer, wondering how she might repay the kindness of the handsome, burly man.

Chapter 13

MELISSA TURNED ON the fog lights as her SUV blindly cruised around a winding curve of a seemingly deserted mountain road. A long valley stretched out below, normally lit with a grid of streetlights, now dark and dismal. The horizon swirled with purplish colors like a giant amoeba. The aurora borealis had moved near the equator, activated by increasing electrons collecting in the magnetosphere, or so the local news had said that morning while she drank coffee. Melissa increased the speed of the windshield wipers to clean the condensate, rethinking her situation.

When electrical power began to shutdown in neighboring communities, and Melissa's cellphone had not received calls, she realized that her daughter could not stay overnight at a friend's house. She couldn't leave her on the mountain with her husband stranded at his business, and prediction of more impending power outages. So, she had rushed out to get her, and now wasn't even sure it had been a good idea.

A transformer suddenly exploded atop a power pole, interrupting her thoughts, sprinkling hot fragments on the hood. Fallen power lines danced on the pavement like attacking snakes, spitting sparks that ignited the dry grass. Flames spread down the slopes leaping over boulders and decayed tree trunks. Birds fluttered from the bush, winging down into the valley. Melissa gripped the steering wheel like a vice, her young daughter in the passenger seat terrified and unable to speak.

The engine chuffed and shutdown. Melissa frantically banged her palm on the gas gauge. Her screaming mind frantically prompted her to disengage the engine, allowing the massive vehicle to coast. But lack of power had thrust her into a battle with the steering wheel. The SUV bounced and bumped, drifting dangerously closer to the jagged edge of the road.

Suddenly dislodged rocks rolled down the flaming slope initiating an avalanche. In that precarious moment, with life hanging in the balance, the two females struggled with their runaway vehicle. The SUV gained speed around the curve, and suddenly slammed into a tree at the edge of the slope; the front bumper wrapped around the trunk, anchoring the vehicle. Airbags popped from the steering column and side panels, squeezing the passengers against the seat, tearing the skin like sandpaper. Nonetheless, the women breathed a nervous sigh of relief; they were alive.

The headlights dimmed out, and they sat alone in the dark silence, only the hissing from the ruptured radiator that disturbed Melissa's chilling thoughts. The dismal truth was obvious and frightening: They had to leave the disabled SUV and hike about two hundred yards to the crossroads down the road.

She leaned against the door and repeatedly bumped it with her shoulder, until the door swung open with a chilling squeak. Melissa stepped out and slung her purse strap over a shoulder, grimaced at the bruises inflicted by the door. She sidestepped the bumper and wormed her way around the SUV, afraid to look down the slope. Melissa reached the opposite side of the vehicle and jerked open the passenger door with the aid of one leg pushing against the doorpost. The daughter's arm was injured and bleeding, and the teenager nervously slid from the seat into her mother's arms.

They finally staggered off the jagged rocks onto the pavement, exhausted, trembling, and frightened. Melissa tried her cellphone once more, but heard only static, no connection. The sudden howl of wolves on the mountain dispelled false confidence, and the women bolted down the inclined road unencumbered by their injuries and vanity. The fragile women waddled down the pavement, protective glances peering into the shadows. Adrenaline had completed its mission, pain returned. The only realty they gratefully felt.

They ran only about thirty yards, huffing and puffing, gasping for air. The cellphone crackled, and then a robust ring and Melissa placed the phone against her ear, hopeful, expectant, and frantic.

"Bob! Oh Bob! It is you . . . yes . . . base of Schuylkill, near the turnoff . . . ten minutes . . . thank you, darling!"

A sudden burst of light lit the mountainside. An eighteen wheel tractor-truck careened around the curve, horns blaring like trumpets, airbrakes hissing, tires squealing. The driver professionally downshifted gears, eyes gapping at the SUV jammed against the tree, and two human shadows silhouetted on the pavement by his bouncing headlights.

Melissa and her daughter whirled around hands clasped against their faces, descending death written across their wrinkled foreheads.

Suddenly the truck jackknifed, the trailer crashed against the SUV, the sound of twisting metal echoed down the alley. Flames leaped into the sky in a billowing cloud of smoke and debris, rising up into the trees in a gust of wind.

The SUV exploded in flames.

Melissa dropped her handbag and ran toward the truck, where the driver sprawled motionless on the pavement. She kneeled beside him and ignored the blood from a gashing wound in his side. She gently cradled his head in her lap, caressed his hair as tears rolled down her cheek. This brave man had given his life to prevent certain death of her and her daughter. Melissa whispered a prayer between sniffs. Surely, he had relatives, she thought. Perhaps he too, had a young daughter.

Chapter 14

REPORTERS GATHERED ON the east side of the Capitol Rotunda and waited for the FEMA director to come to the portico. Gas generators were staged on the grass that fed a bank of lights and sound amplifiers. Messages had reached the news media explaining that Congress had met in joint session to consider emergency funds in the wake of the solar catastrophe. The FEMA director and six other dignitaries arrived a few minutes later, including the Speaker of the House and the majority leader of the Senate.

The FEMA director acted as spokesman. "I am pleased to announce that emergency funds have been approved in a joint session of the House and the Senate. Reports on casualties and the homeless, are filtering into the emergency center. However numbers may not be available until human needs are met and power is restored.

"The utilities across America are in emergency status trying to restore power through gas generators until the power grids are functional again. Restoration of grids that use satellite switching remains uncertain at this time, but TVA reports they will restore sixty percent of its generated power by end of next week."

"How widespread is this blackout globally?"

"The Canadian power grid is linked at New York. It collapsed at about the same time as the U.S. northern tiers. The only communication link we have with Europe right now is by HAM radio. The HAM satellite was apparently hidden behind the earth, and was shielded from damage. The transatlantic cable is scrambled by too many signals that are overloading the circuits. We can confirm that England and parts of Ireland are under a blackout."

"You said the funds are approved. How soon can emergency funds get out to the states?"

The House speaker leaned his chubby face into the microphone. "The bill went to the President within the hour. We expect that funds will be available sometime tomorrow under emergency procedure."

"Sir, perhaps we can use the Pentagon's communication links?"

The FEMA director nodded to a gentleman on his left, and the Senate chairman of the Intelligence Committee shuffled to the microphone.

"Most communication satellites went down because of the solar wind but the Defense Department is now up on generated power. AWACS units can still communicate air-to-surface, but flying without GPS is still hazardous. The Air Force hopes to fix four of the twenty-four GPS satellites but that, too, is doubtful. Right now our mission is to the urgent needs of the American people."

Another hand raised in the center. "We hear from our field reporters that looting and rape are on the rise."

"Yes, President Darcy is quite disturbed by this travesty. The governors have authorized the

National Guard to aid local police in controlling the street problems."

"Mr. Speaker? How did Congress manage to have a quorum on-hand?"

"No one left Washington. We were in session when the lights went out. We know all too well what America, indeed the world, is suffering right now. We are all in this together."

Several geographic sections of the nation finally received power in a necessarily planned sequence of available circuits. Utility companies had worked feverously to restore the power grids. Fortunately, the Y2K event preparedness of 1999/2000 had solved many potential problems. Consequently, one network after another restored electrical power as the atmospherics slowly neutralized. Power outage lasted an average of two weeks for some sectors, four weeks for other sectors. One grid in the northeast sector was still without power because switching circuits in a satellite had resisted corrective signals from its ground-based controller. Utility planners made notes to eliminate satellite switching. One other discovery, not obvious before revealed that most of the ground-based switching equipment was old and outdated. Authorities set long-term goals to design an alternate system.

Curious and weary people finally came out of their homes and hiding places and assessed the damage. Winston Darcy addressed the American people in several TV news conferences from the Oval Office. America had weathered the magnetic storm of the century. Europe, too, had recovered. Great Britain was the last country that returned to normalcy. The suspected reasons were reported as psychological problems within the elderly population and the very young. Yet, lifestyles slowly returned to some semblance of normality. People everywhere could finally rest and sleep.

But one person in the whole wide world knew that Planet Earth was not out of danger. That person had the evidence locked in his desk drawer at Yamato Aeronautics Tokyo. The world was unaware of another catastrophe.

For now, the wounded world slept while it could.

Chapter 15

BREAKING DAWN ANNOUNCED the rising sun over Palo Alto, California, but the city still lay asleep as the evening stars dimmed into a gray atmosphere. Monique Chevet slept quietly in her bed tranquilized by the effects of two sleeping pills. A ringing phone gratefully awakened her from a nightmare. Dazed by the events of last evening, and lack of sleep, she grabbed her purse from the nightstand and fished for the cellphone.

"Yes," she whispered and yawned with her eyes shut.

"Mademoiselle Chevet?"

Her brown eyes popped open as she threw off the covers. "Jean-Pierre—is it really you?"

"You must come home quickly as possible, madam."

She stood with her knuckles screwing into her eye sockets. "Why?"

"Something's come up, mademoiselle."

"Darn it, Jean-Pierre! What is it?" she demanded as she stomped her foot.

"Extortion, for one thing, somebody is trying to pull off a hostile takeover of Chevet Energy."

"What's that!" she exclaimed as she flopped into a chair, now widely awake. "What—"

"That little matter with your grandfather," he hinted as he cut her off.

Her eyes popped open. "Grandfather's diary, oh, Jean-Pierre, you've been harboring this devilish secret for twenty years and never told me."

He bowed his head. "It was never your problem until now, mademoiselle."

She wilted, head in her hands. Slowly she raised her head with resolve. "What does Claude want me to do?"

"He suggests you confer with him immediately upon your arrival. He'll explain the options."

Monique deeply sighed, wondering just what to do, what to say. "I'll let you know when I book flight, Jean-Pierre. Thank you for calling. And be careful my old friend."

The troubled young woman went to the bathroom and splashed water on her face. She stood looking into the mirror, then pinched her arm, and wondering if it were all a bad dream. The pain tingled deep within her muscles, instantly surging to her brain. It was no dream.

She left the bathroom and sat down with the cellphone on her lap considering an impulsive action. Although she had known Spencer for only a few precious weeks, she trusted him implicitly. A smile filled her face as he answered the call.

"Ah-oomph! If this isn't you, Monique, I'm going back to sleep."

"It's me, you crazy American," she chuckled.

"Monique! It is you! What are you doing up so early?"

"Want to take me out to breakfast?"

He scratched his skuzzy head, rose on his elbow, stretching the impression on his face left by his pillow as he searched for his wristwatch twisted in the sheet.

"Uh, say in about an hour, no make it forty-five minutes," he said sleepily squinting at his wristwatch.

"I'll be waiting."

"Uh-huh."

Breakfast in the waterfront cafe made the eggs and bacon more scrumptious, especially gratifying with Spencer at the table facing Monique. The California sky hung like a blanket in misty gray. The Pacific coastline awaited the appearance of the dawning sun's beaming rays. A sunburst silently exploded over the lofty ridges of the distant Continental Divide. The surf quietly swelled and gently splashed onto the sandy shore below the restaurant's support pilings. The sun poured down the mountain slopes like a gigantic floodlight and lit the dawning desert. A silhouette of the tower parapets cast its shadow onto the watery surf like some medieval scene from Shakespeare. Flags on the roof waved in the dawning breezes. Seagulls swarmed over the foaming surf as if on cue from the life-giving rays of the injured sun, little turtles scooted back into the sands of the retreating surf.

Monique musingly sipped her orange juice gazing at the man she loved seated across the table. Reality crushed her spirit, realizing she had to break some bad news.

"Spence, darling, I'm going back to Paris."

Spencer choked on his coffee, and wiped his shirt with a napkin.

"You're leaving?"

"Just for a while," she promised, grimacing at the wrinkles in his disappointed face.

Spencer recovered from the spill, no time to worry about the stain on his shirt. "I can't let you—I won't let you go alone, Monique!"

"Oh, Spence, I can't make you leave graduate school."

"Dr. Randall will understand. I'm sure I can get his permission."

"I could never forgive myself if I got you into trouble."

"We won't discuss it any further. I'm going with you, and that's that," he demanded, clasping her hands across the table, "now, what's the reason for this urgent trip?"

Her eyes glowed, not at the question, but his caring smile. "Legal tangles: It seems there's a run on corporate stock. And something's screwy about that deal with the Japanese company. You remember that reference in the diary?"

Spencer's head bobbed. "The company your grandfather hired."

"Yes, apparently, somebody has leaked the story to the press. There's some kind of investigation underway."

"You want a sabbatical?" Randall chuckled with amusing disbelief. He rocked back in his chair, arms clasped behind his neck, puffing on his pipe. "But why?"

"Monique is going back to Paris, sir. I can't let her go alone," Spencer explained, but unspoken words stuck in his heart.

"You'll be missing a golden opportunity to study this historic upheaval on the sun. It isn't over yet," Randall advised, chewing on his pipe stem.

Spencer shuffled boyishly, "Right now I can't seem to concentrate on this project," he said, gently sighing.

Randall counseled him like a father. "Signs of love my young friend."

Spencer hung his head. "I'm sorry to let you down."

"Nonsense, there is one matter you could check for me while you're in Europe."

Spencer's eyes kindled a glimmer. "Yes sir?"

"That Japanese company: I'd like to know exactly what isotope of uranium they loaded on that rocket."

Chapter 16

A BOEING 767 CRUISED well above a raging storm cloud at thirty-three thousand feet over the Atlantic. The seeming quietness outside the double-paned porthole relaxed Monique, but her heart pounded with anguish and despair. For the misery and pain unleashed upon the planet, she harbored undeniable quilt; for economic collapse of mounting numbers of industries, she desired to make restitution. Yet, she knew the news from Jean-Pierre meant the chaos was not over. Alas, the looming trouble awaited her in Paris unnerved her spirit. Through it all, she could only rest in the reality of Spence's presence seated beside her. This kind and gentle young man was her one glimmer of hope, her reason for pressing on despite the insurmountable obstacles stirring in her mind.

"I'm so confused. What could have happened?"

Spencer felt her anguish, and tried to compensate. "It seems plausible that the Japanese company who launched that rocket must've leaked the story."

Squirreling around in her seat, she touched her index finger to his lips, and then kissed him. "It's all beyond me. I'm just glad you came along."

He kissed her slender fingers. "I'm not letting you out of my sight."

She smiled. This was the man she had learned to respect and she trusted his judgment. "I had to cross an ocean to find you, Spence. I wonder if I really deserve someone like you."

Her head suddenly bowed, sulking like a lost gamine wandering alone in some distant land. She had never really had a beau, Marquee was only a friend, and there was no romantic attraction on her part, his part obvious.

Spencer gently gripped her shoulder. "What's troubling you sweetheart?"

Her face slowly rose, lacking its usual luster and splendor, her confidence, and even her arrogance no longer a crutch, as if she were stranded on a fantasy island. Out of the scars in her heart, cut deep by the message from Jean Pierce, she finally spoke.

"I see mountains that we must cross before this nightmare breaks into daylight."

Spencer's compassion surfaced as he lifted the mid-divider between their seats and cuddled Monique in his arms. Gently stroking her short bangs, his heart confirmed that she was indeed the only one he could ever love. Then and there he determined in his heart never to let her go. "Don't worry, darling. We'll cross those mountains together."

A flight attendant squatted by their seat. "Say, could I interest you two lovebirds in some refreshments?"

As if a dark cloud had been lifted, Monique managed a smile. "How about two coffees?"

"Make mine two creams, hazelnut," Spencer injected, broadly smiling, his ruddy complexion aglow with confidence when he saw the smile on Monique's face.

Presently, steaming coffee sat on the pull-down shimmering with tiny ripples from a slight turbulence. As Monique watched the curling steam rise into the air conditioner, a chill shivered through her tingling muscles.

"I hope Jean-Pierre meets us at the airport. I'm so rattled I can't seem to remember the way to my château."

Spencer's smile broke into a grinning chuckle. "You women are so complex."

A sparkle glittered in her doe eyes. "Life is complex, Spence. But women experience life. You men only taste it."

His face spread a masculine grin. "Come here. I'll show you how experienced I am."

Spencer knew in his heart that Dr. Randall was correct; he was in love with the fascinating woman.

He enclosed her into his strong arms and tasted her ruby lips. They embraced in the silence of ecstasy heard only by two youthful lovers. Wispy clouds streamed by the porthole like the distant past rushing toward the turbulent future.

Monique's heart swelled with hope. These precious moments were all she had, all she needed, to weather this storm. Oh, how she loved this man. "I like that. Do it again."

He embraced her again, caressing her hair, stroking her back. She purred like a kitten as he released her. "You taste mighty good, sweetheart."

"Sweeter than honey, darling, and don't you forget it."

The sleek aircraft lowered below the clouds on its descent to the Charles De Gaulle Airport in Paris. She made two vectoring turns in the sky highway and lined up with the distant runway, descending like a graceful eagle. Her wheels screeched and gripped the pavement as turbines reversed. Screaming turbine fans idled down to taxi speed. The swaying airframe crossed the airstrip onto the tarmac crossing onto a taxiway.

People stood in the aisles crammed together like sardines. They took short, ungainly steps toward the exit into the Jetway. Security checkers slowed the disembarking passengers to a snail's pace, and open luggage lay on inspection tables on either side of the line. The bags moved through a scanning machine and exited through the opposite end. Passengers walked through a sensor station with their pockets and purses emptied into little plastic bowls.

A security guard waved a mobile metal scanner, moving the wand up-and-down their torsos and extremities. Several dogs jerked and dragged their trainers on taunt tethers, eagerly sniffing for hidden explosives.

"There he is—Jean-Pierre!" Monique shouted, releasing Spencer's hand.

The little French filly galloped through the milling crowds like a mustang released on an open range. A security guard in the distance raised a mobile phone and said something. She twisted her slender body through the maze of people and popped to the other side under the scrutinizing eyes of the security guard who had watched her every move. She zigzagged around tall, alabaster pillars dodging streams of humanity.

She surged into the aging valet's arms. "Oh, dear, dear Jean-Pierre," she whispered, embracing his wizened, lanky body hugging him with waning strength. Her arms finally released and she slowly slithered to her feet. "Thank you for meeting us," she said placing her hand on his wizened face. "This is Spencer Jenson, a good friend."

"Master Jenson," the valet gestured with a slight bow, as he critically gazed at the young stranger.

"Put her there, Johnny," Spencer said, extending an open hand. He gripped the wrinkled hand of the surprised valet and pumped it several times.

"Ah-hum, oh, ah, thank you, sir, this way, please," he said. The befuddled valet briskly led the couple out of the busy terminal. They passed several parked cars along the curb, finally reaching a black limousine. Jean-Pierre opened the back doors and the passengers stepped inside the plush interior. After loading the luggage, the musing valet drove away from the crowded terminal. He took several turns and entered the snarled expressway toward downtown Paris. It's good of Monique to bring home her friends. But what's with this American cowboy?

Twilight faded into dusk as the black limousine cruised down a black asphalt street. Nighttime gathered splendor over the historic city, the sky a pale gray, the air misty and cool. A chilling fog hazed the skyline of the tall structures rising in the distance. The familiar shadow of the Eiffel Tower protruded majestically above the haze, her straight lines bent by light refraction. The blinking light atop her pinnacle looked like a harbor light in the dense fog, but it had no effect on the ever-increasing traffic approaching the basin city stretched out along the Seine River. Spencer glanced out the window at strangely familiar scenes zipping by the limousine. So this is Paris! Although his historic knowledge of Paris came by books and movies, picturesque shops and streets poured from his richly stored memory. The graphic scenes triggered his imagination as floods of reminiscent pictures and fantasies replayed through his mind's eye. The square on the left looked pale and cold in the dusky light, but there sat a painter working at his easel, and there, too, a woman baking bread for market. Spencer could even visualize Gene Kelly splashing along its flooded streets with an umbrella; the scenes changed as quickly as they appeared, new things, yet aged dismally old. Crumbled buildings stood starkly in a bombed-out district left for historic remembrance.

As the ghastly scene prodded his mind, memories began to spill out like faded snapshots a half-century old. Tanks had paraded these streets, and soldiers had goose-stepped along these narrow ways during a period of dark history, when the people of this city had suffered under siege by the Third Reich. It seemed that an angry bellicose Grecian god had filled the sky with smoke and thunder and vowed the total destruction of Paris.

Chapter 17

THE ARISTOCRATIC DISTRICT of Paris lay in the original site described as *Ile de la Cité* in the Seine, where the law courts were established around 1250 AD, *Sainte Chappelle,* and Notre Dame.   The left bank contained the university quarter, most of the remaining medieval buildings and, far west, the Eiffel Tower built in 1899 at 988 feet, raised to 1,052 feet in 1959.   Yet, many historic homes had been left undamaged by retreating occupation forces of the German Army during World War II.   Ironically, some of these homes had entertained the likes of General Charles De Gaulle before he became president, and others had been used as headquarters for allied forces

A black limousine swayed around a curving driveway, and parked at the front entrance of a sprawling château. The architecture dated from the 17th century, and this is where Monique had grown up under the tutorship of Jean-Pierre. She loved the aging Frenchman, even his pragmatic personality. And somehow she was glad to be at home again. The valet opened the back door of the limousine and assisted her exit.

"Wow!" Spencer exclaimed. "So this is your grandfather's estate?"

She mused for a moment. "It's mine, now," she said, displaying a smile, but her eyes suddenly withered. "That is, of course, if this investigation doesn't take it away."

Spencer sensed her familiar depression. "Soon as we get unpacked, we'll have a parley with Jean-Pierre," he promised with a comforting hug.

Jean-Pierre entered the room laden with luggage under his long arms. Spencer ran to his aide.

"I'll take that, Jean-Pierre."

"Thank you, sir, but I can manage."

"Jean-Pierre, would you please put those bags down and sit over here with us for a moment?" Monique demanded in her not-so-quiet persuasive voice.

"Yes, mademoiselle, as you wish."

The tired, old Frenchman looked into the familiar eyes of Monique. The child he once knew was all grown up. Yes, she was an adult now. Somehow he was glad that she had found a friend she seemed to trust. And in the light of the room he saw a handsome, intelligent young man.

They quietly sat in a circle around a period fruitwood table with flowers in a vase releasing its fragrance into the air.

Spencer found the valet quite a friendly sort; in fact he liked his attitude. "Jean-Pierre," he called. "Who first contacted you about this investigation?"

Gray, wiry eyebrows arched. "He was an inspector of the police."

Spencer persisted. "He has a name?"

"Inspector Parquet, I've got his card somewhere," the valet remembered, bony fingers fumbled with his inside coat pocket. When he found the card a mysterious thought entered his mine. *What is it he thought, nothing perhaps, but there was something about Parquet's face—probably that beard. Oh well. I can't think about that now.*

Spencer took the card from his outstretched hand. "It says here on the back that a legal suit has been filed."

"Yes. That's my scribbling. I think Marcus Fragnet, the district judge, signed the suit papers."

"Who is the plaintiff? Someone had to file this suit!"

"That's the problem, sir," the sulking valet replied.

"Problem," Spencer injected?

"Yes, I think a payoff is involved somewhere, and that judge is my candidate. He has a long history of taking bribes."

"And do we have a lawyer?"

"Claude Moreau, the senior corporate lawyer of Chevet Energy," the valet advised.

As they drank wine, Monique shared her experiences in America, and Jean-Pierre listened with thankfulness in his heart. His prayers had been answered. God had used a young man named Spencer Jenson.

Chapter 18

A RED FERRARI evaded slower cars as it cruised through the evening traffic of downtown Paris. It seemed that Monique acted like a robot at the wheel simply to push her beloved Ferrari to the limit. She drove with a nonchalance attitude that struck Spencer as rather dangerous, if not a bit mad as she zoomed through intersections and shot into narrow cross streets.

Afternoon showers had drenched the historical streets, and long lines of commute traffic slowly merged into the freeway. Spencer calmed his beating heart now that the heavy traffic finally slowed the sports car to normal speed. Flooded potholes splashed beneath the Ferrari's radial tires like burst balloons filled with water. Monique crossed over the Seine to the right bank and steered behind the *Louvre* and the *Tuileries* garden. The major financial and commercial sections stretched along the riverbank laced by the system of squares and boulevards laid out by Haussmann in the 19th century, notably the *Place de l'Etoile*, surrounding *the Arc de Triomphe* and the *Place de la Concorde*, with the *Avenue des Champs* connecting them. Government buildings were located throughout the center, sprinkled with patches of green grass and an occasional patio.

"The corporate offices are just ahead," Monique said, over the hum of the motor as she shifted through lower gears. The windshield wipers smeared a grimy haze that obscured her vision, and she carelessly fumbled for the washer lever.

Spencer sat in the passenger seat mesmerized by the historical buildings all draped in the misty morning haze. Although his long legs were cramped in the bucket seats, the passing scenes gripped his attention. He wondered how these historical relics had survived the consistent bombings of World War II.

"Here it is," Monique said, then double-clutched the transmission and swung the Ferrari into a parking garage. She down-shifted into lower gears and the sports car transaxle whined and whirred around the ramps to the fourth level. The Ferrari finally steered into a tight spot and switched off the ignition. "The elevator is over there," she said, pointing over the ramp.

The quietness was uncommon. "What building is this?" Spencer quizzed, after recognizing some of the architecture.

"I think it's part of the old *Louvre* Annex that moved into renovated quarters several years ago. Chevet Energy purchased the building about ten years back for its corporate headquarters after agreeing to restore its museum quality."

They finally reached the elevators located in the far corner of the parking lot. As they waited for the lift, Spencer smiled into Monique's glowing face, pleased by her quick adjustment. Being back in familiar surroundings had calmed her fears. "Feeling better now that you're home?" he asked.

"Yes, I'm a little anxious. This corporate stuff is not my . . . how you say—bag?"

Spencer smiled again, holding open the elevator doors for her to enter. Monique punched the keypad, suddenly clasping Spencer's hand. "Come here, you misplaced American."

She surged into his arms pressing his body against the wall. She kissed him warmly, desirably. As Spencer held her embrace, he glanced over her shoulder. He saw a human shadow slip behind a concrete pillar just as the elevator doors closed. That was not unusual, he thought, unless the man conspicuously hid himself for a reason. "Don't get me nervous, now."

Her pixy face wrinkled recalling a forgotten thought. "Almost forgot for a moment about that dreadful rocket."

"It will be okay, honey."

She kissed his cheek. "You're the kindest, most thoughtful man I've ever known, Spence."

His thumb massaged her dainty chin as he stared into her adorable face with high cheekbones and smooth tanned skin. Her alluring smile formed a confession that poured uncontrollably from his lips.

"I love you Monique," he admitted, as he planted an irresistible kiss on her warm lips.

Monique rested her head against his chest at peace for the moment, more confident in his arms. There was a glow on her face—the glow of a tranquil moment.

The elevator suddenly stopped and bounced the couple apart. The doors opened onto a wide and magnificent corridor. Several large tapestries draped the walls with enormous appeal and beauty, yet strangely lacked in monotony, despite their repetitious designs. These fine examples were made during the sixteenth century showing colorful figures and elaborate scenes interwoven with gold thread.

They walked down the long corridor passing period French furniture neatly lined beneath the wainscoting. A bombe chest sat against a wall. A backgammon table sat by a window with exquisite designs carved in the side rails. Tall, arched windows formed the ends of the corridor all crowned with lambrequin valance and matching scalloped fabrics woven in the Louis XV period.

They finally faced a large entrance with two massive doors adorned with brass and fruitwood inlay. Magnificent bronze urns sat on either side of the doors poised like knightly guards. Spencer pushed open the mahogany doors with great anticipation of continuing the tour of French antiques.

"May I help you—why Monique! How good to see you, darling. Claude is expecting you. The executive board worked all night to prepare for your visit," a pert and bubbly receptionist greeted.

"Thank you, Gigi," Monique replied, smiling.

"It'll be only a few minutes. Will you take refreshments?"

"No, thank you. We'll wait, Gigi."

They sat on a gilded settee arranged in a conversation circle of authentic antiques. Spencer had only started to admire the beauty when the buzzing intercom disturbed his thoughts.

"Claude will see you now, Monique."

Monique stood ready to see Claude, but Spencer's eyes had been unconsciously seized by the lure of antiques. "Come on, Michelangelo," she smiled.

"Huh?"

She took his hand with a sassy smile, and led him to the office door. Spencer pushed open the door, warmly grinned at Monique. A distinguished man sat behind a Louis XV bureau plat. The senior vice president of Chevet Energy, a lawyer by profession, stood and walked toward the couple with an extended hand.

"Monique, my child, how good to see you, again," he said, bowed and kissed her hand. The lawyer was a rather handsome man, mid-forties, slightly balding black hair, and cleanly shaven.

"Claude," she replied.

"And who is this fine gentleman?" he asked as he pumped Spencer's hand.

"Spencer Jenson, from America, he works with the director of Wilcox Solar Observatory," Monique said, amusingly beaming.

"That would be Dr. Bruce Randall," Claude surprisingly replied, having attended the Brussels meeting as an astronomy novice while in the city on business, but greatly surprised by the subject of radioactive waste launched into space. Only by chance was he in the city during the meeting? Nonetheless, it had caused him to open up the corporate files dating back to 1982.

Spencer quickly responded, flexing his gnarled fingers, squeezed by a vice-like grip. "Why yes. Dr. Randall is tutoring me on my doctorate."

The lawyer smiled, gesturing to a table, "Won't you please sit over here? We have much to discuss."

They sat at a large console accented with veneer inlays. The edges of its four rectangular legs were gilded with bronze trim. On the table laid an open briefcase surrounded with scattered papers. A gold label glistened above the handle: Claude Moreau.

"I don't know what Jean-Pierre was able to tell you, Monique. But a hostile takeover is underway, attempting seizure of Chevet Energy," he said matter-of-factly.

Monique leaned forward in her seat, her back straight, adrenalin flowing into her veins. "Jean-Pierre mentioned a district judge, Marcus Fragnet."

"Yes," he nodded, "Fragnet has the dubious reputation of illegal actions. His escapades are well known in legal circles."

"Do you think there's a conspiracy here?" Spencer bluntly injected.

Moreau's bushy left eyebrow arched, surprised at the insight of Spencer, but then after hearing Randall's speech, and this young man as Randall's understudy, he decided that the youngster must be intelligent

"I do. But proving it is difficult," he turned facing Monique. "And the board hesitated to pull our stock from the open market without the approval of its chief executive."

Monique glared at Moreau with resolve in her pixy face, and the blood or her grandfather flowing in her veins. "Nobody's going to steal this company. You have my permission to fight. In fact, I demand you fight!"

Moreau smiled, nodding. "I thought you'd see it that way, Monique. The board put together a strategy last night, hoping you would approve it today."

"What's your plan?" she defiantly asked.

He inhaled a deep sigh, searching for some papers spread on his desk. "We will, of course, deny the charges that Chevet Energy tried to prevent release of that report from Japan."

"Whose charges," Spencer asked.

"Undisclosed, that's our best defense. Yamato Aeronautics even denies the release of its records. Obviously, someone is trying to drive down the stock price with the release of this Yamato news. We've been buying our own stock to keep the price stable."

Monique's defensive posture shifted to offensive tactics. "I think Spence and I will just pay a visit to this Japanese company. I want you to look into this bribing judge angle. There has to be someone smarter than Fragnet behind this, and we need to uncover the reason for releasing this information."

Moreau's waxed left eyebrow arched. "Those are two good starting places. I have already engaged a private investigator to shadow Fragnet. Here's the news clipping," he said, sliding the newsprint across the desk, bumping against Spencer's hand.

Spencer could only make out a few French words, but Monique solved his dilemma. "Give me that," Monique demanded, winking a smile as she quickly read the article. "Here's an address of Yamato Aeronautics outside Tokyo proper. The owner is Asahara Sakamoto."

Moreau gazed across the bureau plat. "Sorry we don't have time to discuss your Dr. Randall. He's done the world a great service," he said and rocked back in the leather chair, thinking. "I knew something was bothering Dr. Chevet. The nuclear waste had been hauled off but there was no official manifest that documented that it went to an approved dumpsite. The Atomic Energy officials seemed satisfied to see that the waste was gone and surprisingly didn't inquire further."

"Yes, but wouldn't it have been cheaper to pay the hauling cost rather that launch it into space?" Spencer returned.

Moreau tapped a letter opener against his thumb. "Dr. Chevet did not hold the popular idea of burying nuclear waste. For one thing, it makes spent waste readily available for terrorists groups to steal. I think, too, Dr. Chevet had to act quickly. The company stock was rapidly falling. I'm not condoning his actions, only observing his reasons."

Spencer nodded.

Moreau leaned forward in his chair and opened his briefcase. "Here's the file on Yamato Aeronautics. The corporate jet is at your disposal."

Chapter 19

MONIQUE AND SPENCER left the Chevet Energy headquarters and wandered toward the elevators. Their minds puzzled over the frightening prospect of a conspiracy to take over the corporation. The elevator suddenly opened and the dazed couple stepped inside. Spencer punched the lobby icon. His memory reminded him of the mysterious man.

When the elevator doors finally opened on the parking garage level, Spencer suddenly extended his arm against Monique. "Wait a minute," he whispered. He surveyed the lobby like a turtle with his head stuck out of its shell, and saw no sign of the mystery man.

"What's the matter?"

"Thought I saw someone tailing us as we came in, guess it's nothing."

"Well, let's get out of here. We'll drive back to the château, if you don't object—I need a few things for the trip to Tokyo."

As the external doors opened on the parking lot, Spencer spotted his mystery man standing in the shadows across the way. He watched with peripheral vision as he opened the Ferrari door. He took one final glance after seating Monique but the man had vanished.

Monique glanced at his watchful eyes. "See something?"

"Nah," he fibbed.

The Ferrari exited the parking garage just as the sun sank into the distant and hazy horizon. Paris at night was historically astounding. So many familiar things emerged from the shadows as they whizzed along the narrow streets. But Spencer was more concerned at whether they were being tailed, although he was quite certain nobody could catch Monique with her foot on the accelerator, and 570 horses under the hood. He watched the rearview mirror with the eyes of an owl, ready to challenge the mystery man at the first opportunity. But the car was no longer following the Ferrari.

Finally, the flashy classic pulled into the private driveway of the château, but Jean-Pierre did not meet their arrival. Monique always carried her essentials in a flight bag: Makeup, credit cards, and French perfume of a special blend, and hopefully they wouldn't be long anyway.

The large four-foot front door swung open as they scaled the steps. Jean-Pierre met them with a rare smile. They followed him into the spacious front foyer with vaulted ceilings where hung three beautiful chandeliers. He sat the luggage on the floor by the winding stairway, and led them into the anteroom. Monique seemed a bit exhausted by the trip and sat on the sofa; Spencer took his seat next to her and watched the expression on the valet's face.

"Is something wrong, Jean-Pierre?"

His wrinkled face answered the question before he spoke. "The office called and left a message. I wasn't at all sure you would return here—that's why I failed to call you."

Monique didn't hear his reasons for not calling; only that someone had called. She stirred. "What message?"

He replied straight forth. "Your pilot has been released for the night. I gather the airplane needs to be service before your trip."

Spence seemed relaxed, but not Monique, so he responded jokingly, but with a bit of American slang. "Well that's a nasty bit of news."

The joke had not aroused even a comment, and Spencer sat silently consulting his mind. A trip to Tokyo would expend most of the night, and they had just crossed an ocean. Perhaps a rest is in order he decided.

Jean-Pierre seemed always cognizant of what to say, and this was the time for his elderly wisdom. "Why don't you two stay overnight and I'll fix dinner?"

Spencer finally voiced his honest opinion. "You took the words right out of my mouth, Jean-Pierre."

"Well, then. You two freshen up, and I'll start dinner," Jean-Pierre advised. The valet walked off to the kitchen where a cook and a maid were waiting for is orders. He gave the cook explicit instructions for the menu, sent the maid to prepare rooms for the guests, and he went to his room for a moment; there were some things about the estate that he wanted to settle with her before she left.

Finally the dinner was ready and the couple went into the dining room when the announcement was given. Jean-Pierre appeared and served the pates. He waited until they were settled to ask his questions, dutifully standing by the table, a napkin draped over his arm.

"Mademoiselle, we may lose our gardener, his wife is having surgery and desires to be with her."

Monique wiped her mouth with the cloth napkin and laid it by her plate. "Would you see that he gets a sizeable bonus? And don't allow him to spend his savings on this surgery. Take care of it would you, Jean-Pierre?"

He nodded affirmatively and stood. "Thank you, mademoiselle that is very kind of you."

After dinner, the couple settled on the sofa discussing the events of the next day, but suddenly realized they were tired, and had to rise early. It took little persuasion to convince them to retire. Jean-Pierre led Spence to a bedroom upstairs across from Monique's suite.

Late in the wee hours of predawn silence, Spencer was awakened by the sound of running water. He sat up in the bed, looked around the room, wondering if he was just dreaming. The sound seemed to emanate from the armoire standing against the far wall. Curiosity wrestled him out of the bed, and he ambled to armoire. Although the sounds were no louder, it did seem to resonate from inside the armoire. He opened the doors but the sound did not change in volume. He craned his neck to one side, gripped the backside of the furniture, and pulled a corner from the wall. Suddenly a door slid open in the wall; some sort of pocket door activated by the armoire movement, he surmised. He stared through the opening into total darkness, a myriad of questions surfaced in his mind. Quickly he spun around and retrieved a flashlight from his overnight bag, then followed the beam into a cavern deep down into eerie blackness.

As he slowly walked he wondered what or why this secret passage had been built. Was it during the 16th century, or, perhaps, much latter? Why?

He rounded a slight bend as the sound of flowing water gained in volume. Then the flashlight beam glistened on the surface of rippling water as he entered a sort of underground cove. Mystified at what he saw, Spencer slowly strode toward several crates stacked against a rugged wall. Mechanically, Spencer's eyes traveled over the several wooden crates, twelve, he counted. His curiosity rose to unbridled imagination, as he ambled toward the mysterious crates, cursory searching for some kind of marks on the sidewalls that might identify the contents. And then, he saw it. On the end of each crate a Swastika was stenciled in bold black. Without hesitation, he unconsciously dislodged a wooden top, and the glitter of gold bars petrified his thoughts.

Jean-Pierre stood in the shadows, but Spencer was so intense on his discovery he had not noticed him. In that moment of dark silence the valet's mind suddenly recalled the day he had found this cavern but had never told anyone until he had finished his research. An echoing voice suddenly pierced Jean-Pierre's ears, and his thoughts vanished.

He whirled. "Jean-Pierre, what is the meaning of all this, where did this stuff come from?"

The stalwart valet, now awake and alert, marched toward the crates knowing this young man had strong feelings for Monique. He sat on one of the crates and crossed his legs.

"When Monique left for America, I stumbled upon this mystery much as you have tonight."

"It's a mystery, all right, but what is it—who put these crate here?"

Jean-Pierre paused momentarily. "That, too, had puzzled me, and so I did some research."

"Yeah?"

"It seems that this very château was occupied by German soldiers as a field headquarters during the German occupation of Paris in World War II."

The information froze his mind. How often he had read books about the Civil War and the German blitzkrieg, the occupation of Paris, its liberation by General Patton, although the credit had gone to the pompous Montgomery.

"That's incredible! Any idea how much gold is here?"

Jean-Pierre hesitated, although he had counted the crates and the bars, he was altogether unsure of the weight. "I'm not quite sure, sir."

Spencer nodded. "Well you do understand that gold is weighed in troy ounces."

This young lad knew history and Jean-Pierre played along. "Yes, I understand the Roman system is retained to preserve the standards previously set across time."

"That's quite correct, Jean-Pierre. The troy ounce is heavier than the American ounce, known as the avoirdupois ounce."

That was a fact of French weights. "I see, and how does one equate the two?"

Spencer consulted his memory. "A troy ounce equals 1.09714286 of one avoirdupois ounce, although he remembered only the first three digits, the rest he guessed."

Then we must estimate the weight to gain the value"

"Yes, did you count the bars?"

"There are twenty-five crates containing twenty bars each."

"Holy Moses, that's five hundred gold bars!"

"Yes, I quite agree, sir . . . how much would you estimate that in your American dollars?"

"Gosh, let's see. If we estimate the current market price of say 1,500 dollars an ounce . . . 392 ounces per bar at 250 bars is about 98,000 ounces . . . if my math is correct that's $38,415,000 Million American dollars.

Jean-Pierre sat on the crates flabbergasted.

Spencer finally regained his composure with a million questions buzzing in his mind, most of which concerned the survival of Monique's company, and her safety.

"Do you think Dr. Chevet knew about this gold?"

Jean-Pierre's wizened expression mirrored his resentment at hearing the comment. "Certainly not, had he known, he would not have launched the radioactive waste into space, nor did he ever mention it to me."

Spencer persisted with his questions, eager to hear the truth. How else would he discover why he and Monique were being followed by a mystery man?

"But didn't this history you discovered show up in the records of the sale?"

A cognizable smile stretched the valet's wrinkled face. Perhaps the French laws should be explained to this young man who knew next to nothing about the background of Chevet Industries, he thought.

"Master Spencer, I don't expect you to understand our laws. You see, Dr. Chevet bought this château through a mortgage agency. He wasn't concerned with historic details, just put down the money for a cash sale. In fact, I am reasonably certain he purchased it for his terminally ill wife to die in honorably."

Spencer gripped his chin remorsefully deciding not to go into Chevet's personal family concerns, but the expression in Jean-Pierre's face reflected the same question that nagged him.

"Master Spencer, what are we going to do with this gold?" the valet sighed.

Spencer didn't know the answer only the danger involved. "We cannot assume that someone else has not stumbled onto this mystery, too."

"Yes. Then maybe we should guard it someway," the valet offered.

"Seems probable," Spencer thought aloud, still querying his mind for valid answers and concern for the safety of Monique; after all, she was the CEO, and somebody was just too darn curious, probably about the gold, he suddenly realized, remembering the stalking mystery man. "Is there anyone, Jean-Pierre that you can trust in this household?"

Jean-Pierre stood mute for a few moments, his mind searching the list of employees. "I can trust the chef, he, and I were hired the same day by master Chevet. If you like, I'll ask him not to allow any stranger near the bedroom, and I'll lock the door, and keep the key."

"That should do it, Jean-Pierre. We have no other recourse at this time, but we'll have to discuss it with Moreau."

The valet nodded affirmatively but was not entirely satisfied with the temporary plan. He placed a finger aside his nose. "Master Spencer, I would not reveal this discovery to Monique just yet, she has too much on her mind."

Spence agreed. He and Jean-Pierre were on the same page. Monique must be protected.

Chapter 20

A LONELY SWALLOW flew out to meet the dawn as the sun laid its misty blanket upon the old French city; the dewy slopes sparkled like diamonds seemingly alive with dancing fairies. The metallic color of a red Ferrari glowed in the early morning light as it cut a pathway to De Gaulle airport. Its bright red colors gleamed as if it led a parade of chariots, armies, kings, and queens from history's ancient pages.

"Jean-Pierre is a really nice guy," Spencer mused.

Monique's head tilted in a coquettish pose, high cheekbones, and smooth tanned skin as she shifted the gears around traffic in the narrow streets. "Yes, and I love him almost as much as you."

Spencer's heart melted, her words had set a fire flaming in his heart that would burn forever, just for her. A canny smile curved his lips. "You just wait until I get you alone again."

Her laugh fogged the windshield that quickly cleared, but her response fogged it again. "I heard voices last night. What were you and Jean-Pierre discussing?"

Spencer twisted in the leather bucket seat and faced Monique as he rehearsed in his mind what he would say. Nothing had changed the decision that he and Jean-Pierre had made, and their secret concerning the gold hidden beneath the château, therefore he fibbed. "He questioned my intentions about you."

Her left eyebrow cocked. "You must be joking."

"No," he replied wagging his head. "He loves you like a father. I've got to play my cards right if I intend to properly court you, Monique."

She pinched his thigh; a wrinkled nose expressed her approval. "You Americans, you're so out of touch with European women."

Spencer answered with a broad smile.

Finally the airport sprawled across the distant horizon, and Monique took an exit off the expressway. After a series of turns, she drove directly to the Chevet private tarmac where they saw the corporate plane sitting on the pavement in the morning shadows. Monique parked the Ferrari, and Spencer took out the luggage. The pilot was not seen around the aircraft, so they went into the terminal. Monique decided she needed a few toiletries she had forgotten, and Spencer excused himself to go to the restroom.

They parted with a few brief words and waved. As Monique walked toward the shops on the opposite side of the terminal, Spencer followed the international signs to the restrooms. He finally entered a long dimly lit hallway, and brushed past two smiling French ladies. Her gulped as he thought perhaps he had entered a unisex restroom, even though there were none in France. Regardless, he took but a moment and left as fast as his legs could transport him.

The lanky American sighed deeply as he returned to the main floor of the terminal through the narrow hall. His anxiety vanished as he spotted Monique coming out of a bath shop on the far side. He stopped and smiled at her girlish strut and curvy figure; if only he could voice the words in his heart.

She caught his wave and rushed toward him across the lobby, her face a flood of excitement. His pleasant thoughts quickly shifted to fear when he glimpsed someone cloaked in the shadows behind a marble pillar. Suddenly he realized it was the mystery man aiming a gun.

A shot rang out!

Monique staggered and fell! Crowds swarmed like an upset hornet's nest, alarmed by the image of frequent bombings in large crowds.

"No!" Spencer screamed at the top of his lungs gripping both sides of his head with his hands.

He rushed toward her and fell to his knees beside her motionless body. Nervous hands lifted her torso into his lap; he brushed a tress of hair from her silent face. Tears cascaded down his cheeks as he pressed her against his chest. He rocked her in his arms like a baby, thoughts crucified his inner being. The stark realization that he'd never see her alive again exploded his mind. Shattered dreams erupted, of no importance now, only her life. He gazed into the face of the one he loved, the pain of recent memories, the joy of her vibrant presence, now empty and barren. All reality vanished; he was alone in his misery, his face as empty as a sheet of cardboard. A single regret remained in his barren mind: Why had he not known her longer? He embraced her limp body and those trembling words uttered helplessly.

"Don't leave me, darling" he whispered, hugging her silent face against his wet cheek. "Oh, God, please don't take this woman," he pleaded.

The limp body faintly flinched!

Muscles weakly twitched. Spencer tightened his grip, she was alive!! His heart leaped with hope, thanksgiving, and praise, a thousand memories returned and filled the vacancy of his heart. He stood cradling her in his arms, his heart thumping wildly. He looked left then right, and then ran to the front frantically screaming. "Help, I need medical attention. Please help me, someone!"

An attentive policeman rushed in from somewhere. "I've called the airport medical unit. It's on the way," he said in broken English.

The officer had seen the shooting incident, quickly surmised the situation, and barked a message through his lapel mike.

A medic finally arrived and dropped his bag beside the patient. He checked her pulse as trained eyes traveled her body and searched for the wound. She had a bullet puncture near the pelvic bone but no exit wound. He looked up at Spencer. "We need to move her to the hospital at once, can't seem to stabilize the shock, it could be internal injuries."

Another medic busily set up a gurney and placed a mini-pack of breathing oxygen over Monique's nose and mouth. The two medics gently angled Monique's traumatized body about three inches and cautiously slid the gurney underneath, secured her with straps.

Spencer watched every motion like a hawk tracking its prey. "I'm going with you," he demanded.

"But that's not allowed, sir."

"It is now, buster. Move over," he said, and tugged at the pistol in his pocket. The mystery man had dropped the weapon, and he'd inadvertently picked it up, and then decided he may need some kind of protection in this wide open city.

The medic grinned. "Put that thing away. If she where my woman, I'd go with her, too. Get in."

The ambulance raced toward a hospital in the nearby district. Spencer cared only that Monique was alive. Paramedics attached monitors to Monique's prostrate body as the ambulance whizzed through Paris traffic as the siren blared.

Her vital signs steadily blipped on a tiny screen: pulse, blood pressure, and temperature. The same data flashed on a monitor at the hospital. The busy paramedics conversed by radio directly with a physician. Monique rested in good hands, and that was all that mattered. Spencer deeply sighed, his heartbeat almost normal, and lifted a cellphone from a side pocket. He punched a code as his face grimaced at Monique's condition. "Jean-Pierre, this is Spencer. Listen closely. Monique has been shot."

Garbled sounds resonated over the tiny speaker.

"Hold on, Jean-Pierre. I'm in the ambulance— hey, you there at the wheel, where're we going."

The medic turned his head and watched the road by peripheral vision. "Bernadette Hospital."

"Did you get that, Jean-Pierre? All right, now try to meet us there. You'll have to stay with Monique. I'm going on to Tokyo, alone."

The ambulance finally screeched into the emergency entrance. The two paramedics pulled the gurney out; wheels dropped and locked, and they pushed Monique into the waiting trauma unit. Spencer closely trailed on their heels like a Tennessee bloodhound sniffing the trail of a fox.

A despondent and fatigued young man stood with his eyes glued to the porthole of the operating room. Spencer had read the diagnoses report. It was a simple procedure that removed a slug, and then cauterized an artery. The x-rays revealed a white line which displayed the path of the bullet. The slug had miraculously missed vital organs and had lodged in the pelvic bone. Monique was not in the OR extremely long, although it seemed like an eternity.

The bed rolled out of the OR in about forty-five minutes, and Spencer followed the orderlies to the elevator, still numb with anxiety. They got off on the sixth floor, and put Monique in Room 605. A floor nurse stood by the foot of the bed reading the chart, cast in the shadow of a tall young man.
Her chocolate eyes peered over the chart.

"And who are you?" she asked, in average English. Spencer ignored her question. "That's my fiancée," he replied and pointed at the bed. "Somebody took a shot at her. You will take good care of her, won't you?"

She winked as she walked out of the room to the desk, not annoyed, although somewhat jealous, if only her husband cared for her as this man obviously cared for his woman, she thought.

"Just fill out this form," she said with professional calmness, brownish eyes glowing with sudden compassion as she smiled. "I'll look after her, don't you worry."

Monique was under anesthesia and slept soundly with blood plasma dripping into her vein. Spencer sat by her bedside while he busily scribbled information on the form. He read a question and his eyes narrowed: *relationship to the patient?* He blushed and wrote fiancé.

The door slowly creaked open. A lanky and wizened man barged in without his usual finesse. "How is she, master Spencer?"

Spencer stood and took the valet's hand. He stretched his other arm around his neck, patting him on his curved back, grateful that he was there. "She's medicated, Jean-Pierre, probably will sleep for a couple of hours."

His leathery face wrinkled. "What's going on here, master?"

Spencer grinned at the valet and understood his fatherly interest in Monique. "First, Jean-Pierre, don't call me master. It's Spencer," he grinned.

"Ahumm, yes, uh—Spencer."

As they talked, a black-suited man with a mustache walked into the room unannounced. His mandrake beard was neatly trimmed, and he wore a cape with a cane, although he had no noticeable limp. Highly polished shoes supported his rather robust frame with a barrel-shaped torso. He said not a word as he quietly panned the surroundings. Finally the mysterious man spoke. "I'm told there has been a shooting at De Gaulle."

"And you are?" Spencer inquired.

He clicked his heels. "Inspector Parquet of the 14th Precinct at your service," he replied.

Parquet had grown up in the filth of existence on the dirty barges along the Seine River in the central Paris basin, the younger of two boys. He discovered his plump body as a chubby junior that gave him the more laborious tasks, especially after his brother had been killed in Vietnam. He abhorred barge existence, no fun, only work morning till night. The haunting memory of how his family had eked out life in a daily struggle could not be erased; it was indelible in his mind.

Parquet had buried the brutal memory deep in the matrix of his mind and sealed it with years of scars and torment. The death of his mother had faded the light in eyes of his aging father; he sat day-by-day in the shade guzzling wine, never bathing, a stench greater than the barge gunk. That was the day that Parquet had left the barge life, and found a position in the automotive factories in the suburbs.

Three years in an assembly plant had gained him favor with a security guard who had served alongside his brother in Vietnam. This favor finally had transpired into a position as a motorcycle policeman in the local district who kept thieves out of the market districts who scared away the customers. The more seasoned motorcyclist had "grease guns" slung over a shoulder that were reclaimed from the French Underground—the *resistance*.

One fortunate day finally arrived, a day that Parquet marked as the pinnacle from which his life had launched to a more desirable lifestyle in governmental politics. Though fortunate it, too, was a hapless accident that resulted in a broken leg and required the use of a cane for life. While in a chase of an old rusty Renault, he laid done his motorcycle to avoid hitting a child in the street, the granddaughter of the *Commissionaire de Police*.

In gratitude, the high-ranking official appointed Parquet to lieutenant *général de police* in the detective branch. Although he harbored extreme gratefulness, he also had deep-rooted ambition fired in the crucible of barge existence. He steeled his mind to play the game of politics and gained a sizeable income through corruption, the motive of political occupation. Yet, addictive greed had mingled with his vaulting ambition, and thrust him into the prospect of early retirement. And yet, he desired more, more to pad his retirement nest, more for a lifestyle of his dreams. Through the years, he had gained the reputation of the ever vigil opportunist—Inspector Parquet.

Parquet's searching eyes leveled on the valet, whom he had met several years ago on an investigation of one of Dr. Chevet's nuclear plants. "Jean-Pierre," he greeted with a nod as he extended his hand.

Spencer focused his attention on the French inspector as he inquisitively peered into his dark eyes. "Monique was shot by a man who followed us."

Parquet casually twirled the pointed ends of his mustache as his piercing eyes locked on the young American's countenance. "Can you identify this man?"

Spencer wagged his head trying not to form an opinion of the inspector just yet. "He wore a trench coat and a hat, couldn't see his face," Spencer replied, continued to size the officer, his demeanor, his eyes, and his mannerisms. He trusted no one now.

"We'll find him," the inspector said assumingly, with an index finger laying aside his pointed nose. "Why please excuse my arrogance! Monique is well, I trust."

Spencer smugly played his hand mainly because he had experienced the drama of being in a foreign country. "Do you know Monique?"

"I knew her grandfather, casually. I haven't seen Monique since she was a teen."

Jean-Pierre thought the remark strange, since he had not remembered the visit of the inspector when Monique was an adolescent. Of course, he thought, neither was he around every moment of a day nor was his mind as sharp; the maids had cared for Monique while he was often away from household duties as he attended to the old master.

Spencer hesitated to even mention the diary or its contents, and certainly not the hidden gold.

Yamato Aeronautics was on his mind. "Inspector, I'm afraid you'll have to excuse me. I have urgent business."

He raised his cane. "Sorry you have to leave so soon. I had hoped we might have a cocktail together. There are some things I wish to say to you," he surprisingly responded, lowering the cane.

Spencer reconsidered the inspector's request and rethought his decision. "Think I could use that drink after all. Jean-Pierre, you stay with Monique. I'll be in touch my friend."

Spencer turned to Monique who lay peacefully asleep in the bed like Cinderella. He kissed her cheek, as if he expected her to awaken. Spencer winked at Jean-Pierre, and left with the inspector.

Inspector Parquet escorted Spencer to a casual café just outside the hospital. They took a shortcut along a narrow walkway trimmed with wrought-iron railings that surrounded the hospital building. A bridge walkway spanned a wide moat overlooking a calm waterway bubbling over rounded rocks. Climbing roses entwined around the bridge rails in a scene reminiscent of the Venice canals. Spencer's eyes seemed captured by the flickering shadows on the waving leaves.

"Do you plan to be in Paris long, Mr. Jenson?"

Spencer blinked, his eyes refocused. Had he even mentioned his name? Somehow the man's attitude bothered Spencer. "Uh, I've got business in Japan while Monique is convalescing."

"I see. Then I'll trouble you for that weapon."

Spencer's eyes brightened with surprise written on his face. "The man who shot Monique dropped it," he explained as he handed a Beretta to the inspector.

"You understand I can't have my guests running around the city with weapons. And I believe the fingerprints of your assailant are smudged by now."

Spencer nodded. Of course, Parquet was right. He had tampered with evidence. Then and there he decided the Inspector should handle the police work after all.

A quaint little outdoor café appeared at the base of a wrought-iron bridge overlooking a moat. Two men entered an open courtyard basking in filtered sunlight. The younger man towered over an officially dressed policeman. The inspector pointed his cane at a small round table on the veranda. Each man pulled out a chair with curved wrought-iron backs.

"Is this sufficient?" Parquet asked, laying his cane by the chair.

Spencer nodded and sat down.

"Cognac," Parquet told a waitress, "bring the bottle."

Spencer sat silently waiting for the Inspector's next move; after all, he had decided not to damage any more evidence nor meddle in police work. He only hoped the meeting would not last too long, it was it was a long trip to Tokyo, and the pilot was waiting, so much to do, to answer so many questions now.

The inspector crossed his legs and lit a long, thin cigarillo, watching Spencer's countenance. He'd often used the silent treatment in his interrogations. But this young man was no one's fool. There was much he needed to know about his exploits if he were to solve this baffling case.

The magnificent surroundings recaptured Spence's imagination as they waited, unscathed by

Parquet's penetrating stare.   The bottle of Cognac finally arrived and the waiter poured two glasses.

"I'll post a guard at the hospital. Your mystery man may decide to finish the job."

"Thanks Parquet, that's very kind of you."

"Spencer Jenson. That's your name, isn't it?"

"You seem to have all the answers."

"Come now, Mr. Jenson. I know why you're in Paris. It is my business to know."

"Then you tell me."

"If you insist," he responded, while he sipped his liquor.   "Monique's grandfather kept a diary. Although he never confided in me, I knew what troubled him. We traced a fax he sent to Yamato Aeronautics in Tokyo twenty years ago. The rest is international news, as you Americans say."

Spencer seemed impressed and persuaded himself not to be so antagonistic with the inspector since he seemed fair about the case. "So? Tell me what is so interesting about me?"

"Only what your work means to the safety of this planet."

Spencer relaxed.   Parquet seemed genuine, certainly cognizant of his situation.   "Maybe the worst is over."

"Don't be too sure, my young friend."

Chapter 21

JUST BEFORE SPENCER'S taxi arrived at the De Gaulle terminal he glanced at his wristwatch for the umpteenth time. *It's midnight. Let's see, now. Tokyo is waking up to hot tea about now.* The taxi finally squeezed into the left lane and stopped at the passenger entrance. Spencer got out, and paid the driver, surprised by the activity around the entrance. De Gaulle was a hub terminal, and even at this late hour, the several concourses bustled with international travelers. He spotted the corporate pilot who waited just beyond the ticket counter but Spencer vectored to a telephone booth, instead. He crammed his lanky frame into a tiny space, and punched a series of numbers on the keypad. The lateness of the hour and all that had transpired revealed that he had forgotten the cellphone in his coat pocket.

"Is this Yamato Aeronautics?"

"Yes," a tiny female voice responded.

"Is Asahara Sakamoto available? This is Chevet Energy in Paris calling."

"I'm sorry. He's out for lunch, sir."

"I see. Then, could he meet me later today in his office? It's important."

She sat her morning cup of tea on the desk. "Could I have your name, sir?"

"Spencer Jenson."

Pause.

"You're on his calendar for five o'clock this afternoon, Mr. Jensen."

"Thank you so very much."

Spencer hung up the phone and wiggled from the tight confines of the telephone booth. His cellphone suddenly fell from a pocket and bounced on the pavement, landed at the pilot's feet and produced a blush on Spencer's face.

"Everything okay?" the pilot asked as he picked up the cellphone.

"Think so," he replied. "Could we make that flight to Tokyo now? Monique is not going."

The pilot handed over the cellphone. "Sure thing if you don't mind flying all night. We'll have to sit down in Bombay to refuel."

Spencer smiled. "That's just fine. You have to get me there in time for a five pm appointment."

"Get aboard, Mr. Jenson."

Spencer finally settled into a plush, window seat aboard the Lear jet and rethought his mission. Asahara Sakamoto was a prime piece in this puzzle, and it was important to meet him personally. Suddenly his frazzled mind remembered Dr. Randall's request to clarify the uranium isotope, and he left a reminder note on his cellphone. He refocused on the news clipping, it specifically said the report originated in Tokyo, he recalled as he took the news article from his shirt pocket, but he had forgotten it was printed in French. The thought sent his mind back to the hospital with the memory of Monique when she had read the clipping and told him the name of the Aerospace Company. A sudden sigh closed the thought. Oh well, he thought,

Sakamoto had questions to answer, hopefully answers that would solve this riddle. He sighed once more, and snuggled into the window seat, gathering his arms across his chest, and finally rested for a few moments. Besides, he had always done his best thinking while relaxing. Two nagging questions still stirred in his mind: Would Sakamoto know about the mystery man? Would Monique's wealth prevent her from loving him as he loved her?

Nippon towers rose majestically in the Asian sky somewhere in south-central Honshu, and its glass windows shone in the afternoon like an obelisk. Spence wondered why the address was here and not in proper Tokyo, but the cabdriver knew the company location.

A cab stopped at the front entrance of a tall, glass building. The smallish cabby ran around the hood and opened the back door for his patron. Spencer unfolded his lanky body out the door towering above the cabby.

"You're sure this is the right address?"

The cabby went ballistic. Animated arms gyrated; his voice chattered something in Japanese, all the while one hand pointed at the shiny building. Spencer hunched his shoulders, casually wagged is head. He overpaid the cabby just to satisfy him.

The tall, glass building reflected the long shadows of afternoon, the sun hung low in the western sky mirroring Mount Fujiyama in its reflection. The streets were jammed with compact cars, bicycles, and mopeds, a few compact cars. The familiar noise engendered by a western occupation permeated the atmosphere, lights, food, loud music, videos on large outdoor screens.

Spencer entered the front lobby and found the elevators located beyond the information desk. The sprawling lobby rose a majestic forty feet enclosed with vaulted double-paned glass panels. Spencer stood in a crowd of people who patiently waited for the elevator, but never allowed his eyes to stop its roving.

In sudden amazement, he spotted the mystery man reading a newspaper on the opposite side of the lobby. Just as suddenly he lost the man in the maze of people that crowded around him. The moving crowds wiggled toward the elevators and squirmed through the lobby in a moving mass of humanity, but Spencer pushed inside the elevator cabin at the earliest opportunity. The mystery man suddenly lunged from nowhere and squirmed into the elevator, side-stepping to the rear corner. Spencer craned his neck, an attempt to see the man who stood somewhere in the back but couldn't see his face, nor could he even turn in the packed group, but he caught a brief recognition of a wide-brim hat that covered the man's face.

The doors finally opened, and the exiting crowd staggered like penguins and bumped along Spencer's body, although the mystery man had not gotten off. The man crammed behind several passengers, and Spencer only knew the man had not exited as the doors closed. He dashed upstairs, all the while hoping to catch him when he exited. But when the doors opened on the next floor, the man wasn't in the elevator. Spencer took the stairway to the next floor, hoping he might find the man in some dark corner. But no such luck. He pounded a fist into an open palm. Just once he'd like to cram his knuckles into the mystery man's face.

On the next floor he opened a door labeled 'Yamato Aeronautics. He found himself in an open area with dozens of desks in small cubicles lined row-after-row. Busy Asian engineers faced their computer consoles fingering the keys like concert pianists. Clicking sounds of busy keyboards echoed over the cubicles like tickertape machines.

"May I help you?" a cute Japanese receptionist asked in fluent English.

"Oh, uh, yes! Is Mr. Sakamoto available? He's expecting me."

She glanced down at her itinerary. "You're Mr. Jenson, who called early this morning?"

"Yes."

"One moment, please," she said with a slight bow, and addressed an intercom. "Mr. Jenson from Chevet Energy is here to see you, sir."

A long pause persisted. "Send him in," said a voice on the intercom, again in English. She pointed to a brassy door in the far wall.

"Through that door, sir," she replied.

Spencer rehearsed his questions as he strode the long distance. He gripped a brass knob, and the door swung open into a large, executive suite. A distinguished Asian executive sat behind a glass-top mahogany bureau. The Asian stood as Spencer approached the desk.

"Mr. Jenson," Asahara Sakamoto said, bowing politely. "How may I help you?"

Spencer minced no words despite his politeness. "I want your testimony on this story that leaked to the press," he said and handed him a news clipping.

"I see. Won't you please sit down, Mr. Jenson," he said in a quiet voice while he glanced at the news clipping. "I have this same clipping in my files."

"Can you tell me who leaked this story?"

Sakamoto settled into his chair. "I'm afraid not. I certainly did not," he replied with his hands pressed together finger to finger.

Spencer leaned forward in his chair, two pair of eyes met across the desk like opposing daggers. "Then who did? You must know something about this."

Sakamoto acquiesced. "I cannot be sure, you understand, but the Yakuso has many eyes and ears in Japan."

"Yakuso," Spencer asked as he sank back into his chair?

"A Mafia group operating in the islands; they are interested in acquiring spent nuclear material from which to make dirty bombs for sale to terrorists groups. It is a very lucrative market, you know."

"Let me get this straight. You're saying the Mafia released that story?" Spencer returned, traumatized by a vision of a Mafia mystery man who had followed him.

"I am only inferring. Someone broke into my office about two weeks ago. They could have copied my files on the launch of those two rockets."

Spencer's face exploded with questions. "Did you say two rockets?" he gasped!

"Yes. Two, launched thirty days apart," he puzzled.

As Spencer sat gaping, Sakamoto opened a locked file drawer and rustled through several papers. He opened a file, laid it on the glass top and read: "Uranium 233 waste, one thousand drums, on the first rocket, and Plutonium 239 waste, two thousand drums on the second."

Spencer gulped, desperately assimilating the meaning, indeed, the consequence of this horrible discovery.

"Tell me uh—how did you manage to launch such massive weights?"

"First, Mr. Jenson, I must tell you that I did not launch the waste. It was my father, Mikki

Sakamoto, who negotiated with Jacque Chevet in October of 1982."

"But the records, do they show the launch vehicle?"

Sakamoto leafed through the file of several pages. "They used two Vostok-K boosters that the corporation purchased from Russian black market."

"The Moon Booster?"

The Asian's head nodded, although he still scanned the pages of a set of engineering drawings for design changes. "Yes, it was stripped down to the instrument unit and booster engines, with a longer cylinder section for drum storage. The company built specials fairings that surrounded the drums which were strapped to the superstructure."

"Then the tracking transponders were removed, too?"

He read further. "The drawing shows no tracking gear," Sakamoto answered, spinning around the blueprint.

Spencer gazed over the instrument package and looked for the guidance computer. "Then they didn't perform a midcourse correction?"

"Apparently not, the customer made the decision not to contact the launched package."

"I'd say the flight program went for a looping orbit around the sun," Spencer concluded.

"Probably, that kind of booster power would send the rocket directly into the deep solar system."

Chapter 22

SPENCER FLAGGED a taxi cab, his mind still lingered back in Sakamoto's office viewing the blueprints. He slumped in the backseat not even remembered that he had told the driver the address. The cab drove off through the narrowed, crowded streets, his direction headed twistingly to the airport. Although tired and perplexed, Spencer squirmed against the back window in a soft position. His troubled thoughts were on a second rocket still in orbit somewhere in the planetary system.

The cab finally cleared the city traffic and raced along a wide stretch of open land bordered by a chain-link fence. In the shadowy distance of evening, Spencer saw the terminal lights of the airport but his mind continued its probing questions. Where is that second rocket hidden? Who is the mystery man? He released a deep sigh of carbon dioxide from his lungs and refilled with new air. And how is my dear Monique progressing? He thought.

He retrieved his cellphone and punched a button; a tone buzzed twice, then clicked. "Jean-Pierre, how is Monique?"

"She's progressing just fine, Mast—uh, Spencer."

The familiar sound of Jean-Pierre's voice somehow cleared Spencer's mind reinforced by the good news. "Oh, that's just great, Jean-Pierre! I'm headed for the airport now, should be taking off in a few minutes. We should be in Paris by midmorning, Paris time."

"I'll tell Monique. Thank you for calling, sir."

Spencer offered a plea from his heart. "Watch over Monique, Jean-Pierre, she's in a delicate position."

"I will, sir. Was your trip fruitful?"

"A bell-ringer, Jean-Pierre," he replied to a confused valet puzzling over American slang.

The cab stopped at the main terminal, and Spencer overpaid the cabby without the usual squabble. His tall frame assisted a look over the milling crowd through the glass windows. The sleek corporate jet sat on the Chevet private tarmac all fueled and ready for a fast trip back to Paris. Spencer rushed thought the lobby, and raced to the tarmac striding next to the waiting the pilot. He opened the jet door with a smile.

"Buckle up, Mr. Jenson. We're cleared for takeoff."

The private jet taxied down the runway, streaming upward into a star laden sky. Spencer sat next to the window looking out at the broad, expansive horizon. The Lear jet turned through its prescribed corridors, and snaked out of the crowded airspace. They finally climbed into their assigned highway at thirty-six thousand feet, vectoring toward the European continent.

The stars suddenly burst into striking brilliance. Gazing out into the Orion constellation, Spencer's mind drifted back to his high school days. Many nights he'd wandered out in the Kansas wheat fields and lay on his back sucking a straw, looking at the stars stretched majestically horizon to horizon.

Sometimes he lay there all night, just watching for a meteor shower. Those early formative years had won him his scholarship to Stanford University. Youthful ambition drove him into the doctorate program under the tutorship of Dr. Randall. The name Randall sent terror through his mind. Omigosh! He'd forgotten his call to Dr. Randall, he thought.

He pulled out his cellphone though he'd not realized the differences in time zones. The phone buzzed and buzzed through a myriad of satellite channels, searching for an open link. A buzz and a click; a connection was finally made, but the party still had not answered—suddenly an answer.

"If this is not the President, you have three seconds," a yawning voice said.

"Dr. Randall it's me, Spencer!"

He popped upright in the bed, reaching for the lamp switch. "Spence, my boy, wondered when you might call."

"Just listen carefully, sir. I have little time and vital information. There are two rockets—two, not one!"

"Two?" blurted out the professor as he threw the covers off his body and sat up on the bedside.

"That's according to Sakamoto at Yamato Aeronautics in Tokyo."

"You'd better come home, son. I'm going to need you. Things are really going ballistic here."

"I know, sir. The news is full of doomsday stories over here, too."

"When can you leave, Spence?"

"Monique needs me right here for a couple of days, sir, she's been shot."

"What? Holy Mother of God! Is she all right?"

"Nothing too serious I'm told."

"What's going on over there, Spence?"

"I'm not totally sure, but it seems there's a conspiracy underway to seize control of Chevet Energy by extortion, hostile takeover, and now attempted murder."

"Better let the police handle this, Spence."

"Inspector Parquet is on the case, sir. Soon as Monique can travel we're coming home. Oh, and sir. You were right about U-(233) being on the first rocket; it's the light-water breeder, uranium-thorium variety. The second rocket is loaded with two-thousand drums of plutonium 239; it's the decaying variety generated in a fast-breeder process."

Randall's forehead wrinkled, as he closed the phone and sank back into the bed.

"Why does bad news never come in small doses," he mused as he sucked on an unlit pipe. Spencer had supplied another cog in this wheel of mystery, and now the world was faced with double jeopardy: two rockets, not one.

The jet finally touched down on the runway in Paris. The Charles De Gaulle Airport basked in the morning sunlight although its brilliance was dispersed in a few clouds. Airliners were moored at every available Jetway, and after a few turns on taxiways, the jet finally reached the private tarmac of Chevet Energy. Spencer roused from a dozing sleep, stretching his arms skyward with a deep yawn.

"Just keep your hands up, Jenson," the pilot barked, pressing a Berretta against his temple.

Spencer's eyes narrowed, his mind rapidly sorted events.

"What the hell, you . . . you're the extortionist." His body coiled like a rattlesnake. "You shot Monique!"

"You two lovebirds just had to come along and gum up the works, didn't you?"

Spencer could see it all clearly now. The pilot was the mystery man. He probably had ransacked Sakamoto's office, too, and released the story to the press.

His anger turned to wisecracks. "What'll we do now, bubba? You hold all the cards," Spencer responded with malice in his eyes, rage in his heart.

"Shut up," he snapped, waving the Beretta. You're going to be my ticket out of here."

Chapter 23

TWO MEN GOT off a parked Lear jet at Chevet Energy's private tarmac adjacent to the Charles De Gaulle Airport. They approached from the aircraft's shadows into the brilliance of the morning sunlight, their backs to the sun. The distant glare made their faces unclear.

Suddenly a black limousine pulled to the curb and parked illegally, hazard lights flashing. Monique sat in the backseat, overly excited. Her wounds were tightly bound with surgical tape, pain desensitized by drugs. Her physician had warned her to stay immobile. However, the prospect of seeing Spencer had electrified her desire to go with Jean-Pierre to the airport. Without another thought she stepped from the limo. Jean-Pierre supported her with his long arms, and her face registered obvious pain as she twisted through the crowds. A technician offered a wheelchair, but Monique denied it.

She and Jean-Pierre rounded the corner of the private tarmac, the sunlight in their eyes. In her excitement, she only saw the tall black shadow of the man she loved. She collapsed into Spencer's arms and hugged him with all the waning strength the tight bandages allowed. She said nothing.

Words were inadequate to express her emotions. Jean-Pierre stood huffing and puffing, his alert eyes recognized a gun in Spenser's hand, but the pilot's hands were tied behind his back. Question marks flashed on the valet's wrinkled forehead.

"What's this about, sir?"

The uncertainty of the location of the second rocket had numbed his hearing.

Although he heard the valet's voice, he could only smile with Monique in his arms.

Jean-Pierre persisted with his question. He had known the pilot for several years and now he was Spencer's prisoner.

Spencer released Monique who threw her arms around his waist. He explained the sordid trip, including his brush with the pilot. How he'd wrestled the gun from the nervous man without too much effort. He wasn't a professional killer, probably never even killed a snake. When the pilot had learned that Monique was alive, he logically decided that turning states evidence outweighed a charge of attempted murder. He concluded his explanation.

"And so the riddle is solved, I think. Your pilot here planned the whole thing."

"He shot Monique?" Jean-Pierre screamed; adrenalin surging into his cholesterol laden arteries.

"Yes and probably conducted a little extortion, too," Spencer added.

Monique whirled to the pilot with eyes ablaze. She slapped his face, winced at the sudden pain that traumatized her side. "You . . . you—you're fired!"

Spencer pulled Monique into his arms. "He'll pay, honey. Save your strength," he grinned.

Her fiery eyes lowered, revenge vanished as she wrapped her arm around Spencer's waist and laid her dizzy head on his chest. Her strength was gone, trapped by her pain. "Oh Spence darling . . .

take me away from all this," she whispered in his ear.

Spencer's heart swelled with reassuring hope but the image of a second rocket loomed in his cortex like an avenging devil. Finally he faced the faithful valet. "Where is Inspector Parquet, Jean-Pierre?"

Before the valet replied, a man with a black mustache and cane emerged from the shadows. "And what do we have here?" Parquet asked, waving his cane.

Spencer's exhausted body relaxed at last. "It looks like this pilot is your man, Inspector."

Parquet nodded and greeted Monique, and then turned to Spencer as he stroked his mustache. "Good work. We have another man down at the police station. He could be an accomplice. It is not likely this man acted alone. You must come with me to press charges, Spencer. And bring along your prisoner."

Spencer nodded at the valet. "Jean-Pierre, will you take Monique back to the hospital? I'll finish this thing and get back to you." He suddenly kissed Monique. "See you later, honey," he said shaking his head. "Gosh you look good to me."

She smiled alluringly, weak, dizzy, and disoriented from the pain medicine. Oh, how she loved this gentle man. She managed a weak whisper. "I'm not staying in that blasted hospital, you know."

As Parquet drove the car along the freeway with the bound pilot in the backseat, Spencer's tired mind reflected on the second rocket. He wondered if Dr. Randall had discovered the plutonium's orbit. There were so many dismal questions that must be faced. He longed to be back at Wilcox.

Parquet glanced through the rear mirror and steered the car left at the next light. "So Jenson, what did you learn at Yamato Aeronautics?"

Spencer sighed. "We've got bigger problems than anyone imagined."

Parquet nodded. "I warned you this might be the case, but surely things are not so insurmountable that your American whiz-kids at NASA cannot solve, or Dr. Randall."

This guy knows everything, he thought. "There's a second rocket somewhere in space, loaded with plutonium waste."

Parquet's eyes squinted but he never flinched or turned his head. His white knuckles tightly gripped the steering wheel, beady eyes stared straight ahead. "Maybe it's headed into deep space," he wistfully replied.

"Don't count on it. The gravity of the sun is too great."

"Then there's nothing to worry about; perhaps it has already hit some other planetary object, nonetheless, just a little inconvenience for this planet like the first rocket."

"That may be a comforting viewpoint but hardly scientific."

The exhausted young man dozed, but struggled against the mounting desire to sleep. He paid no attention to the direction, neither the cars that whizzed by, nor the historic scenery nestled along the fairway. Spencer was too tired, too depleted. Parquet's judgment offered him some relaxation and he realized now that European policemen were often mysterious and closed-mouth. Finalization of this sordid matter was all he cared about, all he dreamed about. He wanted to return to the Wilcox, to the U.S.A. And yes, he had decided to ask Monique to come to America with him.

The police car finally pulled up to an old vacant building and stopped. Parquet got out of the sedan, and pointed his pistol at Spencer who dozed against the door. "This is where you get off, Mr. Jenson."

Spencer's eyes fluttered open, startled by the muzzle pressed against his forehead, but somehow not surprised, for this had been a day of surprises.

"You're in this, too!" But Parquet's malicious smile answered his question, and the situation was not advantageous. "Why you slimy bastard," Spencer growled.

"The odds have changed, Jenson. You changed them, and now you must pay. Get out," he replied as he pointed the pistol.

He opened the back door and untied the prisoner with the muzzle in Spencer's back. "Take him inside," he ordered the sneering pilot.

A single bulb illuminated a dim and empty space. Spencer sat on a wooden crate with his hands tied behind his back, his knees under his chin. The room was empty except for a few boxes and debris scattered on the floor. Some window panes were broken out, a straw broom stood in a cobweb corner, a mouse wiggled into a hole. A dog's howl in the distance caught his ear. What seemed an obvious truth at the precarious moment struck him with an embarrassing force of damaged pride. He couldn't believe he had underestimated Parquet. He didn't even suspect the pilot.

The pilot paced back and forth before the prisoner like a nervous panther that contemplated his dinner. Sweat beaded on his brow. The task of execution troubled him immensely. The gravity of the matter seized his conscience. "I didn't sign on for murder, monsieur," the pilot confessed.

Parquet laid the point of his cane on the shoulder of the nervous man. "If you had done your job, he would be silenced now. You could have pushed him out of the jet. That's the easier way for a coward to kill a man."

The pilot gasped dryly, unsure of what to say to this man who had been his benefactor and arranged for his position at Chevet Energy as the corporate pilot. "I told you about the diary, even gave you all the information on Yamato Aeronautics. And what about that gold under the château—wasn't that enough?"

"You blundering idiot! After all I have done for you, gave you a chance to better yourself—better than I had at your age," he snorted, his eyes suddenly flashed red. "And I purchased stock in Chevet Energy on the strength of your advice, would have had controlling interest by now, if not for your incompetence. Give me that gun!" he ordered.

Parquet snatched the pistol from the pilot's hand and pressed the muzzle against Spencer's head. "I'll show you how to kill a man."

The pistol fired!

The startled pilot slumped to the floor in a puddle of blood. The gun had moved too fast for his reaction.

In the same instant, the door burst opened. A blinding flash of sunlight filled the room.

Parquet whirled and raised the pistol but Spencer surged from the crate and rammed his head into the inspector's stomach. The two bodies sprawled on the floor and wrestled for the gun like tumbling cats. Spencer corralled the gun with his foot and awkwardly kicked the weapon out of reach, all that could be done with his hands tied behind his back. Parquet's lame leg prevented his reach for the gun.

Claude Moreau rushed into the room, picked up the gun as he lifted the inspector from the floor. Spencer erected himself and stood with the blinding sunlight in his face.

Monique limped out of the brilliance and fell into Spencer's chest. "Oh, Spence, darling, thank heaven, you're safe!"

She hung on his neck, kissed him repeatedly. Spencer stood helpless with his hands tied behind his back. But he enjoyed the moment, contented and relaxed, still ached but unencumbered by the pain, the antidote hung around his neck. Her touch, her smile warmed his heart, a feeling that he'd learned to expect from this dear woman. The wound only hampered her mobility, not her emotions.

Monique whispered into his ear. "I told you that I would not stay in that hospital. It's where you are that I belong."

Tears flooded Spencer's eyes. Now he knew that she loved him, too.

Jean-Pierre untied Spencer's bonds, babbling more words than he'd spoken in three days. "Wish I were a younger man Spencer. If these actions continue, I'll have to take karate lessons."

Spencer wiped the sweat beaded on his brow and looked into the face of a man he respected, even admired. The valet had performed masterfully. At times he seemed too old, yet his spirit was young and viable. There was a vibrant man beneath his aged guise. Jean-Pierre had been but a young boy in the French underground during World War II, and yet he had been a father to Monique, too. Therefore, Spencer valued this man, esteemed it a privilege to know him, and would forever remain grateful to him.

"You *are* a young man, Jean-Pierre, young as you feel."

Claude tightened the bonds on the inspector's hands, and looked up at Spencer. "It was Jean-Pierre who became suspicious of Parquet, finally remembered his younger face when he had attempted to purchase the Chevet mansion."

"We'd give him a medal in America," Spencer replied, gazing into the valet's soft eyes and gently gripping his shoulder. He turned and faced the Chevet lawyer. "I've got to get a flight back to California immediately. Can you help?"

Claude snorted. "I know a judge who would like to take this man into custody. Load him into my car. I'll take care of him and the pilot's body, too. You folks can head to the airport," he said, as he pushed Parquet toward the car.

Spencer wasn't sure of the French law. "Is this legal? I mean, he can't wiggle out on a technicality. Can he?"

Claude threw back his head, suddenly laughing. "I'm an officer of the court. His fingerprints are on that gun, and the slug in the pilot's body will match ballistics," the lawyer explained. "A charge of first-degree murder will do nicely, I suppose."

Chapter 24

SPENCER FAILINGLY ATTEMPTED to reprogram his cluttered mind while Jean-Pierre drove the limousine to the De Gaulle airport, although nagging fatigue had made it difficult to concentrate, especially with Monique beside him in the backseat. So many things swirled in his tired brain recalling all the dismal events in Europe, yet nothing was dismal about Monique; he could wait to tell Dr. Randall. Reality stretched beyond his comprehension and created more questions than answers. Had Randall found the second rocket? What was its trajectory? And what were the drag coefficients? But as important as these questions were, none were as vital as the person seated at his side. Monique nestled in his chest, and he tightened his arms around her warm and slender body.

"Are you able to leave the corporation in Claude's hands?"

She smiled. "Now that the plot of hostile takeover is solved, Claude is the best man to handle the corporate image."

"And this trip back to America, do you really want to go?"

Her soft eyes looked into his expectant face. "Spence, darling, my life is where you are. This second rocket is more important than us both. We'll see it through together."

Spencer drew her shoulder under his right arm and kissed her, rubbed his hand up-and-down her warm back. Somehow he wished he held her for eternity, never released her again, and then the sun telescope flashed in his mind where it had relentlessly lingered and his final thought voiced.

"Dr. Randall must be in hog heaven looking for that needle in a haystack."

"But twenty years have passed," she responded with lingering remorse in the tone of her voice. "Why have those rockets just now appeared?"

"A little thing called apogee and perigee mixed with celestial mechanics."

Her pixy face wrinkled, this romantic man had lifted her from despondency again. "Give me that in your best English."

"Physics terms that describe the height and width of an elliptical orbit, apparently, the trajectory on launch required midcourse correction to hit the sun directly. Without course correction, the rockets went into a wide loop around the sun."

She frowned. "You mean those two rockets have been wandering in space for twenty years?"

"Not exactly wandering, it's a complex orbit, affected by every planet the rockets approach. The greatest pull is from the sun; at times the larger planets like Jupiter overcome the drag. It's a tug-of-war with gravity."

"It's Greek to me. You're as bad as Marquee."

"Who's Marquee?" he asked in a jealous tone.

"He's just another astrophysicist who tried to explain this terrible thing."

"An old beau," he queried, as the limousine motored through a green light.

"Nah, just someone who wanted my money," she replied, turning in her seat. "You never knew about the Chevet fortune."

Spencer gently nudged her cheek not cognizant that Jean-Pierre had told her about the gold, but of course he had, he thought.

"With those doe eyes of yours, who could see anything beyond? I like you just as you are, impulsive, like me, sometimes arrogant, like your grandfather. But still, I fell in love with you, Monique. I wouldn't ever want to change you. You're beautiful to me just the way you are."

Tears welled in her eyes. "Don't ever leave me, darling."

The sudden muffled ring of a cellphone vibrated on Spencer's belt, the sound camouflaged his beating heart. Reluctantly, he lifted the cellphone. "Spencer here," he said and winked at Monique.

A tiny voice responded. "It's Dr. Randall, Spence, just checking on Monique. How is she?"

"Sitting right here," he smiled, and handed the cellphone to Monique. "It's Dr. Randall," he whispered.

She pressed the phone against an ear. "Hello, Dr. Randall. How is my favorite stargazer?"

"Well," he chuckled. "I can see that you're doing just fine. I'm delighted . . . uh, Monique, I'd like to ask you a question, if I may?"

"Shoot—that's Spencer's word, you know."

"How to say this: I, uh, I made a mess of my marriage, even lost my son in the split up. Spencer is like my own son. And while you were here, I realized that you and Spencer were growing closer together. What I mean to say is . . . darn it, I'd like to consider you as my own daughter, Monique!"

"Why, Dr. Randall! I'm touched. You just hold on to that dream. Your daughter and your son are on their way to the airport now. We'll be there tomorrow in your, how you say, hog heaven—want to talk to Spencer?"

"Why, why—yes," he stammered and waited for Spencer's voice.

"She's a jewel isn't she, sir?" Spencer smiled.

"Spence my boy, how did you ever merit a girl like that?"

Spencer chuckled.

Randall sniffed.

"Listen Spence, neither me nor Goddard has been able to find that second rocket. I'm anxious to have you back here."

"I've missed Wilcox, too. Then there's no sign of the plutonium rocket?"

"Not yet," Randall replied. "Incidentally, I like that girl. Glad you brought her along."

"Right on, see you soon, Dr. Randall."

Monique wiggled her nose as Spencer closed the cellphone. "He's a sweet man," she said. "He must have led a lonely life, like me."

"He's a brilliant man. I've learned much."

She warmly snuggled under his shoulder as he pulled herself against his chest. "You and Dr. Randall can handle the astrophysics. I'll provide the encouragement. And darling, if you behave yourself, I might add some entertainment," she said with a sassy voice.

Spencer beamed. "Can't ask for a better arrangement; Randall by day, Monique by night."

She suddenly twisted around in his grasp, bangs swished across her forehead. Sparkling eyes stared into his ruddy face. "That midnight ride of your Paul Revere is true enough. But let me tell you about Lafayette. Your George Washington saw in Lafayette a brilliant military strategist. And I see Lafayette in your eyes, Spence. You're a fighter and so am I."

The limousine pulled to the curb of the airport terminal and stopped. "Here we are," Jean-Pierre announced.

They stepped out of the car and waited for Jean-Pierre to get the luggage. Monique took the valet's hand, unable to find the words. She stood on her tiptoes and kissed him on the cheek. "My dear ole friend, how will I ever repay you?"

Jean-Pierre placed her hand in Spencer's hand, as if he gave away a bride. "Just be happy, my child. That's all I need."

The valet placed his hand on Spencer's shoulder and winked with a rare smile. "You two enjoy your flight to America. And take good care of Monique, Spencer." As the couple walked into the terminal, Jean-Pierre bowed his head, and whispered a prayer. *And God did I not thank you for answering my prayer? Double thanks, Lord.*

Chapter 25

DR. RANDALL STUMBLED into his condo at high noon with an exhausted body, and peeled off his clothes. His tie fell across the chair. Both shoes flew under a table as he collapsed on the bed and pulled up the covers. His eyelids fluttered closed.

A sudden low-level beeping sound popped open his eyes. One eye squinted at his coat hanging on the back of a chair. He erected himself and slid off the bed. He stumbled to chair and fumbled for the cellphone. Although his head reeled from lack of sleep, he managed to punch the button.

"Dr. Randall?" the tiny speaker responded.

"Yes, this is Randall," he stuttered between yawns.

"Randall, this is Dr. Brown at NASA. Bo Stringer asked me to forward some information to you."

"What information, Dr. Brown?"

"Goddard has located the second rocket."

He quickly slumped into the chair, his mind awake and alert. "Where?"

"It appeared on the last Hubble digital picture we downloaded this morning. It's about ten million miles out, near the orbit of Venus, barely visible, obscured by the shadow of Venus. Darn lucky we found it."

Randall's fatigued muscles stiffened as he reached for his tie draped over the chair.

"That's super, Dr. Brown, fantastic work."

"The pictures are scanning now to your observatory e-mail address, along with the coordinates," he said, and paused, "there is one other observation."

Randall finished lacing his shoes. "Yes?"

"The 3-D computer imagery suggests that the rocket made a sweeping swing around the sun. Too bad it didn't have video equipment aboard, would've been colossal pictures."

"Yes. And curious wonder that it didn't collide with something out there, too."

Dr. Brown's bottom lip stiffened, his chin wrinkled. "The guys here in the center are taking bets that it'll hit the sun, just like the first rocket."

Randall stared at the sleepy man in the mirror, and swept his fingers through thinning hair, the cellphone pressed to an ear.

"It isn't over until the fat lady sings, doctor. It did manage to avoid planets and asteroids for the last twenty years," he dropped the comb, "have you called the President?"

"Not yet. Bo wanted me to check with you first."

Randall fought his fatigue. "Listen, Dr. Brown. You and I both know our chances of stopping that rocket are thin as my hair. I suggest that you give Bo Stringer all the slack you can. His shuttle crews are our best bet. In my mind, they may be our only hope."

A silence hummed over the line.

"Bo Stringer is a good man. He'll think of something. Trust me."

"The people of the entire planet trust us Dr. Brown. Thank you for the tip. As soon as I see the data, I'll call you."

Randall put down the phone gazing at the calendar posted on a corkboard. Time was the enemy. Wagging his head, he gathered papers scattered over his home office desk and rushed into the garage. The garage door opened with a push on a remote.

As Randall zipped down the freeway, he reflected upon the second rocket as he tried to imagine what a one-two punch would do to Sol's stomach. Where's that rocket going on a slingshot swing around the sun, he thought? He punched a preset number on his cellphone, while continuing his thoughts. Now that Spencer was back from Europe, maybe they could decipher that rocket's orbit.

"Put on a pot of coffee, Spence. We've found the second rocket!"

Spencer's tan face grinned from ear-to-ear. "One cup black coming up, sir."

Randall burst into the observatory threw off his jacket and tossed his briefcase on his desk as he loosened his tie. His eyes quickly saw the mail and a few documents on the desk, but where was the e-mail?

"Where's that coffee, Spence?" he asked as he picked up an e-mail lying in a basket.

"Right here sir."

He took a sip of steaming coffee while shuffling through the photos. Randall sat the mug on the table as he gripped a data sheet and scanned the columns of numbers. Riveted eyes read the coordinates from the tabulation of numbers, and suddenly he bounced up the gantry steps like a giddy kid. A touch of his trained fingers programmed the equatorial mount that held the 60-inch reflector telescope. The equatorial mount finally stopped on the exact coordinates. Randall stared into the eyepiece expectantly.

"Spence, plot the trajectory of this thing. The numbers are coming down now."

Spencer sat down at a console and gripped the mouse. The cursor double-clicked on an icon, and a window appeared on the monitor. He entered a code that actuated a stored series of equations.

Randall turned to Spencer while the computer crunched on the numbers.

"How's Monique, today?"

"She's got an appointment with a doctor this afternoon, should be the last visit. Her wound is healing just fine."

Randall nodded. "You know, we really haven't discussed your trip to Europe."

"Yeah, I just thought this second rocket was more important."

"Well, it is. But you're important, too, Spence."

His head wagged embarrassingly. "I talked with Claude Moreau yesterday, he's Chevet Energy's new president. The courts have indicted Inspector Parquet on two counts of extortion and second-degree murder, plus an embezzlement charge. Seems he stole money from the police coffers to purchase Chevet stock. In fact, they have arrested a ring of Parquet's men."

"You sure fell into a hornet's nest."

"Yes, but Monique is the one who was stung.

Randall rolled his eyes to the bowl of his pipe and lit the tobacco with a few gentle sucks on the stem. A cloud of aromatic smoke exited his mouth, and he watched it curl to the ceiling. He shifted the stem to the corner of his mouth.

"She seems like a sharp girl, certainly has lots of determination."

"She thinks a lot of you, Dr. Randall."

"Well, the world owes her a great deal of thanks for having the courage to step forward with this information."

Spencer nodded as he refocused on the console, eyes suddenly narrowing. "Dr. Randall! Better take a look at this. That thing is not heading for the sun."

Randall leaned over Spencer's shoulder and gazed at the monitor.

"Hum. See what you mean. Let's see if we can estimate the decay rate of that orbit."

Randall approached another console, and punched in three codes to bring down the data from the microprocessor attached to the motorized mount. Several punches on the keyboard activated the coprocessor output. The computer hard drive churned and crunched digital numbers into gigabytes of information.

A window flickered on screen. Randall hit a key and a chart of the solar system overlaid the plot that showed the trajectory in real time. His eyes popped wide open as he fumbled for his spectacles that still sat on his head. A curious silence slipped by his mind as if a millennium, while they both studied the plot.

Then time seemed to stand still.

Randall aggressively chewed his pipe stem. Spencer sat in amazement mentally calculating. Randall finally sat down at a keyboard, still thinking. He entered several codes. The computer crackled and hummed as if protesting the command. Greek symbols flashed across the monitor involved in long, complicated equations. A series of numbers finally appeared in rows of tabulations.

"I've computed the sun's drag on the rocket's orbit," Randall reported.

The program flashed through a series of windows. A trajectory plot appeared on the screen.

Faces grimaced.

Spencer gasped. "It looks like it's bending into a collision course with the earth!"

Silence—the aggravated type.

Randall removed his pipe as his mind rapidly computed a maze of numbers. "I'd say about 28.5 days before impact," he whispered.

Randall's Hotel Room
Rockville, Maryland

Chapter 26

GRIFFIN ENTERED THE parking lot of Randall's hotel about high noon and went straight to his room. Randall had called him earlier, and had already placed a disk on his computer that featured a widescreen as Griffin entered the room.

"Great Jehoshaphat! Griffin exclaimed as he reviewed Randall's plots of the plutonium rocket's trajectory. "You're sure about the computations?"

"Absolutely," Randall responded.

Griffin massaged his chin thinking aloud. "Not much time, is there?"

"It'll be close, that's for sure."

"I came directly to Washington anticipating a taskforce meeting when I received your call, but LaCroix is out of the country," Griffin remarked with his eyes glued to the plots.

"Then we'll have to tell the President."

"Yeah, and I've got to catch a plane to the Cape," Griffin replied as he grabbed his briefcase. "I'll do some homework during flight and call you in about two hours to see how it went with the President."

Randall only nodded as Griffin left the hotel room, and quickly punched a private code into his cellphone. He cradled his pipe with the phone against his ear. The words just had not materialized as he hoped. The President had asked to be in the loop for all information but this was devastating. The cellphone buzzed twice and clicked.

"Office of the Chief of Staff—how may I direct your call?"

"This is Dr. Bruce Randall. Could I speak with the President?"

"Please hold, Dr. Randall."

The phone buzzed, and then a voice spoke.

"Dr. Randall, this is Andrew Evans. How can I help you?"

"It's imperative that I speak with the President, Andrew."

"I see. Hold on, Dr. Randall."

A moment dragged by like an hour as Randall tried to find the words, only thoughts materialized, thoughts that no President should hear. How would the President respond to this report, fresh on the heels of the first rocket? Was there really anything anyone could do on such short notice, he thought

"This is Winston Darcy, Dr. Randall."

"Mr. President. I'm deeply sorry to interrupt your schedule."

"Nonsense, Dr. Randall. What's on your mind?"

"Since General LaCroix is out of the country, Colonel Griffin and I agreed that you ought to know what we've discovered."

"Yes, I'm expecting a call from LaCroix when he arrives in Israel. Now what is it you wish to tell me, Dr. Randall?"

"Sir, that second rocket Goddard located—"

"Yes!"

"I'm afraid it's on a collision course with the earth, sir."

Agonizing silence gripped the Oval Office as the President rose from his chair and gazed out the window into the rose garden. It was his personal therapy in times like this that he usually watched the insects as they buzzed around the roses. President always stood with his hands clasped behind his back, his stance before he made an important decision. Finally he strode three steps to the desk and punched the conference button.

"You're sure about this, Randall?" he replied almost in a whisper, not as a question but a confirmation.

"There is no error, sir. I'll fax the photos and computations."

"How long before impact, would you say?"

"About twenty-eight days, sir."

More silence.

"Well," Darcy groaned with a deep sigh. "You and Griffin continue your investigation. I'll have the Pentagon alert LaCroix. And Randall, keep this confidential until we can decide on a course of action."

"Yes, Mr. President."

The White House office of General LaCroix seemed small and cramped with maps and strange objects scattered about the room. He'd just returned from Israel and had canceled his meeting with the Security Council, after a call from the Pentagon. While somewhere over the Atlantic on his return trip, LaCroix had instructed his staff to schedule Dr. Randall and Colonel Griffin for an emergency conference in his office at the insistence of the President.

His staff had located Griffin at the Cape in Florida. Randall was in Rockville, Maryland where he had spent the afternoon rechecking his computations at the Goddard Solar Center in Bethesda. After his meeting with the director, Randall checked out of his hotel room, and drove a rental car down the Washington Expressway to the Pentagon. Colonel Griffin had taken the first flight back to Washington. Bo Stringer's secretary reported that Stringer was in Japan where they were discussing a joint venture in space, a plan that Stringer knew was doomed to failure. All outgoing aircraft were grounded because of an unusual storm that had flooded the airports. Bo asked to be reached by conference call unless he could be briefed when he arrived.

The taskforce sat around a conference table deep in the Pentagon. The battle-hardened Joint Chief gazed across his desk at Dr. Randall and slightly grinned. "The news media seems to be revising their opinion of you, Dr. Randall. You're the talk of Europe."

"Yeah, not long ago I was a crackpot. Today, I'm a nutcracker."

"We've got a helluva' nut to crack now," Colonel Griffin sighed, having arrived an hour before Randall.

"What's the trajectory look like today, Grif?"

Griffin pulled a fistful of papers from his briefcase. "As the gravitational forces stand right now, that plutonium rocket should impact earth in about twenty-six days."

"Hell, you're not implying it might change trajectory are you?" LaCroix barked.

"After it clears the gravitation of our moon, the earth's gravity will grab it. But we have no exact numbers on the rocket; we won't know the degree of change until that happens."

The feisty old General chewed down on his cigar and wistfully pondered his briefing with Winston Darcy at an early morning breakfast in the White House. He was somewhat pissed because Stringer was out of pocket. Yet the secretary was ready to connect a conference call if desired. He removed his cigar.

"The President wants a realistic assessment of what will happen when this thing hits earth's atmosphere?"

Griffin nodded. "You've seen the heat shields on the Apollo capsule and the ceramic tiles on the Shuttle nosecone. Well, sir, this rocket has no heat shield."

His eyes squinted. "Won't it just burn up on reentry?"

Griffin faced the General thinking he had better clarify the situation; this general had a short fuse like no other commander he had ever served under.

"The angle of reentry will bounce the rocket around because of its center of gravity. The booster engines will become the heat shield, sir. The mounting heat of reentry will explode the waste drums somewhere above, or in, the Pacific, depending on how long the booster shielding holds."

LaCroix grunted, chewed down on his cigar. "Are we dead sure this thing will splash into the Pacific?"

Randall removed the pipe from his mouth. "It's a fairly safe bet according to the computer model," he said, thinking. Randall thumped the pipe stem on his notepad. "Yes General LaCroix, it will hit the Pacific."

"I hope you're right, Randall. There will be hell to pay if any part of that superstructure hits a populated landmass."

Randall stoked his pipe with a pair of nail clippers. "That's not the worst of it General. If it does impact one of those Pacific islands, the force would set off a massive earthquake and initiate a tsunami. We might even see the eruption of Mount Fujiyama, Mount Aloha, plus many other dormant volcanoes in the Pacific Ring of Fire. The undersea volcanic ridge would crack open along the Mariana Trench, spilling out magma. In such an event, the seas would boil for hundreds of miles around the blast. There wouldn't be a living thing left alive for a thousand miles along that trench."

Faces became solemn. Brains churned. Colonel Griffin finally broke the deathly silence. "There's too much we're unsure about, to start postulating gloom and doom. How much plutonium waste are we really talking about, Dr. Randall?"

Randall puffed aromatic smoke, eyes staring into the distance, "Two thousand drums," he rocked forward in his chair and removed his pipe, "but, gentlemen, there is another danger. Radioactive particles will soar upward from the blast, and enter the troposphere. From there a surge of particles will follow magnetic lines to the poles."

LaCroix absorbed Randall's assessment while he stirred in a stack of papers on his desk. He finally found a file and laid it opened. He quickly moved his nicotine-stained finger down a column of numbers printed on a nuclear mass/weight conversion chart. His finger stopped at one set of numbers.

"The active plutonium waste in two thousand drums would weigh about forty thousand pounds roughly, plus the weight of inactive mass, empty drums, capping water, and superstructure. That's about a hundred and fifty tons in payload," he calculated as he looked up from the chart. "Who had a booster in 1982 with enough thrust to lift that thing into space?" but LaCoix he knew the answer.

"The Russians, of course," Griffin replied. "The Vostok can lift two hundred and eighty seven tons, sir."

"Yes General, but that's twenty tons of fissile plutonium," Randall reminded him.

"That's a helluva bomb, all right," the General reasoned as he wagged his head.

Randall stood, not convinced the General really understood the seriousness of the problem. "Gentlemen, we're wasting time. We have a target and a mission, so let's get to it," Randall barked.

LaCroix surprisingly nodded in agreement. "There aren't any earth-based rockets that could intercept that thing in outer space. We'd have to have a rocket in orbit with restart capability."

Heads turned. "There is one possibility, sir," Griffin announced as heads whirled around like fans watching a tennis match.

LaCroix balanced a fresh cigar between his fingers pointing directly at Griffin. "We're all ears, Colonel."

"The Shuttle is in orbit now. In her cargo bay is an experimental unit that might do the trick," Griffin speculated.

"What experiment, Colonel?"

"A solar-powered laser cannon, sir. She's dubbed SPLC."

LaCroix's wrinkled face suddenly erupted. "A damn pea shooter, Colonel, there's no laser capable of exploding that rocket," he growled, his teeth gnashed his cigar.

Griffin dared not launch a rebuke, but the General had no knowledge of celestial mechanics. "We don't have to destroy it, General. Just bump it off course," he replied with a slight grin.

Randall's eyes bloomed as he bounced from his seat, gratified that he finally heard information he could work with. "That's it Grif! We alter its trajectory! Can this laser withstand solar wind protons?"

Grif seemed startled at Randall's quick assessment. "That's a question for Bo Stringer and his engineers," he inserted.

General LaCroix's mind locked on the laser cannon. "How does that thing work, Colonel?"

Griffin ran his long fingers through his hair, rethought every angle on the engineering drawings, the test results, the revisions, and finally related them from his memory. "The SPLC is equipped with massive solar panels that feed into the generator, bringing the output up to giga-watt range. The turret that houses the laser cannon is computer-controlled from either the spacecraft or from Houston."

The Generals leathery face frowned. "But can it hit that rocket, Colonel?" the General barked.

Griffin bobbed his head. "Again, we'll have to ask Bo. She should pack a helluva wallop. But we've got to convince Bo Stringer."

"Humph. That's your job, Colonel. He left Japan four hours ago. See that you brief him on this meeting," the General commanded as he dusted the ashes from the cigar in an ashtray.

Chapter 27

KIM MARSHALL STAGGERED lazily into her townhouse after a frustrating afternoon. She had spent most of the day interviewing displaced people trying to put their lives back together. Her lead story for the telecast tonight involved human-interest situations arising during the solar maximum, and the ominous rocket that had plunged into the sun. As she entered the door, she heard the phone loudly ringing in her home office. She dropped the door keys in her open purse and ran toward her desk.

"Hello," she puffed.

"Is this Kim Marshall?" a voice asked.

"Yes it is. Who's calling, please?"

"Can't tell you that, Ms. Marshall, but you'll want to hear what I have to say."

"Not without a name."

"Let's just say I work in the Pentagon."

Her tanned face brightened. "I'm listening."

"It's too important to discuss over the phone—could you meet me at the Lincoln Memorial in one hour."

"How will I know who you are?"

The phone went dead.

Kim gazed into space thinking about the mysterious caller. Was it a viable message, who really was the person? "Oh well, she thought aloud, "he did say he's in the Pentagon. Guess I'll follow up." Kim walked out of the office to the parking lot and got into her car. It would be a long night, she thought.

Dusk descended over the capital city as Kim parked her Jaguar below a grassy knoll just fifty yards from the Lincoln Memorial. Before she got out, she panned the grassy area looking for her contact. Not knowing what the caller looked like, she locked her car and climbed to the crest of a sloping knoll. Pockets of lingering tourists were milling around the park, taking their last looks at the historic monuments. Some were already boarding their buses and the crowd was thinning out.

A sudden evening breeze rustled the tree as she strolled toward the famous monument. Fruit blossoms were in bloom and released a hint of sweet aroma that floated over the Mall. Kim finally reached the Lincoln Memorial and entered the open rotunda. Her thoughts strangely digressed as she sat alone on a stone bench in the quiet shadows of the vacant memorial gazing at the historic stature.

Although she'd been in this very spot many times before the awesome statue of Lincoln consumed her awareness. Flashes of historic words from the Gettysburg Address curiously emerged from her mind. The phrases pounded her conscious as memory forced her reflection on the Civil War, and how this great nation had risen from the burning coals of conflict against the nation's own people: brother against brother. She'd seen that kind of patriotic resolve even today in the faces of countless Americans hammered into their minds by the solar maximum and the uranium rocket. They had faith in President Darcy; they'd seen his resolve before—so did she.

A near voice startled her revelry. "You're very punctual, Ms. Marshall."

She whirled. The voice belonged to a man of average height, maybe six feet, neatly dressed in sharply pressed trousers, and a windbreaker with open collar and a tasteful tie. He wore dark sunglasses that obscured his face. Kim's hazel eyes caught a glimmer of highly polished shoes with dangling tassels—expensive.

He sat down beside her, eyes staring straight ahead.

"You're the caller," she asked.

"Uh-huh."

"And what's this important information about?"

The informant faced the Lincoln statute as if rethinking his statement. "There's a second rocket in orbit."

"What!" she gasped and almost fell out off the bench.

"It's loaded with two thousand drums of plutonium."

Her eyes closed, her mind screamed in defiance. She struggled to regain her composure. "Heading toward the sun, I presume" she hedged.

The face behind the dark glasses remained silent for a moment. Teeth gnashed. Jaw muscles rippled a cleanly shaven face, wondering why or even if he should divulge this confidential information; yet, he reasoned that the public should know that the earth was in dire danger.

"I'm afraid not. It's on a collision course with the earth."

Kim dropped her hands in her lap; she sat numb and speechless, glued to her seat. Her moisture laden eyes gazed at the Lincoln stature, the image a shadowy blur. Her pulse elevated, the heartbeats rang in her ears like clanging bells. Her heart cried out within her chest, thumping with erratic beats. "NO! This can't be! Not another calamity," her mind screamed.

"I can't go on the air with hearsay."

The man produced an envelope from the inside pocket of his windbreaker. "Will this do?"

She took the envelope with morbid thoughts still sizzling in her subconscious. Nervously opening the flap, she pulled out a two-page document. The top sheet had the embossed imprint of official Pentagon stationery. The title caption identified the document as the minutes of the President's taskforce. The front sheet had the security stamp: 'Secret.'

She suddenly whirled to the man seated beside her with questions on her lips.

But the man had vanished!

Her glowing, red hair swished right, then left. She bounced from the seat, and ran outside the memorial. Only a few students were boarding a bus out near the Vietnam exhibit in the distance. The informant was nowhere in sight.

Kim released a deep sigh, and strolled to her car in a captivated daze, while reading the document over and over again. She finally unlocked the car door and slid behind the steering wheel, still in a trance. A glance at her wristwatch prompted her to drive to the TV station; there were documents in her files she must see.

Kim powered up the computer in her TV office, searching the files for a story she vaguely remembered but couldn't recall. Somehow she knew it had a bearing on the information in the taskforce minutes. She focused on a logo and double-clicked the mouse. Suddenly an article flashed on screen! Her hazel eyes speed-read the contents. A tensed face smiled, not from joy, but satisfaction in finding the article: *Neutron bomb and Plutonium fusion, alternative to uranium.*

"Good grief!" she barked.

Her journalistic senses reeled as steady fingers traveled the computer keyboard with remarkable accuracy. She knew next-to-nothing about nuclear bombs. Nonetheless, she quickly composed the lead story for tonight's news telecast. Her nimble fingers stopped at two paragraphs into the narrative, she had already decided that the human-interest story would have to wait.

Kim locked the Pentagon document in her desk drawer; her mind just couldn't release the devilish information. As she removed the key, an impulse seized her active thoughts. She punched an intercom button. "Brad, could you come by my office, please?"

She studied the copy for telecast but momentarily. Brad entered the office with a puzzled face. "What's on your mind, Kim?"

She handed him the computer printout on neutron bombs. His deep, penetrating eyes read the contents, and then gazed into Kim's glowing face. "What's this flesh-eating nuclear stuff about?"

"Remember that symposium I attended last month discussing neutron bombs and plutonium? Listen Brad, a neutron bomb attacks flesh, not buildings, or structures."

"And?"

She quickly unlocked the drawer and tossed the taskforce document on the table. "And this."

Again he did a cursory reading, but the explosive information about a second rocket surged into his mind with churning perplexity. "Who gave you this," he snapped.

She rocked back in her seat. "A man called me and identified himself as being from the Pentagon."

An eyebrow arched. "An informant—do you know his name?"

"No, but it's on official stationery, Brad," she persisted.

"It's classified Secret, Kim," he insisted as he tossed the document on her desk. "Can't let you air this flesh-eating neutron bomb stuff."

"Bu—"

"You're not an expert on neutron bombs, Kim. And you can't verify the source of that taskforce document. If there is a second rocket on a collision course with the earth, that's your story."

Kim slumped in her seat, quietly evaluating Brad's advice. "All right, then I'll sit on it. But if that taskforce doesn't inform the public about the payload on that rocket, I will."

Brad nodded. "Thanks, Kim. The public is worried enough. No need of stirring their misery."

Her ruby lips spread into a captivating smile. "You know, Brad. Should you ever leave the broadcast business, you'd make a good press secretary for the White House."

Brad chuckled under his breath. "Get out of here," he said with a jerk of his head. "You're on the air in ten minutes."

Technicians hurried around the set, checking mikes and loading the TelePrompTer. Kim Marshall sat at her news cubicle reading the modified press release, while a makeup technician touched-up her face and hair. The program manager raised a hand and pointed a finger at Kim. The camera light flashed red, a musical theme flooded the audible airwaves, and a logo filled the screen: WOFF ALERT!

"I'm Kim Marshall and this is Washington Drumbeat. The nightmare of the past few weeks is about to be eclipsed by a second rocket discovered by Goddard Space Flight Center. That's right. Another rocket is in orbit. WOFF NEWS has learned within the hour that Goddard is tracking a second rocket on a collision course with the earth. You heard correctly. The rocket will hit the earth. More details when we return. How does NASA fit into this new development? This is Kim Marshall reporting. Stay tuned to WOFF NEWS."

Phones began ringing in the newsroom. Kim's earpiece buzzed. "Kim, the White House is hysterical, you struck a nerve. We'll have to defend your report at ten thirty tonight. I've called the lawyers. You and that 'Secret' document have to be there," said a tiny voice.

Her face beamed. "To recap our exclusive story tonight: WOFF NEWS reports a second rocket is on a collision course with the earth at this very moment. Impact has been estimated by Wilcox Solar Observatory, and confirmed by Goddard Space Flight Center, to occur in twenty-six days.

We'll return with a special panel of nuclear experts after these messages. You're tuned to WOFF NEWS."

Within the same hour, news agencies around the globe picked up the WOFF telecast. The talk shows buzzed with expert discussion groups dissecting every morsel of the electrifying news. The world could be destroyed, humanity annihilated. That was the story of yellow journalism and tabloids.

Thick plate glass surrounded the sealed conference room at WOFF NEWS, although verbal sound still penetrated the three-ply panes. Rumbling voices reverberated from the conference room, starkly audible in the news bullpen. The night shift had just settled into their cubicles working on the late night news stories. They tried not to stare at the meeting, without too much success.

Brad Crenshaw, managing director of WOFF NEWS, sat beside the corporate legal advisor with his hands folded, watching the tempers of two lawyers clash like gladiators. Stinging words slashed the air like piercing swords. Kim Marshall sat silent, arms folded in her lap, her face smugly smiling.

"Release of that 'Secret' document is totally irresponsible!" the federal lawyer charged, pounding his fist on the table.

"Watch it, counselor! You're treading on freedom of the press," the WOFF lawyer countered.

"Freedom of the press—you must be joking! It's not just a question of national security. The whole damn planet is at risk here!" he snarled.

It was their fourth exchange of charges. Two opposing lawyers finally sat down, peering across the table with poker faces. The air slowly cleared, verbal dust settled. The audience on the opposite side of the glass went about their duties, hiding any awareness of the unfolding scene.

"Good grief, Brad. You know better than to release that document," replied the federal lawyer.

Brad rustled in his seat. "You know as well as I, that the only incriminating information in that document are the flesh-eating remarks about a neutron bomb. Kim's telecast purposely eliminated that information."

"I realized that, Brad. Your editorial staff does a better job of reporting the facts than most news agencies. Just wish you had cleared it before going on the air," he wistfully responded.

"It's a judgment call, counselor. The news of a plutonium rocket heading for Planet Earth cannot be hidden from the public, especially after that uranium bomb hit the sun."

"Can't argue with you there," he admitted. "The taskforce is concerned about a panic."

Kim sat quietly absorbing the conversation but could no longer hold her silence. "There's a fine line between inciting panic and withholding the news story of the millennium."

The lawyer rose from his chair, sternly poised. "The White House intended to hold a news conference, Kim."

"And Kim tipped your hand," Brad injected.

"Hell Brad. There's more to this story than you realize."

The corporate lawyer frowned, and faced the federal lawyer. "That excuse is so thin it's damn near invisible. There's always more to a story. News is today, now!"

"I didn't come to quarrel, but to reason. Andrew Evans is mad as I've ever seen him."

"Then let him vent his wrath on the man who leaked that document!" Brad defiantly suggested.

The federal lawyer adjusted his wire-rimmed glasses. "Don't you think we'd plug that leak if we knew the source?"

"You're not asking me to disclose my source, are you?" Kim argued, releasing her folded arms.

Brad squeezed Kim's shoulder, a warning not to speak. "Kim's informant concealed his identity. We don't know who he is, only that he works in the Pentagon, so he said."

The federal lawyer stared at Kim, beady eyes aligned with her powdered nose. But before he could speak, Kim stood.

"Counselor, I don't like stoolies any more than you. The best way to avoid a panic is to honestly inform the public."

The muzzled lawyer swallowed his response and said nothing, only wagged his head. He knew

Kim was right.   Glancing at his wristwatch, the lawyer slowly picked up his briefcase. Brad opened the door, and the lawyer turned, panning the silent adversaries sitting around the room.

"For what it's worth, personally I'm glad you broke the story, Kim."

He strolled through the maze of computers, every eye in the room quietly staring as he exited the front door.

Reporters in the news bullpen stood with exhilarating applause.

Chapter 28

BEYOND THE BLUE horizon reaching out above the clouds, the final fringes of the stratosphere had changed to a deep indigo hue. Solar I spacecraft hung suspended in the blackness of outer space, circling the earth in a two hundred mile orbit. In her cargo bay rested a secret experiment undergoing testing in the vacuum of outer space.

The crew was commanded by Scott Higgins and Dr. Trevor Wallace, the lead scientific advisor, both had been briefed on a second rocket in space by Houston. They knew their expertise would figure paramount in the precarious days ahead. The mission now was to make-ready the experimental device bolted in the cargo bay.

"Houston. This is Solar I."

"You're five-by-five, Solar I. Go ahead."

"We're having trouble adjusting the azimuth of the payload. The turret is jammed somehow in the vertical plane."

"Copy, Solar I, we're looking into it now," the flight director replied. He rotated in his chair and stabbed a pointing finger at Station #6.

Engineers huddled around a 32-inch monitor, assiduously punching keys on laptops and calculators. The brainstorming exercise lasted only about three minutes. The senior engineer finally spoke through his headphones. "It'll be a spacewalk, Scott. You've got to replace a receiving module."

The flight director leaned into his mike. "Confirm that, Solar I. Module E-16A has to be replaced."

"Roger, Houston. Replace E-16A module."

Scott and Trevor floated into egress positions dressed in moon suits. Scott opened the airlock on the egress chamber. They weightlessly floated into the chamber and locked the vacuum-seal door. The outside hatch finally opened with faint vibrations of escaping pressure. Both space walkers entered the open cargo bay. Their white suits contrasted with the darkness of space like diamonds on black velvet. Although the awesome reality of the vast universe could not be ignored, these astronauts were trained to concentrate on the mission.

Scott attached a lanyard to a hitch on the railing. His task was safety and assistance in a standard buddy system. Trevor moved along the handholds on the railing until he reached the instrument for repair. The weird sort of Gatlin gun bolted in the cargo bay was 'Top Secret.' It didn't use regular ordnance or any type of explosive projectile. The project name was Solar Powered Laser Cannon (SPLC), code name Blue Streak. The strange cannon looked much like a stovepipe studded with wavy heat sinks. The mechanism had only been activated twice while in space: once to verify the design, another to dry-run the operational program. Intensity of the laser beam in outer space was amplified ten-fold greater than its earthbound trials, mainly because of zero gravity and uninhibited solar energy feeding its power cells.

Trevor carefully attached his lanyard to a U-bolt and anchored his satchel. Suspended in space, he effortlessly floated around the SPLC until he spotted the defective module. He retrieved a spark-resistant spanner from the satchel and snugly fitted it over the module. The unit silently unscrewed from its socket with little resistance. Trevor crammed the defective module into the satchel, and grabbed the replacement.

"Check your oxygen," Scott warned.

"That's affirmative. O2 is low. Almost finished here," he gasped, pulling on the spanner.

"Okay. Check continuity," Trevor advised.

Scott flipped a toggle switch inside the spacecraft to 'VERIFY' mode. "It's okay. Good installation," he squawked though the intercom.

Trevor relaxed while he gathered his tools and freed the satchel from the attach point. He disengaged his lanyard and glided along the handholds on his retreat to the air lock. As he floated with the sun to his back, he raised his sunshade and peered into the blackness of deep space. Although the plutonium rocket was not visible with the naked eye from his location, he did see the Hubble just above the curvature of the earth. His mind flooded with a sea of questions, sparked by the message from Houston: How would they alter the mission? Could they stay in orbit with dwindling supplies of food and oxygen? Did they have enough fuel to descend to a lower orbit without risking deorbit?

Huston barked an order. "Solar I, we detect rising solar wind. Trevor, need you back inside the Shuttle."

"Roger, Houston, entering airlock now."

"Copy, start your sleep sequence, guys. Beddy-bye."

Chapter 29

TWO FORMER NASA astronauts were in conference at NASA/Houston, studying a potential problem with the orbiting Shuttle. Recent studies indicated that massive solar wind could disrupt communications with Solar I. Not only that, it posed a health hazard to astronauts aboard the Shuttle. Bo Stringer, the NASA Shuttle program manager, wrestled with a decision he alone could make concerning the safety of his crew in orbit.

"It's too risky to leave Solar I in orbit with that nuclear bomb out there," Bo advised.

"But that laser gun may be our only hope of altering its trajectory," Colonel Griffin rebutted.

"Those boys are my responsibility, Grif," he barked, pounding his fist on the table.

The air seemed to go out of the room. But before two friends could get caught up in the sudden change of pressure, Griffin moved the conversation back on point.

"And the American people are the responsibility of the President, Bo."

Griffin's statements deeply stung the program manager. Bo nervously doodled on a yellow legal pad, his mind wrestled with the many programs under his direction. He rested his elbows on the

184

table, methodically tapped his Cross pen on his index finger.

Griffin didn't interrupt Bo's thoughts. They'd once been teammates in the Gemini program, and he knew Bo was a whiz at logistics. He sat in stillness and patiently waited for Bo's response.

Bo finally dropped his pen on the writing pad and rocked back in his chair. "There may be an outside chance to achieve both goals." he said, rising from his seat and walking to an erasable board. "Suppose we program the Hubble mirror to reflect the laser beam onto the target?"

"You're going to cut a hole in Hubble tube?" Griffin goaded jokingly.

Bo remained silent as he replayed his thoughts. Several unchallenged ideas ran through his mind, but he needed a workable idea and soon. His face brightened in sudden awareness as he gripped a red marker and drew a sketch.

"I'm thinking we can move Solar I behind the earth to shield the astronauts from solar wind. And we can mount a mirror on the Hubble's outside tube to triangulate the SPLC laser beam from Solar I to the target."

Griffin's countenance mellowed, seeing the genius of Bo's plan—why had he ever misjudged this guy, he thought. "It just might just work. It'll take some fancy image targeting, but it can be done."

Bo nodded. "Okay, I'll run a program to determine where the sun/earth positions will be in this exercise. We'll need a good target window relative to the Hubble, Solar I, and that rocket. I think the angle will allow triangulation."

"It's pure genius, Bo. Go for it."

Bo's eyes kindled a spark gratified by the smile on his friend's face. "Okay. I'll authorize a team to begin work on the computer program and a crew to refurbish a launch pad. We'll send up a shuttle with the new equipment in its cargo bay."

"Maybe you could stage two shots by selecting the maximum window to activate the laser. That'll give you time for a second shot, just in case that rocket requires another kick."

Bo nodded as he gathered his papers. "Okay. You win, Grif. I'll ramrod this project myself."

"The President will be pleased, Bo."

"We're still having satellite problems. Can you call Dr. Randall and get the current trajectory numbers of that rocket?"

"I'll do better than that. I'm due to meet Randall this afternoon."

He stood and pushed his spectacles to the top of his head; only his engineers knew he used the things, and now Griffin knew, too. "That's it, then. I'm going to call Goddard and bring them up to speed on the Hubble's new mission. They're not going to like it."

Griffin chuckled. "Tell them we all need funding, and the President's watching this project, and by the way, I've known for years that you're farsighted."

Chapter 30

THE COUNTOWN STOOD at twenty-one days until the plutonium rocket would collide with the Earth. The trajectory of Rocket No. 2 progressively degraded as expected because of the sun's constant drag. Every major observatory on the planet had its astronomical eye trained on the rocket. The news media telecasted updates around the clock. The shocking news did not show in the faces of the people on earth, but it rocked the philosophical and religious beliefs of countless millions.

"Here come the latest figures, Grif. We can extrapolate a trajectory precise enough for target practice," Randall said puffing on his pipe.

"That's what the program manager asked for. Would you e-mail these numbers to the Shuttle directorate? Re: Bo Stringer," Griffin asked.

"Sure thing," he said flagging a secretary in the hall.

Grif pulled on an earlobe with thumb and index finger as he thought of a subject he wanted to mention.

"Randall, I've been doing some number crunching on that uranium/plutonium fission problem you mentioned the other day. It occurred to me that Japan's Institute of Space and Astronautical Science did some work on that question. It seems like they built a scale model breeder reactor for the experiment."

"Hum. I'll look into it. The only thing I remember about U-(233) is its half-life and peculiar action with U-(239) in a breeder reactor," Randall suggested

"I would get that e-mail off right away," Grif advised.

"Bo's a pretty ingenious fellow, isn't he," Randall remarked handing off the paper to the secretary.

"He could have the only solution to this calamity."

"My conclusions exactly, Grif," Randall admitted.

Spencer and Monique returned to the observatory about high noon, casually laughing about something which they had rarely done during this fretful search for the second rocket, and now that it was found things really looked more dismal than before. Randall sat reading an e-mail from Kim Marshall. He removed his pipe and gazed through the curling smoke at the jovial couple. These two were resilient youth. They could withstand the pressure of life. He tossed the e-mail on the desk. His mind drifted to the memory of his divorced wife and his teenage son. When the son had chosen to live with his mother, something inside Randall had died. In many ways, Spence had taken his son's place. And now this couple reminded him of all the right things he should've said and done. Spence had a gift of doing and saying the right things that mattered most to women.

Randall had not found the time to be a model husband during his study for a doctorate, even though his former wife had held a job to finance his career. Remorseful actions of his previous mistakes had seared the scars within his heart. More and more each day he had somehow found the strength to release those burdens by staying glued to his work. And watching Spence and Monique just now, allowed him some joy and peace of mind.

"Well, you two. Had your dinner, yet?"

Monique's eyes sparkled. "I've forgotten even to eat lunch."

"Me, too," Spencer replied.

Randall puffed a billow of aromatic smoke and removed his pipe, "How about dinner on me."

"You're on!" Spencer exclaimed, surrounding Monique in his arms.

"There's a little French cafe down by the ocean. We'll let Monique order and surprise us," Randall said, suddenly laughing.

A threesome sat quietly in a quaint little cafe waiting for the surprise dinner Monique had ordered. The dusk suddenly burst into golden shades of copper glowing outside the glass window by their table. Spencer chewed on cashew nuts from a bowl at the table, and the glow from his window caught his attention. The ocean gently washed upon a sandy shore, then rolled back into a surging sea. The timelessness of the ocean set his mind thinking. The girl he loved sat by his side, and the thought turned his head as he watched her pixy face. Monique curiously played mental Scrabble with the nutshells, and felt his eyes surveying her face. Her doe eyes rolled upward and she smiled. He winked.

Randall sipped on red wine and smoked his pipe between sips. The quietness had triggered his active mind, and his thoughts wandered to the second rocket. This beast could end all careers if Bo's engineers couldn't alter its course. And what of Monique and Spencer; their lives together were shattered, as so many other countless millions. He sat his glass on the table and sighed; maybe Bo was as good as Dr. Brown and Grif thought.

"Penny for your thoughts," Monique said, softly caressing Randall's hand.

"Absent-minded professor," Randall replied, wagging his head. "You know, for the first time, I think we actually have a chance to divert that rocket. No reason for me to conclude such a thought with only twenty-one days before impact. But there it is: a darn hunch."

Spencer grinned. "Battles have been won on hunches, sir."

Monique lovingly caressed Randall's hand. "And wars have been lost by procrastination."

Procrastination, indeed, Randall thought, gazing through the window at the pounding waves that crashed against the sandy shore. Bo Stringer and his shuttle crews were in a race against a solar clock. They had to pull off a miracle if it were even possible to save the planet from chaos. Randall lit his pipe as his thoughts drifted to Kim Marshall's e-mail asking him to confirm information on a neutron bomb.

Chapter 31

NASA PROJECT ENGINEERS gathered around a conference table waiting for the shuttle program manager. They each had received Alert E-mails calling them to this emergency meeting. The cyberspace grapevine had rumbled over the launch facility, whispering news; emergency appropriations by Congress, approved by the President. The center was infused with new life for an historic project. As Bo Stringer entered the conference room, the atmosphere loomed quiet and subdued like the day of final exams. He strolled to the lectern and laid his briefcase on the table. Bo faced the engineers and punched a button on a keypad. A 35mm slide focused on a wall-mounted screen. He picked up a pointer.

"This is Rocket Number Two. It's expected to collide with earth in nineteen days."

Without a word, some engineers punched the keys on their laptops. Others scribbled on notepads. These were professional men who had seen tragedy before: a fire in an Apollo capsule that suffocated three astronauts; an Apollo spacecraft stranded in space without main engine power; a blow-up during launch which killed all aboard the Challenger. Outer space was their element, math their language. Once they had been young aspiring idealists, who harbored the dream of going to the moon. But skepticism had discouraged the nation, until the Russian Sputnik jarred the military strategists. Competition between the prideful military forces produced one humiliating failure after another. The final humiliation collapsed into roaring flames as the Navy's Vanguard exploded again at liftoff, its third successive failure on the launch pad.

Victory had been snatched from the jaws of defeat when an engineering genius, Werner von Braun, emerged from obscurity at Redstone Arsenal in Huntsville, Alabama, a journey all the way from Peenemunde. Desperation expressed by the President had allowed von Braun and his engineering team a chance, and they modified the Army's Redstone Rocket for an attempt to put a satellite into orbit. The Army's Pioneer I flawlessly launched from Cape Canaveral on the first attempt and inserted America's first satellite into orbit. America had entered outer space with celestial egg on its face. Dr. von Braun's name reverberated around the world. The German genius had advanced rocketry science to a household word. And Bo's engineers were students of von Braun. Yes, these were men of the right stuff.

"What's the payload on this bird, Bo?"

He lifted the second page on his clipboard. "Plutonium waste, two thousand drums, about twenty tons of fissile material.

Faces looked up from their laptops. "Give us something we can understand like the thrust of the Saturn V boosters."

Bo smiled. "I'm told the blast would be the equivalent of a 40-kiloton bomb."

"And the timetable, Bo?"

He had the answer to that question in his mind. "We'll need twelve days to preflight the Shuttle after the modifications arrive. We have a tight envelope to put her in position before that rocket enters the stratosphere. And remember, our satellite networks are still heavy with glitches since that solar storm. Greenwich has worked out a makeshift."

"Has Goddard cleared the Hubble for retrofitting the mirror?"

"They're flying a mirror from the manufacturer tonight. We're calling the mission Planet Rescue. The rescue Shuttle is in countdown now at Kennedy. We had to do some rush work this past weekend to refurbish the pad in time for this launch."

"And the crew?"

Bo nodded. "Woody Crossfield will command. Butch and Joey are at Marshall training on mirror retrofit procedures and practicing the space walk."

Even as a veteran of space flight, Woody had never gone to the moon. Astronauts in the current crews had only flown the Shuttle. When NASA funds had steadily decreased after the Vietnam conflict, space exploration dwindled to exercises in the International Space Laboratory and the Hubble Space Telescope. Contact with deep space probes had revitalized Mars phobia which had financed two habitats, one in Utah, another in Devon, Canada that studied the viability of living on Mars.

Butch and Joey were new recruits with over one hundred hours in spacecraft simulators. Both were test pilots from Northrop Grumman. They had been selected because of their test-pilot experience. This launch was too risky for a complete crew.

"Bo, my team is working on the SPLC program alterations," an engineer replied. "If that modified mirror mount can rotate at least fifty-five degrees, we can achieve the desired range for collimation."

Bo recited the specifications of the engineering drawings. "Houston says that yoke has a forty-two degree pitch, with seventy-four degrees of rotation. However, we've got to nail a tight launch window to achieve triangulation from behind the earth."

An engineer made a note. "What's the target time on retrofit?"

"When Rescue I achieves orbit, ninety-three minutes remain to dock with the Hubble. The new yoke and mirror should be mounted by the next revolution. There is no time for checkout or practice runs. We'll have to do this right the first time."

A senior project engineer stood. "Assuming preflight goes well, we'd only have two, maybe three days left to achieve the launch window. That's mere hours, gentlemen. These precious hours will quickly vaporize with schedule interruptions, delays, and a million unseen anomalies. There is no margin for error."

Bo tucked his shirt into his pants while gazing at the group of engineers he'd trained, and few had advised him. "You've all been there before. The world is depending on you guys," he said quietly looking into their faces. "There's enough experience in this room to thread a needle with that laser. Let's roll!"

Chapter 32

THE PRESIDENT'S PRESS secretary stood behind a curtain and waited for a signal from the security director. The conference had been hastily called because President Darcy was due at the UN in three hours. News reporters and dignitaries crammed into the East Wing of the Whitehouse. Noise in the packed room began to build to a roaring pitch like a group of magpies feuding with a flock of crows. The press secretary had to cup his hand over his ear to discern the message in his earphone.

"Ladies and gentlemen: the President of the United States."

The buzzing crowd silenced and scrambled for their seats. Many others packed along the perimeter wall while some craned their necks for a clear view of the President.

Two people followed the President, including Bo Stringer, NASA Shuttle program manager, and Dr. Bruce Randall, director of Wilcox Solar Observatory. The FEMA administrator had not arrived as yet and Evans was busy on his cellphone. Two secret service agents stood on either side of the line.

Winston Darcy cleared his throat while he looked across the crowd. He gripped the edges of the lectern and leaned forward.

"We've got another bombshell to drop I'm afraid;" he said gazing at the reporters in the front row. "I want you to listen very carefully, but hold your questions and let these men talk. As you know, a second rocket is on a collision course with the earth. We have an update," he turned to the rear with a nod, "Dr. Randall."

While Randall approached the front, the crowd had rumbled when they heard the phrase 'hit the earth.' Kim Marshall's telecast on the existence of a second rocket had electrified the world. Literary talk groups speculated that Kim might be nominated for a second, unprecedented Pulitzer for television reporting.

Randall reached the microphone from the end of the line of guests and took a moment to adjust the sound. "My assistant, Spencer Jenson, recently returned from Japan, where he talked with Asahara Sakamoto at Yamato Aeronautics in Tokyo. Sakamoto discovered from his files that two rockets, not just one, were launched into space twenty years ago . . .

Kim Marshall's mind silenced Randall's voice. She thought of the story Brad had pulled from her telecast, and the hot discussion between two lawyers in Brad's office. Her efforts to find the Pentagon informant went unsuccessful, blind allies at every turn. Even her several conversations with the federal lawyer were fruitless. And Dr. Randall had not answered her e-mail. She lowered her head in deed concentration. Randall's voice echoed in the shadows of her mind.

. . . Goddard found the second rocket and has calculated its orbit. The taskforce has been working around the clock trying to devise a way to prevent the rocket from hitting the earth. There is hope. Bo Stringer and his staff at NASA have found a unique way to veer the rocket off course," he concluded, nodding at Bo.

Stunned faces blankly stared as the NASA engineer ambled to the front. This unmarried man had a monumental task thrust into his hands, and if he failed, there was no other recourse. The planet, the people, the way of life, and freedom would return to the jungle of survival of the fittest.

Bo wormed his way to the lectern, passing several engineers he knew, but did not expect to be at this meeting since they should have been in Houston.

"It's too hazardous for the astronauts to remain in orbit with solar wind at maximum strength. Solar I spacecraft now remains in orbit and is testing an experimental laser cannon, which my engineers think could veer that rocket off course. We decided to change the orbit of Solar I to shield her behind the earth. And we took the HST off its study of black holes, and Douglas is modifying a yoke-mount to attach a mirror to the outside tube of the Hubble. Our plan is to send up another shuttle with the modified mount and a mirror. We expect to focus the laser from Solar I onto the rocket by using the HST mirror to triangulate the beam. We're calling the mission Planet Rescue."

The President moved toward the lectern amid a rumble from the assembled crowd and shook Bo's hand, placed the other hand on his shoulder, as the exchanged a few encouraging words. A reporter in the front row flagged his attention. "Mr. President, will you ask the United Nations to censor Japan for launching nuclear waste into space?"

Winston Darcy had his answer before he reached the microphone, "I think that course of action would be counterproductive. We have monumental problems to solve in a miniscule of time. America is the only country capable of veering that rocket off its course," he shifted his stance and walked to the opposite end of the dais, mobile microphones followed his every move, "I have received word from many of the leaders around the world. They all send their hopes for our success, indeed the world is looking to America to save this planet."

He nodded at the FEMA director. "Thank you, Mr. President," the director said, "we have gained extensive experience over the past few weeks when the first rocket hit the sun, although this second rocket will undoubtedly be more severe. As before, we are considering this action like a class F-5 storm. We expect another power-grid blackout and loss of communications. I'm told that flooding will also become a more severe problem. Many of our medicines and supplies that were consumed during the first disaster have been supplemented by gracious donations from Great Britain and Australia. As before, the state emergency agencies are tied directly with federal networks. Law enforcement agencies will go on highest alert. We've made one critical change: this time, we will enforce a strict curfew. Looters will be given only one warning. If that warning goes unheeded, police officers are authorized to shoot on sight."

Darcy stepped to the podium as he surveyed the reporters; his keen insight knew their question before it was asked. "Our embassies in Japan and Australia have briefed those nations in the Pacific basin to prepare for unusual storms, including tidal waves, possibly a tsunami. And now I'll entertain more questions."

Hands went up all over the room, the first question bypassed the President, and he was not surprised: The reporters wanted technical answers.

"Dr. Randall. If NASA is successful in veering the rocket, how will it affect the earth?"

Randall waited for reasonable silence before he responded because he wanted every man in the room to hear this important information. "You must remember that the solar maximum is still with us, and may continue for several weeks. And we can expect the solar wind to continue bombarding the magnetosphere. Atmospheric storms could form in the westerly trade winds around the Rockies with profound effects on rainfall in the east."

Another reporter stood. "Suppose that laser beam doesn't veer the rocket off course and it explodes in the earth's atmosphere. What then, Dr. Randall?"

"Here we must speculate, and no scientist likes to do that. But I'll give you the opinion of the taskforce. First of all, the heat of reentry would provide the detonation source. An explosion in the atmosphere would be equivalent to a 40-kiloton nuclear bomb."

"I'm confused, Dr. Randall. We're discussing kilotons at liftoff and kilotons released by a nuclear explosion. How can these numbers be equivalent?"

Randall smiled as if he addressed a graduate class. "That's a good question. I'd give you high marks in my astrophysics class."

A humorous chuckle rumbled over the crowd, releasing mounting tension. Randall put on his professor's hat.

"On liftoff, we're talking kilotons of weight exerted by the force of gravity. As to a nuclear explosion, we're expressing kilotons of yield. Now, yield is also defined in terms of force; a kiloton has the force of 1000-tons of TNT—"

"Whoa, Dr. Randall, I yield. Forty kilotons it is."

Laughter roared from the crowd. When the chatter quieted to murmurs, a question came from the floor.

"What about the Rescue Shuttle and Solar I, how long can they stay in orbit?"

Bo moved to the microphone as Randall stepped aside. Stringer was familiar with fielding questions from his engineers but questions from reporters were a different thing altogether. He chose his words carefully.

"We'll have to bring down both Shuttles," he replied, and then paused. "But I'm not going to test you on space mechanics."

Again, the reporters robustly laughed chattering with their cohorts.

A hazel-eyed woman sternly sat at the rear of the amused crowd without a smile on her pristine face. The rumble gradually subsided as Kim Marshall stood and momentarily panned the group. Strangely, the crowd quickly became totally silent. She faced the speaker.

"Mr. Stringer, we've heard a runaway rocket loaded with plutonium described like it were a computer game on a kid's cartoon show. Isn't it true that we don't have a prayer in neutralizing radioactive fallout?"

A deafening hush settled over the East Wing. Dr. Randall suddenly realized that he had left Bo standing in the breach of an attack by Kim Marshall; he quickly took the microphone from Stringer.

"You said the right word, Kim: Prayer. This reporter is right. We have only a prayer," he pleaded and looked into the TV cameras. "Pray that we might make the right decisions in the precious time we have left, before this planet vanishes into oblivion."

Chapter 33

THREE ASTRONAUTS TUMBLED weightlessly inside the cabin of Rescue I orbiting at three hundred seventy-three miles above the earth. The launch from Cape Kennedy had been flawless: Countdown at liftoff went uninterrupted, the tilt program was on cue, and the boosters disengaged at the exact altitude. The rocket escaped the force of gravity gliding at twenty-four thousand miles per hour through the target launch window without a hitch. No astronaut could've asked for a smoother launch, certainly not these three. This scientific mission had not required a normal crew compliment. Indeed, Rescue I carried a skeleton crew of three trained to do a specific maneuver. The planet's existence depended on the success of their mission. In the cargo bay were two vital pieces for retrofit to the Hubble space telescope: a modified yoke-mount and an eight-foot diameter mirror.

Only a week ago, Congress had granted additional funds to launch Rescue I, Bo Stringer's brainchild. Engineers at Houston had worked around the clock to modify a yoke for mounting on the Hubble's external tube. Goddard had located a mirror that had failed the resolution tests requirements. Engineers decided that the flawed mirror could function as a reflector in the mission, saving precious time. Practice sessions were conducted at the Marshall Space Flight Center in Huntsville until the last possible minute.

On the second lap around the earth, Rescue I had eased into a docking position with the Hubble space telescope.

"Houston, this is Rescue I," Woody announced.

"We copy, Rescue I."

"We're having trouble attaching the yoke assembly. The Hubble seems to wiggle a bit."

"Roger Rescue I. Hold for conference." The flight director flipped a switch on his console and listened through his earpiece as he waited for the decision of the engineers.

"Hold on Rescue I. Goddard is attempting to adjust Hubble's gimbal frequency on the stabilizing platform. Do you copy?"

"Roger, Houston. We copy," Woody replied.

"You guys look awfully insignificant down there on that blue and white bowling ball," Joey reflected, jokingly.

"That's the first time I've heard the earth called a bowling ball, Rescue I, sounds a little poetic."

"I'm no poet," he chuckled, "how's my pulse rate?"

"You'll live. Estimated time to install yoke assembly is thirty-four minutes. You're behind ten minutes, Joey."

Bo String gazed critically at the big screen, and punched a button on the console, "Woody, watch your oxygen."

"Keep your shirt on, Bo. It isn't easy holding this baby stable."

The ground crew smiled at one another busy punching keys on their computer keyboards, those guys were professionals—they'd need all the grit they had.

Bo managed a weak smile, rechecking a few calculations. The reality of the task had begun to test his manhood, to test his courage, and his strength to stay focused.

The senior astronaut of the rescue crew studied the gages on his monitor; the spacewalk had neared its completion. He flipped a switch on the console.

"Okay, Joey, it's time to wrap it up. Oxygen level is red," Woody advised, as he watched the gages on the overhead module.

"It's done. Yoke installation complete," Joey puffed. "I'm coming in."

"That's a copy, Rescue I," Houston replied. "Take thirty, and then start the mirror mount exercise."

Somehow the urgency of the mission had not mandated a break, and the astronauts voted to begin the mirror installation without a breather.

"It's your baby, Butch. Joey will assist and release the mirror from the cargo bay hold downs," Woody commanded.

"Roger, egress in progress. We are going through the pressure chamber now."

Joey untangled his lanyard, and then positioned his body to support the mirror in the cargo bay. He released the mirror hold-downs and the mirror slightly wobbled. Both he and Butch gripped the eight-foot diameter primary mirror and gingerly pushed it through the blackness of outer space.

They finally floated the mirror alongside the Hubble telescope tube like an ant stealing away with a potato chip. Nearing the sidewall, Butch gripped one of the seventy-six handholds and stabilized his body by stuffing his foot in a grapple fixture embedded in the sidewall. With gentle nudges of his fingertips, the massive mirror softly settled into the saddle of the modified yoke as if it were a feather silently gliding to the ground. Joey attached the hold-down clamps and they both removed the protective covering from the mirror. "Okay, she's mounted—it's time for checkout of the motorizing electronics."

"Roger, Rescue I, checkout in progress."

A ground signal from Goddard activated the axes electronics. Woody observed a blinking green light on the command console.

"She's active, Houston!"

"Roger, Rescue I, understood. Mirror is active. Good work guys, you completed the entire spacewalk exercise in one hour and twelve minutes. Not bad, guys, not bad at all!"

Applause from planet earth was heard with the clarity of a telephone conversation from across town, three hundred seventy-three miles up and three thousand miles downrange.

"Rescue I, this is Houston."

"Go ahead Houston."

"Button up you guys, you're coming home on the next revolution."

"Copy that, Houston. We'll spend the orbiting time to ready the cargo bay."

"Roger. You're next window is 89.75 minutes, Rescue I. Do you copy?"

"Roger. I make it 88.67 minutes on the cabin clock."

"Understood, Rescue I: 88.67 minutes."

Woody tightened the Velcro on his gloves. "Okay guys let's get ready for de-orbit, and remember Houston, Bo Stringer is buying lunch," he said while

---

gloved hands flipped the toggle switches above his head.

Butch and Joey spent most of the remaining orbit in a preparation for de-orbit, while Woody checked every detail of the reentry calculations. Finally they sat in their seats buckled and ready for countdown procedures for main engine restart. Woody went through the restart checklist as if he was in the simulator back at Houston. What time they had, they rested until the window materialized. That moment came all too soon. Woody rustled in his seat as he flipped overhead switches.

"Okay Houston, we're going to put it right down the slot, like a straight-in pool shot. And maybe we won't lose any more ceramic tiles this trip."

Bo Stringer rocked back in his seat and mused of his plan to hide the Orbiting Laser behind the earth's shadow. Was it really a safety measure as he had told himself, or had he made a critical error?

Chapter 34

SOLAR I COMPLETED its twenty-eighth day in silent orbit around the earth while it endued the cold and loneliness of outer space. She orbited at two hundred-ten miles above the planet, and awaited computations that changed orbital parameters. She looked not like the savior of the earth, but in her cargo bay rested an ominous-looking gadget that figured to be the only hope of earth survival. The spacecraft's oxygen levels loomed dangerously low as well as foodstuffs and water. Solar 1 was scheduled to deorbit in two days, but new orders from Houston had extended the mission, and had pushed the fatigued crew to near exhaustion.

Sketchy news rarely explained the entire situation back on earth. But these men were professionals and had not needed all the details, at least not until now. All their energies had concentrated on the mission if they were to succeed. They understood they were expendable; their mission was vital to the planet's safety and they had been well briefed by Bo Stringer. The purpose of the mission was clear and the risks were assessed. Bo had canceled his plan to place the solar gun in the shadow of the earth to protect the astronauts. His engineers had calculated that the canon's solar power would be robbed of energy since the direct sun doubled the gun's power output. The contractor that had developed the moonsuits assured Stringer that the suits would be sufficient protection during the limited exercise.

Without any error, the spacecraft had to descend into a lower orbit to adequately align with the target. From that vantage point they would triangulate the cannon with the modified mirror that Rescue I had attached to Hubble's external superstructure. Inside the pressurized cabin, onboard computers were cycled through final procedures to alter the orbit of Solar I. This was a normal task in the sense of criticality. The slightest error in attitude, or even a millisecond over-burn, would de-orbit the craft.

"Houston. This is Solar I: Ready for insertion."

"Roger, Solar I, Delta V in process. Activate N2-1 starboard nitrogen jets."

"Copy, N2-1 activated."

"Set the N2 timer at 4.23 seconds."

"Copy, 4.23 seconds."

"Energize N2-1 attitude jets."

The astronaut flipped a switch on the command panel and the spacecraft changed attitude. "We have 2.75-degrees pitch. Yaw is nominal. Roll is stable," Woody reported.

"Copy, Solar I, activate main engine restart."

"Copy, main engine activated."

"Set burn time for 3.65 milliseconds."

"Copy, burn time is affirmative."

"Okay, Solar I, you have a 10-minute window. You are 'GO' for retrograde burn."

Hydrazine and liquid oxygen (LOX) poured into the ignition chamber. The volatile mixture silently exploded into churning gaseous flames. Surging pressure belched from the main engine nozzle like a mute scene from a silent movie. The power of this instantaneous blast could not be characterized by the eerie silence in outer space. Objects in zero gravity seemed to move as if in a dream featured by slow motion.

The spacecraft pitched into a lower orbit like a soaring eagle gliding into the Grand Canyon. Insertion into the new orbit required a course correction. The onboard computers automatically extended the burn time by 40-nanoseconds to compensate.

The spacecraft slid into a lower orbit of ninety-seven miles, hovered within the shadow of the earth. The spacecraft would not remain in this shadow during the solar gun operation; its location was only temporary until the gun was operable. Houston concurred on the orbital data. The new orbit precisely positioned the peculiar experimental gun for alignment with the Hubble mirror retrofit. The astronauts took timeout and readied themselves and the spacecraft for collimation exercises.

"Houston, this is Solar I: We are ready to Collimate."

"Copy, Solar I: Hold for one minute."

"Solar I, this is Bo. You guys have a crucial task. The eyes of the world are glued on your actions. Do this thing by the book."

"Roger, Bo. The ink is still wet on this book. You wrote it only two days ago. Now we'll have to edit your lousy grammar."

"That's the spunk I'm looking for."

"There aren't any heroes up here, Bo. That's our world down there, too."

"You do this one, and I am buying you lunch. I'll even walk your dogs."

"You're on, Bo."

The flight director came online, and the astronauts were busy flipping switches. "Okay, Solar I, Goddard is ready to energize the mirror-mount retrofit."

So far, the flight program had worked, not flawlessly but adequate, the reason for redundancy. But the real challenge now depended on the pointing control system of the Hubble. Would it function with the outboard retrofit? Image-pointing began with a laser focused on a dime two hundred miles away that held the spacecraft steady for hours or days. Once the Hubble locked onto an object, its sensors checked for movement forty times-a-second. The telescope was held in position by constantly spinning gyros that changed speeds on signal from the sensors.

The Hubble mirror finally focused on Rocket No. 2, its computers turning electronic data into long strings of digital numbers. These digital data traveled as radio signals to a satellite that beamed the information to Goddard. From there, it traveled by landline to Space Telescope Science Institute in Baltimore, MD, where digital data converted into pictures and astronomical observations. Goddard's orbiting satellite, critical to success, had been checked and rechecked after the surge of solar maximum. NASA's engineers were satisfied the system should work. All systems had signed off.

"Houston calling Solar I."

"Roger, Houston: Ready and waiting."

"Goddard reports Hubble is ready for mirror alignment."

"Copy, Collimation in progress," Woody replied, flipping a series of switches.

The laser cannon electronics activated in Solar I cargo bay. The turret rotated twenty-one degrees like a robot going through its program.

Simultaneously, the Hubble outboard mirror rotated to align the beam. Hubble's computer locked onto the laser beam and a program activated the controller sensors that stabilized the mirror.

"Houston. Target is acquired! Repeat. Target is acquired!"

"Copy Solar I, target is acquired. Good job!"

A roar of applause rumbled in the Houston Command Center. Tensions melted into jubilation. Cigars, Cokes, and bottled water went around the center. Celebration time! A miracle had really happened.

Although filled with pride, the professional astronauts continued recheck of the spacecraft attitude and made adjustments to the stabilizing platform electronics to remain stabilized in orbit. Outboard nitrogen jets were on gyro auto-control. The spacecraft hovered in earth's shadow with its cargo bay open like a goony bird out of the shadow's range in complete sun. Suddenly the control board flashed a blinking red light.

"Houston? We've got problems!"

"Roger, Solar I. Goddard lost signal with the NASA satellite. Hold your position."

Goddard engineers feverously worked to correct the missing signal. They found a $2.87 faulty relay that had to be reactivated; if not, the circuit had to be circumvented. Neither option was viable. With the link down, Solar I could not fire the laser internally which was far more accurate than ground-based delayed signals.

Minutes crept into terrifying hours.

Time, that illusive thief of livelihood was also the enemy of programming, which directly determined the accuracy of the program performance. The countdown clock moved through twelve hours of excruciating silence. The lack of any message from Goddard spawned confusion and desperation around a stunned world. Leaders of major countries gathered at the United Nations and discussed the impending chaos. World activity geared down and idled. Planet Earth hung in a teetering balance while its final hours ticked away on the clock of eternity. Nations of helpless people turned to God. Churches, synagogues, and mosques called their people to prayer. Kneeling crowds huddled on sidewalks and streets with heads bowed. Hordes of people walked arm-in-arm to their places of worship while they chanted prayers. Street gangs locked arms with policemen and sang hymns. Stock markets closed in the U.S., Europe, and Japan. Traffic slowed to a crawl. Crime vanished. The earth rested. Time seemingly stood still.

The infamous rocket loomed somewhere between the sun and the moon like an avenging angel of death. The U.S. media networks had set up cameras at Mount Palomar, California, and televised the orbiting bomb through the center's 200-inch Hale telescope. Europe linked up the 236-inch telescope on the northern slopes of the Caucasus Mountains. The Pacific basin hooked up the Keck telescope at Mauna Kea, Hawaii, with light-gathering power four times greater than the 200-inch Hale.

Live pictures of the ominous plutonium rocket went around the endangered globe. The media blitz had devastating effects on the populous. Every human soul pondered his understanding of the impending end of humanity. Sane people wrongly rationalized themselves into screaming neurotics. Vain and shallow-minded people reasoned it was just another Hollywood science fiction movie.

With only ten hellish hours left before annihilation, Rocket No. 2 became visible in amateur telescopes, even binoculars. The plutonium rocket hung in space, stretched between the sun's gravity and the earth's ever-increasing gravitational pull like taffy candy. A few weeks ago, it had slowly emerged out of a deep, dark place as if it were locked in a traction beam. First the sun had pulled the rocket into the inner planetary system. And now, the earth's mass had won the gravitational tug-of-war, the kiss of death for Planet Earth.

Late in the evening, with just six hours remaining on the countdown, the word finally came down from Goddard. The Hubble was operational again!

"Wake up, Solar I! The turkey shoot is on, again!"

"Copy, Houston! And who's asleep?" Scott exclaimed!

"Hubble is reassessing the target. Okay . . . we got a green board! Do you still have a window?"

"The biggest, brightest window you ever saw!"

"Activate laser cannon!"

"Roger, Power on."

"Execute."

A thin, blue beam bounced off the Hubble outboard mirror, and stretched straight as an arrow to the target. The Hale telescope reported a direct hit near the booster fins. Goddard plotted the orbit in real time.

No measurable shift in the rocket's trajectory.

"Solar I, first shot negative, repeat, negative. Fire the cannon, again."

"Roger, Houston. Firing a second time," Scott responded, clicking toggle switches overhead to bring online the entire solar-panel output. "Full power, Houston!" he screamed, turning to Trevor. "This ought to kick it in the ass."

Another direct hit!

Goddard reported the orbit had indeed altered. Wilcox Solar Observatory confirmed a new trajectory, vectoring ten degrees off the plane, adequate to miss the earth without affecting the tides.

All across the planet people seemed to sigh in relief. But was planet earth really safe? Psychosis played its mystical tricks with troubled and distraught minds. Many weary people pushed their worries deep into their subconscious minds, trying to forget the calamity. Clinging to science for answers, they forgot to offer thanksgiving to the Almighty for their survival. They wallowed in self-pity.

A curious sort of numbness gripped the world.

Chapter 35

"THIS IS WASHINGTON DRUMBEAT and I am Kim Marshall. Today the news from outer space is one of jubilance and celebration. NASA has announced just hours ago that Solar I has been successful in altering the trajectory of the plutonium rocket. The orbiting laser cannon aboard Solar I performed flawlessly. And NASA confirms that the plutonium rocket has safely veered away from Planet Earth. Stay tuned to this station for my interview with Colonel Griffin of the President's taskforce."

The camera light blinked off. A message buzzed in Kim's earpiece. "Kim pickup on line 2, it's Dr. Randall—says it's important."

A quizzical frown engulfed the redhead's face as she punched a button on the console. "This is Kim Marshall."

"Kim, listen carefully. I don't have much time. Colonel Griffin has to get back to the NASA Building for an emergency meeting of the President's taskforce."

"What's happened, Dr. Randall?"

"I can't discuss that now, Kim. Just get Griffin off that set."

"Okay, Dr. Randall. But you owe me an exclusive on that meeting."

She hung up the phone, emotions sizzling, and her bloodstream flooded with adrenaline as she pushed a console button. "Bobby, run that piece we did on Planet Rescue. Griffin's off the program." Kim pushed another button that activated the phone in the manager's office. "Brad, Dr. Randall is onto something hot. He just pulled Griffin off the set and ordered him back to a taskforce meeting."

"Did he say why?"

"Not a clue. But I think big news is brewing. I'm going to follow up."

"Okay, Kim. Try to make the evening news deadline."

Griffin stepped out the side door of the TV station, and quickly got into his parked car. He left by way of a back road to avoid traffic and headed downtown to the NASA Building. As he entered the main road, he steered through the snarled traffic and caught the traffic lights before they changed. When he was settled in the moving traffic, he punched his cellphone.

"I got your message on my phone, Dr. Randall. What's the new trajectory look like?"

"According to Goddard, it's now on a collision course with the moon."

"Good grief, has anyone told the President?"

"General LaCroix briefed the President about an hour ago."

"Be there in thirty minutes."

Randal hung up the phone on LaCroix's desk set and joined the taskforce as they intently watched the trajectory path of Rocket No. 2 on a large screen gathered around a conference table in the NASA Building. The room loomed quiet and subdued the occupants tense and deeply engaged. Just as Bo Stringer pushed a remote, Colonel Griffin opened the door.   Randal shook his hand and whispered something in his ear.

Bo pointed to the screen on the wall. "Here's an overlay of the new trajectory. You can see the vector now aligns with the moon."

"What could've caused this shift?"   General LaCroix grumbled as he rolled his cigar to the opposite side of his mouth.

Randall sat humiliated as he puffed his pipe. What could have gone wrong, surely his calculations were correct, he chided himself. His ears heard the General's remarks but his mind disregarded the words. A sudden fixation wrinkled his forehead. .He pushed his spectacles to the top of his head and pounded his fist on the table.

"Why didn't I see this before?"

"What is it, Randall?" a chorus of voices replied in unison.

"Nodal tides! That's got to be it!"

"What in the hell are nodal tides," LaCroix growled and removed his cigar as he leaned forward in his chair with both elbows perched on his glass top desk

Randall slowly rose from his seat and stepped to the front, found a felt-tipped marker in the chalk tray, and sketched a diagram on an erasable board, then grabbed a pointer as he gathered his thoughts.

"Every eighteen and one-half years, the sun, the earth, and the moon merge into alignment. It's happening right now," he said pointing at the diagram. "The combined mass has further degraded the rocket's orbit, dragging it into a course toward the moon."

LaCroix's face screwed into painful contortions, ashes fell from his cigar and blackened his hand. "Nodal tides?" he mumbled. "Can't we blast her again with that laser gun?"

Bo responded while still assimilating Randall's theory. "Not possible, sir, Solar I landed on the salt flats an hour ago."

Griffin added a response although he was completely baffled. "And we're out of time, too, General. That rocket will impact the moon in six days."

Randall suddenly announced with striking clarity, something he had done on several occasions when answers were sparse, data unclear.

"Gentlemen, we must prepare for a shower of lunar asteroids,"

"Quite right, Randall," Bo agreed after he'd confirmed the calculations and the logistics.

"I'll alert Goddard. Maybe they can track the larger chunks before they burn through the troposphere," Griffin injected on the basis of Bo's confidence.

Randall faced LaCroix, eyes ablaze, his analytical mind bussing with calculations. "General, I believe we'll see several pieces of lunar real estate large enough to cause some real damage. Can the military help?"

LaCroix scratched the stubby bristles of his five o'clock shadow as he slowly removed his cigar. "Asteroids huh, let's call them lunaroids," he decided. "The only thing operational that could pulverize this stuff is the modified Patriot missile. But how do we target the things?"

Bo offered a suggestion. "Goddard can refine the trajectory of asteroids—ah, lunaroids, sir, and predict splashdown locations. That should be enough time to tell you where to target those missiles."

"Yeah, and airborne jets could radio coordinates way before radar could pick-up the signals," Griffin replied.

Randall was still in deep thought. "There is one other observation, gentlemen," he cautioned, his eyes affixed to the diagram on the board. "The position of the moon in this new alignment will most likely send the lunaroids into the Pacific basin."

General LaCroix stabbed his stubby cigar into an ashtray. He had assimilated the information from his taskforce, now ready to command.

"In that case, gentlemen, I'll activate a squadron of Globemaster jets to transport the Patriots. We'll stage them in Los Angeles, Honolulu, Guam, Manila, Brisbane, Auckland, and Tokyo. Whatever those splashdown locations are, we should be able to adjust. I'll divert three carrier groups from maneuvers in the South Pacific. They can act as mobile rovers using F16s armed with Sidewinder missiles. That should cover most of Polynesia, Micronesia, and Melanesia."

Bo responded. "Sounds like a plan, General. But can those carriers get into position in time?"

"The U.S.S. Theodore Roosevelt has the best chance. But, she's all we've got on this short notice," he replied and clipped off the end of a new cigar.

Kim Marshall rushed into the lobby of the NASA Building and hurriedly looked for someone to question. Her roving hazel eyes spotted a junior administrator who stood by the conference room door on the first floor. She quickly recognized him, and walked over. "Excuse me, Danny."

His face lit up like a jack-o-lantern. "Hello Kim! Looking for a scoop?" he exclaimed, grasping her outstretched hand.

Dr. Randall is in that room, isn't he?"

The facial glow dimmed. "Why yes," he replied with puzzlement. "He's with the President's taskforce, but I don't think you can go in," he hedged.

She moved closer and smiled her best beguiling smile, and then brushed her curves against an excited man.

"I'm just following up on a story. Couldn't you tell me what's going on in there, Danny—please?"

One look into her persuasive eyes, and Danny knew he was trapped; there was no way to counteract this beguiling woman, she would counteract and he'd be in deep trouble, not with his supervisor, but his jealous wife.

"I'm afraid I can't tell you Kim," he nervously replied.

Her hazel eyes stared into his boyish face, her head cocked with red hair aglow in the sunlight now pouring through the overhead skylight.

"The people have a right to know, Danny. Their lives are on the block, too."

Her logic was infallible as usual, the exotic perfume overpowering, and feminine curves warped his thinking. The poor man stood helpless, a slave to his youthful lust. Her mesmerizing hazel eyes were just too much for his manliness. His mind suddenly flashed to the paper in his pocket, eyes still captivated by the sassy redhead's tantalizing smile.

"This message just came in from Goddard," he whispered while he watched the hallway, which took his eyes off her. "If I don't look, I can't see you." He dropped a paper on the floor by her feet and casually walked away.

Kim grasped the paper with a one-hand swoop. She speed-read the contents. In an instant, she knew she had an exclusive of huge importance. Her clinched fist went into the air. "Yes!" she exclaimed. "Thanks Danny," she called.

Danny waved his hand without a look back and entered the restroom. He thought he might vomit.

Chapter 36

KIM MARSHALL PLUNGED into the TV station like a cat chasing a rat. She rushed through the bullpen as she haphazardly dodged several desks and stumbled over wastebaskets. Every eye watched the redhead from the moment she entered the room. Kim never slowed her strut until she burst into the program manager's office and slung her jacket across a chair. "That rocket has changed course again!" she blurted out.

Brad stood. "Then where?"

"The moon, it's going to collide with the moon," she screeched and tossed a paper on his desk.

Brad pushed a button on the intercom while he glanced at the paper. "Bobby, hold that piece on Solar I. Kim's got an exclusive," he said as he read the paper.

His brown, piercing eyes slowly lifted and laid a gaze on Kim. "Now tell me young lady, how did you get this confidential paper?"

Her face guiltlessly blanked as she parked her rump on his desk and crossed her long tanned legs. "Nothing wrong with a girl using her charm, is there?"

"Those hazel eyes of yours could charm the skin off a cobra, Kim. Try to remember you're a reporter, not a belly dancer," he said, suddenly smiling.

She returned his smile with a wink, and strutted down the hallway to her office. The Pulitzer winner sat down at her computer. The clock on the wall warned her to hasten. She had fifteen minutes before the evening news telecast.

"This is a WOFF ALERT. I'm Kim Marshall and you're tuned to Washington Drumbeat. The plutonium rocket in space has changed course, again. I repeat: the rocket bearing down on earth was supposed to miss our planet by a mere ten thousand miles. WOFF NEWS has learned within the hour that the rocket may crash into the moon. That's right. It will hit the moon. More after the break—stay with us."

Ads rolled.

Kim quickly reread her report on the TelePrompTer. A small mirror allowed her to fix her hair and even touchup her lipstick. The warning light blinked and she faced the camera.

"To repeat a WOFF Alert, the plutonium rocket in outer space is now heading toward the moon, not the earth, this according to the latest Goddard orbital data. NASA engineers are huddled tonight in a conference room in downtown Washington preparing a strategy to protect the earth from a bombardment of lunar debris. There is concern that lunar asteroids, dubbed lunaroids by the Pentagon, may hit our planet."

Video aired as she spoke, showing an animated sound-bite depicting asteroids swirling in outer space.

"You will recall the heroic actions of several NASA astronauts, who risked their lives to veer that rocket away from earth. Even then, the best advice warned that the rocket's orbit could change again. And now it has changed. The rocket is bending toward the moon at this very moment. When will we see these lunaroids? Stay tuned to WOFF NEWS. I'll be right back with the answer."

The other networks quickly picked up the story, and within two hours the White House switchboards were swamped with calls.

Chapter 37

"TELEPHONE, SPENCE," Dr. Randall paged through the intercom in his observatory office. The professor released the intercom button and settled back into his chair. He wanted to catch up on his e-mails before Colonel Griffin arrived. In his hands he held an e-mail from Kim Marshall dated three days ago requesting an interview. Wonder who's feeding her information?

"Thanks. Be right there," Spencer responded from the instrument room where he serviced the solar telescope. Randall's call wrestled his thoughts from a dirty gearbox. Who's calling me? Monique was out of town. He wiped his greasy fingers on a shop towel and picked up the extension phone that hung on the wall. "Hello, Spencer here."

At first, there was no answer, only heavy breathing. Then a calm, but troubled voice came over the speaker, a male Asian voice. "Mr. Jenson?" the Asian voice inquired.

"Yes, this is Spencer Jenson."

"This is Sakamoto at Yamato Aeronautics in Tokyo, Jenson."

Spencer's face brightened. "Why yes—

"We don't have much time, Jenson. I've got bad news. I found an old manifest listing the drums on that second rocket."

Spencer's face froze solid. He put down the ratchet, knuckles rubbed raw from banging inside the gearbox. "Manifest?" he whispered.

"Yes. And there's something else besides plutonium on that rocket."

His words gnawed at Spencer's throat. "Something else and what is that?"

"Red mercury: three pounds in a plastic canister."

Spencer stared in disbelief, a raw lump wedged in his throat. "You're sure about this?"

"I'm looking at the original manifest that arrived with the drums from Paris. I thought you ought to know."

Spencer picked up a shop towel and wiped his face, then tossed it in his open toolbox. "Thank you, Sakamoto. You did the right thing. I wonder if you'd fax that manifest to my office."

The young doctoral student could not believe the message, and settled uncomfortably into a chair, the telephone receiver still clutched in his hand. His eyes were glassy and distant, his stare unfocused. The message finally seeped into his mind and pushed him to his feet. He hung up the phone, and climbed the steps to the observatory floor. "Red mercury in the same batch of drums containing plutonium," he whispered to himself.

Dr. Randall sat behind his desk engrossed in a treatise on neutron bombs. He heard the door squeak, and lifted the reading spectacles to the top of his head. "What is it, Spence?" he asked, the question directed at his pale face.

"Red mercury," he replied almost in a whisper. "There's a canister of red mercury on that rocket," he said, lifting a fax out of a tray.

Randall dropped his pipe. "What? How do you know?"

"That was Yamato Aeronautics on the phone. Sakamoto found an original manifest of the drums."

"How much?"

"Three pounds. We've got real problems with plutonium riding on that rocket, sir. Here's the manifest."

Randall picked up his pipe, laid it on the desk, and dropped the spectacles to his nose, as he read the faxed list. A moment of assimilation and Randall voiced his conclusion, "Guess I'd better call Hobart."

He picked up the phone and keyed a private number at Caltech. Dr. Norman Hobart headed the nuclear physics lab, a close friend of Randall's from college days. The signal opened, and he heard Hobart's voice. "Norm, this is Randall."

"Why Bruce, glad you called! Sheila wants you to come—

"It'll have to wait, Norm. We've just learned that three pounds of red mercury are riding on that rocket of plutonium hurtling toward the moon."

A brief silence hummed. "Well! That's a helluva note."

"You're the expert, Norm, what do we have here?"

"Red mercury is the inexpensive detonator for a neutron bomb," he dryly gasped.

"Give me a scenario, Norm, something I can use."

"Well," he said, pinched his bottom lip, and breathed a sigh. "The neutron bomb is Sam Cohen's brainchild. There's a long and sordid history here. Earlier bombs were detonated by using nuclear fission splitting heavy atoms to release energy. Later bombs used nuclear fusion, which fused hydrogen atoms to release energy. Cohen's neutron bomb uses nuclear fusion in quite a novel way."

"But what about detonation, Norm, that's the real issue here."

"Exactly, the detonation of a neutron bomb at first was a laborious process, requiring a plutonium fission reaction to release hydrogen atoms for fusion. But red mercury changed all that."

"So what's the answer?"

"Red mercury will initiate the chain reaction. The quantity of fissile plutonium will determine the force of reaction. I'm afraid it could be a sizeable explosion. Of course, all this is theory you understand. A perfect vacuum can do strange things."

"Can't give the President theory, Norm, I want your best answer."

The phone line hummed in silence for a long moment before Norm gave an answer. "If I were counseling the President about this neutron stuff, I'd advise him to snap a lid on it. Hush it up. Your problem is radiation, not the explosive force."

Randall sighed. "Okay, Norm. How's the encapsulation experiment coming along?"

"Pretty fair Bruce. Dr. Guilderstein and I are giving a presentation tomorrow in Washington. Hope you can be there."

"I sure would like to, but who knows what'll happen by tomorrow. I'll tell the President, Norm. And give my best to Sheila. Tell her I'll have to take a rain check on dinner. Hate to miss her peach cobbler."

As the doctoral student and his tutor sat and puzzled over the fax from distant Tokyo, the thought of the plutonium rocket bearing down on the moon seemed all too unreal. It seemed as if some higher force had orchestrated the path of the rocket. If so, was this force friend or foe? A good scientist considered any and all aspects, no matter how strange or unorthodox. But red mercury was no trivial matter.

Colonel Griffin entered the planetarium and briskly walked toward the office suite. He was on the west coast at Caltech for a debriefing on Hobart's experiment. He had used the opportunity to bring a classified message to Randall. In his briefcase he carried a stunning report from NASA-Goddard. Goddard had been tracking the orbiting rocket with sophisticated x-ray devices that could 'see' through steel.

Their disturbing discovery had been immediately classified 'Secret' because of advanced technology. He pushed open the doors to Randall's observatory office. Voices echoed in the conference room. Griffin recognized the two voices.

"Hello, Randall, and you, too, Spencer."

"Grif, come on in. Got your message but didn't expect you this soon."

"Sorry to barge in like this, caught an earlier flight."

"Sit down, and tell me this urgent news."

"I'm the bearer of bad news, Bruce."

Randall wagged his head, a myriad of thoughts all focused on dismal changes wrought by this plutonium rocket. "Well, let's have. This is the day for it."

Griffin heard the comment but had not listened as he opened his briefcase and pulled out a report. "Goddard has discovered about 50-kiloliters of LOX and maybe 15-kiloliters of hydrazine remaining in the tanks of that Vostok rocket," he said and handed the report to Randall.

"Great gods of Jupiter! You really mean bad news, don't you?"

Griffin only nodded.

Randall assigned a task for his mind. "That's twelve thousands gallons of LOX and twenty-five hundred gallons of hydrazine."

Glassy eyes reread the report. Spencer craned his neck over Randall's shoulder. A strange kind of quietude hovered over the room as if the air had been mysteriously sucked out.

Spencer sat down, his knees weak. Randall lit his pipe as he puzzled over the events. Griffin perched comfortably on the leather sofa steeped in confusion as he pondered what was so confused to his two friends.

Finally Randall cradled his pipe and tossed the report on his desk. "Grif, we've just learned that red mercury is aboard that rocket—"

Griffin leaped from the sofa, his eyes swelled like a kid with his first toy, perhaps Godzilla. "Good grief—you're sure?"

"I'm afraid so. But let's look at this logically. We know those drums of plutonium waste are strapped around the propellant tanks. And now you're telling us there's fuel and oxidizer in those tanks."

"Yeah and how I wish it weren't true," he said scratching his head.

Randall's head slowly wagged face stern and still. "This has to be the biggest dirty bomb ever devised."

Griffin sighed and sat down, his mind swirled with deep, dark thoughts. "Thank God it's in outer space," he said, and slumped back into the soft cushions, his mind seized by Randall's assessment.

He had known of Cohen's work on the neutron bomb and Russia's production of red mercury, including its export on the Black Market. He finally arrived at a conclusion and faced Dr. Randall. "It appears to me that radiation is the real problem here, not the residual fuel."

"That's Hobart's assessment, too."

Griffin managed a slight smile. "This puts more emphasis on Hobart's globular compound. I've got Hobart's report in my briefcase. Want to take a look? It's fascinating stuff."

But Randall dazedly puffed his pipe. "I hope the moon can take that blast."

Chapter 38

ANDREW EVANS, chief of staff, followed Winston Darcy into the Oval office, enraged by a recently printed news story in the Post. Darcy rounded the desk and laid a file on the corner, pushed papers aside. Evans sat on a sofa and awaited the President. He knew better than to interrupt, and allowed him time before he spoke.

"Washington Post is running a story today about a neutron bomb riding on that plutonium rocket, Mr. President. The press will pounce on this like a leopard, and we'll have a paralyzing panic on our hands."

Darcy rocked back in his chair with his hands clasped beneath his chin; an index finger twiddled the ridges of a deep cleft.

"Six days. The same time it took God to create the earth. Now man's stupidity may destroy it in the same space of time."

Evans' spoke quickly with advice. "Kim Marshall lit this fire, sir. We'll have to counter her story, too."

Darcy vehemently shook his head. "Absolutely not, Andrew, Kim Marshall is right, you know. There isn't any more time for business as usual. I'm going to tell the American people the truth. That's the only way to handle this nightmare."

Evans advised. "It'll take an awesome speech, Mr. President."

"The people are tired of speeches and so am I, Andrew. All I seem to get from that pool of writers is spin. I want facts," he said, with fire in his eyes. "Get Dr. Randall on the telephone."

Andrew calmly punched a button on the intercom set. "Sonya, get Dr. Bruce Randall on the telephone for the President."

Evans sat down while the President stood at the window with his hands clasped behind his back. How many times had he seen this posture by the President? Even when he was a senator, Evans had watched this man, a courageous man who never stepped back from a problem; he faced it head-on.

"Sir, Dr. Randall is on line 2," the secretary said through the intercom. The President grinned at his chief of staff, then sat down, and reached for the phone. He stabbed a button.

"Dr. Randall. This is Winston Darcy."

"Yes, Mr. President. How can I help you, sir?"

"I understand we've got six days before that rocket hits the moon."

"Yes sir, give or take twelve hours."

"What do you see happening here on earth, Dr. Randall?"

"Mr. President, nobody knows exactly what a 40-kiloton explosion will do in a vacuum. We certainly should expect a shower of lunaroids breaking off the moon. Just how big or how many, is anyone's guess."

"Lunaroids?"

"Yes sir. That's LaCroix's terminology to prevent confusion with the asteroid belt."

He nodded. "General LaCroix tells me we have a slim chance of knocking out the larger—uh, lunaroids."

"I think it's possible, at least we have to try."

"Yes. We can't afford any mistakes on this one," the President responded lethargically.

The tone of his voice somehow told Randall where the President was going with his questions. He wanted a measure of confidence in his decision by comparing notes.

"What we have here, Mr. President is a horse race against time. General LaCroix is the best jockey you have in the stable. At least, that's my assessment from watching him perform on the taskforce."

The chief executive slightly grinned, "I wanted the truth, Dr. Randall. That's why I called you."

"They're all good men on the taskforce, sir."

"And you, Dr. Randall, have made a sizeable contribution yourself. Whatever happens, I want you to know that America is grateful."

"Thank you, Mr. President. Let's hope that our men and women in the military can pull this off."

Darcy mulled over a response; it was a sticky question, and he had his own opinion.

"It seems always to come down to a military solution, doesn't it? The Constitution requires the President to defend the nation and its people. And now, our military will have to defend the whole planet," Darcy replied and gazed through the window into the rose garden. "What's your take on Goddard's discovery, Dr. Randall?"

Randall took a draw from his pipe. "Residual fuel is not the immediate problem, Mr. President. I've just learned that red mercury is aboard the rocket, too."

"Red mercury?"

"Yes sir, red mercury is a detonation source for a neutron bomb—what we have is a huge dirty bomb. Such an explosion will release massive radiation attached to lunar dust and debris orbiting around the moon."

Darcy closed his eyes. The truth was too bitter to contemplate. He pushed a conference button on the telephone console that opened a two-way loud speaker as he stood and walk toward the window, but refused to clasp his hands.

"Red mercury, huh? You've discussed this with Griffin and Hobart?"

"Yes sir, I have. They concur."

"And what do you think of Kim Marshall's telecast?"

"She's accurate, as far as it goes, sir. But I don't think she'll telecast unconfirmed information about a neutron bomb. And I'm sure she doesn't know about this discovery of red mercury, yet."

"I see. Thanks for that confirmation, Dr. Randall."

"Excuse me sir, if I may. Dr. Hobart thinks it's best to keep a lid on that neutron information. He thinks it's inconsequential, radiation is the problem."

Winston Darcy grimaced. "That's good advice. The question now is how to tell the public."

"Sir, if I may."

"Speak your mind, Randall, you deserve that much."

"The press is looking for a sensational story, sir. Give them the truth to chew on and they won't have to invent news. No need to bring up this flesh-eating aspect of neutron bombs, and reopen the question for debate and panic."

He nodded. "That's sound political advice, Dr. Randall. Thank you for your counsel. I deeply appreciate your work on the taskforce."

"Thank you, Mr. President."
Randall closed the phone and rocked back in his seat, wondering if the President really understood the facts about red mercury.

Chapter 39

THE PLUTONIUM ROCKET finally slammed into the moon's surface, quietly as a kitten, dangerously as a lion. Gigantic chunks of lunar boulders blew into outer space around the moon and swept surface dust from the debris field. In time, many of the orbiting boulders would be pulled by earth's gravity toward the atmosphere. Some lunaroids were destined for the asteroid belt, but those that reached the atmosphere and impacted earth were of immediate concern. Before these boulders arrived, solar wind would transport radioactive lunar dust to the earth's magnetosphere. This stretch of time would be measured in human lives on Planet Earth.

Earthbound infrared telescopes had already reported a cloudy mist encircling the moon. The ghastly mist looked like the creeping death described by Moses in Exodus. Spectrographic analysis gave an electronic pictorial of the orbiting debris, a floating field speckled with lunar rocks, many of immense size.

News of lunaroids whizzed around the globe through hastily repaired satellites. TV networks appropriately billed the historic event as 'Lunar Upheaval.' Some networks televised discussion groups day and night augmented by spectacular footage from their film files. It was the story of the millennium, and they knew it.

Over in the Wilcox Solar Observatory, Kim Marshall sat in a room while she prepared for an interview with Dr. Randall. Hel had finally answered her e-mail and granted this interview. She never liked telephone interviews, and flew out to the coast. She intended to be more personal than professional. Yet what stirred her mind was a new theory proposed by Dr. Randall, another catastrophe! The prospect unnerved her, one catastrophe after another had clouded her judgment. The long flight from Washington, DC to the west coast had compounded her anxiety. And anxiety had birthed her bitter anger. She feared professionalism would take a back seat. But her journalistic zeal somehow reinforced her spirit.

She finally entered Randall's front office totally pissed, in no mood for technical lectures. She wanted plain facts. No spin. A secretary directed Kim to Dr. Randall's office off the planetarium. Randall stood behind his desk as she entered, but before he offered his greetings he detected Kim's anger.

Kim snapped on her tape recorder and laid it on Randall's desk. "Dr. Randall, would you please explain this new theory of yours in plain English?"

Randall lit his pipe unsure of just what Kim wanted to hear, what she would accept. "The moon will be the center of attraction now. The lunar surface has suffered—"

Kim's temper exploded as she cut him off.

"Get to the point, Randall. I don't give a damn about the moon. This theory of yours suggests another astronomical phenomenon on the horizon, does it not?"

Randall rocked back in his chair, calmly stared at Kim while he relit his pipe, and puffed a few billows, which he hoped allowed enough time for her to cool off. "It's not really a theory, Kim. Solar wind is blowing over the moon's surface as we speak, sweeping radioactive particles into the earth's magnetosphere."

Her hazel eyes squinted shut recalling how politicians like to spin their answers, but she was surprised that Dr. Randall had fallen into the same trap.

"Good grief, Dr. Randall! Don't you scientists ever see anything but global catastrophes in those crystal balls of yours?"

Randall puffed aromatic smoke into the air thinking how he could explain a technical matter to a novice, one angered at that. "NOAA is tracking the radiation right now at its Boulder, Colorado headquarters."

"Tracking radiation?" she blurted out in utter despair.

"They're using weather maps to plot the drift," he said warily.

"Level with me, Dr. Randall" the fiery redhead demanded. "Weather maps won't cut it. Couldn't this thing be just another magnetic storm?"

Randall removed his pipe, "I'm afraid that's all I can tell you, Kim."

Kim realized that her uncontrollable temper had quenched her professionalism and she tried to compensate. "What were you saying about weather maps and wind drift?"

"You'll have to talk with the DOD, Kim."

She sighed and realized her temper had scuttled the interview. Kim clicked off her recorder and tried to calm her inner rage.

"Sorry, Dr. Randall, guess I'm just so tired of catastrophes," she openly admitted.

"So is everyone else, Kim. Don't let it hit you too hard. We still have time."

A hazel eye arched as she wagged her head. "I hope you're right, I really do."

The redhead reporter left the observatory with her active mind spinning. She wasted the rest of the day while she called her contacts in the Defense Department but to no avail. Later that night someone from Fort Campbell called her cellphone. The message intrigued her journalistic mind. This has to be it, she thought. *That's what Randall was trying to say; secret germ warfare maps. Surely we aren't facing mass destruction by a terrorist attack. What's the purpose? The world is about to destroy itself.*

Chapter 40

IN THE WAITING AREA located somewhere behind the pressroom, Winston Darcy and his chief of staff discussed a vital point in his upcoming speech. Four secret service agents flanked the pair as they strode down a narrow corridor toward the pressroom. Evans angled his head near the President's ear.

"I'd take Randall's advice and not say anything about Kim Marshall's telecast or that Post news article," Evans counseled.

"For once we agree, Andrew. Both the Majority leader and the House speaker concur," he replied as he briskly walked. "Could it be that Kim Marshall has upstaged your staff, again?"

"Humph. She's sitting out there right now, sir. Don't let her upstage you on national TV."

"I'll take it under advisement," Darcy chuckled.

"I'm serious, sir. The point is you've got sane and wise counsel," Evans whispered to Darcy as he brushed against two secret service agents.

The Present walked into the pressroom and stood behind the Presidential Seal. Cameras flashed like a million fireflies on a summer's night. His penetrating eyes gazed across the group of waiting reporters while a technician arranged the maze of microphones. A hushed silence floated over the crowd like the calm before a storm.

"We're tracking sixteen lunaroids that left lunar orbit last night, caused by a nuclear blast on the moon's surface."

A murmur rose from the crowd but no one interrupted.

"So far," he continued. "We've only detected smaller debris that burned out as harmless meteorites, but I'm advised that any massive lunaroid that plunged into the ocean could initiate a tsunami."

"Mr. President, the military has been unusually active at Fort Campbell. Our sources say that three carriers have been diverted to the Pacific."

"General LaCroix is pulling together a plan to intercept the larger lunaroids with Patriot missiles. I understand that launching batteries are being set up on the carrier decks."

The crowd rumbled with whispers.

"Sir, Dr. Randall thinks the splashdown point is the Pacific basin. Can the military get out there in time?"

"General LaCroix believes the U.S.S. Theodore Roosevelt has the best chance—she's already in the Pacific conducting maneuvers."

"Sir, does anybody know about the moon's surface condition following that nuclear blast?"

"NASA is on top of that question," he responded, and moved from behind the lectern. "My purpose tonight is to make America aware of the possibility of lunaroids entering earth's atmosphere. But let me assure you that the North American continent is in no danger."

Darcy spotted Kim Marshall with her hand raised. He nodded. His eyes displayed the thoughts in his mind as he prayed she would not open the question of a neutron bomb's affinity for flesh.

"Mr. President. WOFF NEWS has reported that the DOD is using some sort of germ warfare maps. Do we have any reason to suspect a fanatic or some terrorist group is about to release mass destruction agents into the atmosphere?"

Darcy took a swallow of bottled water. "No, it's nothing like that Kim. Dr. Randall believes we may experience some radiation fallout from that plutonium blast."

The crowd rustled, but no one interrupted the WOFF reporter who seemed always to have breaking news.

Kim rebutted. "I assume these germ warfare maps will be used to track the radiation drift in the atmosphere. Is that correct, Mr. President?"

"Not only track it, Kim, but predict the locations of fallout."

"That's pretty advanced stuff, Mr. President. You're not suggesting these maps are that sophisticated, are you?"

"The DOD project goes back to Hiroshima. Thank God somebody had the foresight to initiate this project. Try to understand that massive numbers of people around the world would die if we could not predict fallout with some advanced warning."

A CSN reporter stood in the aisle. "Can you tell us now when you do expect fallout?"

"NOAA is tracking the atmosphere and NORAD is managing the program. That's all I can report at this time."

Kim Marshall stood again. "Mr. President. Isn't it true, that even if we know the points of fallout, we still have no way to contain the radiation?"

Darcy reached for the water bottle that rested on a shelf beneath the lectern. "That's quite true, Kim."

He gulped a swallow of water. "However, Caltech has developed something on this question. We should have a report by tomorrow morning. Thank you for your attention."

Winston Darcy promptly left the lectern and exited through a side passage, and resisted further questions that still rumbled from the crowd of reporters.

The press secretary moved onto the dais. "That will be all, ladies and gentlemen. You'll find prepared statements as you leave."

Reporters crowded around Kim.

Chapter 41

A SPECIAL MEETING of the National Geographic Society convened on the ground floor of its Washington, DC headquarters. TV networks from around the world crowded into the lecture auditorium for an historic presentation. The aging governor of the foundation stepped to the lectern. The crowd quieted with great anticipation.

"Ladies and gentlemen, welcome to our presentation today. It has been the society's pleasure to fund a project of incredible importance to the planet's environment. Without further delay, let me introduce two imminent scientists: Drs. Norman Hobart of Caltech and Rufus Guildenstern from the University of Chicago."

A tall, robust man with wiry and bushy hair pushed aside his briefcase and stood. "Four years ago, Dr. Hobart approached me with an extremely simple method for eliminating nuclear fallout. His theory adapted the phagocyte mechanisms existing in the human blood. This scavenger engulfs foreign particles and releases them from the body as ordinary waste. Dr. Hobart and I have formulated a unique gel that encapsulates radioactive particles. But let me introduce the inventor, Dr. Norman Hobart."

A nattily dressed bespectacled man about five feet five with a receding hairline stepped to the microphone. Dr. Hobart humbly bowed at the resounding ovation of applause. The audience was electrified by the thought of encapsulating radioactive fallout. In their minds the idea translated into lucrative dollars.

"Thank you, Dr. Guildenstern, thank you very much."

The ovation refused to subside. Finally he leaned into the microphone, removed his spectacles, and spoke.

"The gel formulation which has been mentioned by Dr. Guildenstern is produced as an ionic spray that can be released into the clouds as a mist. It gels into a semi-solid globule on contact with atmospheric dust particles. I first envisioned the concept while studying the manufacture of silicon conductors by ion implantation. This is a conventional method of implanting impurities by directing a stream of ions onto the chips. In the final stage of our testing phase, Dr. Guildenstern experimented with isotopes of Uranium (233) and Plutonium (239) at his laboratory in Chicago for reasons I think you will understand in my remarks.

"Although the nuclear age came in our lifetime, it was short lived because of environmental issues. But the growing realization among nuclear physicists is that breeder reactors, a cleaner and more efficient process are the technology for fuel production in the future. The brief revival of breeder reactors in 1987 opened a door of opportunity to use U (233) since reserves of U (235) are quickly vanishing. Admiral Rickover's success with the light-water breeder has shown that fissile U (233) can convert to Pu (239) with a slow release of proton energy.

"The calamity facing the planet today has been succinctly stated by Dr. Bruce Randall of Wilcox Solar Observatory. We can, as he predicts, expect fallout from the plutonium explosion on the moon's surface. A massive radioactive cloud will plunge into the troposphere. Gentlemen, I believe my spray can encapsulate most of the radioactive fallout in a harmless gel."

The crowd sat mummified.

"Thank you, Dr. Hobart," the MC said. "The chair is open for questions. Would you please find one of the microphones posted around the auditorium?" People popped from their seats all over the auditorium. "You, sir, in the back," the MC pointed.

"How does your spray work in application, Dr. Hobart?" a reporter asked.

The professor rubbed a tissue over the thick lenses of his spectacles, puffed his breathe on the lenses and wiped them once more.

"The radioactive fallout will travel on dust particles in the atmosphere, much like raindrops or snowflakes. These particles will fall by gravity when heavy enough not to be carried aloft by the winds in the upper atmosphere. The matrix of my spray has an ionic binder that forms a globular gel of lead and polymer ions. The ionic gel electro statically attracts and surrounds the nuclear particles much like the phagocytes attack foreign particles in human blood. These heavy globules will fall harmlessly into the ocean."

"Harmless doctor? Would you please expand that thought?" Kim Marshall interjected from her seat near the front.

The professor removed his spectacles searching for the hazel-eyed reporter with his squinting eyes.

"Ah yes, Ms. Marshall," he said and replaced his spectacles. "Preliminary laboratory studies with rats and rabbits show that the gel passes through the waste system without any harmful effects. However, the product has not achieved medical approval, nor was that intended. The purpose of the spray is to encapsulate the harmful radioactive particles."

Kim Marshall stood and seized a microphone from a man standing in the aisle. "Dr. Guildenstern, do you concur with Hobart's findings?"

"Why yes, I think I do in this case, Ms. Marshall. Many people across the globe will consider Dr. Hobart's remedy as their only hope. Others may not. It will be up to Congress and President Darcy to make that determination."

Kim rebutted, "I see, doctor. Then we can eliminate this radioactive hazard, if those globules do exactly what you say they will do?"

Mumbling sounds rumbled over the crowd. But Hobart raised his hands and answered her question. "There is one other feature of the globule," Hobart clarified. "We've added a calcite component that causes the globule to harden, much like Portland cement. When immersed in water, a complex chemical change occurs similar to hardening cement, causing the gel to extend its drying time, resulting in a stable globule. Also, the lead binder provides some shielding from radiation."

Winston Darcy clicked off the TV in his Oval Office pondering Hobart's globule fix. The Chairman of the Joint Chiefs leaned back in his leather chair anticipating the President's remarks.

"Boswell, where are we now on getting that Caltech product into the atmosphere?"

General LaCroix chewed down on his cigar, grinding his teeth. Darcy was the only person alive besides his mother who dared to call him by his first name: Boswell, God, how he hated it. He'd even had it stricken from his military records, changed the initial "B" to Broderick.

"We've had a stroke of luck, sir."

"Oh. And who is the bearer of gifts?"

"Exxon. National Geographic funded two modified gasoline-cracking plants in Houston. Exxon has been producing Hobart's spray for the last two months."

Darcy's face mellowed into a smile. "That's not luck it's a blooming miracle, Boswell! How are you going to apply the spray?"

LaCroix gripped his cigar between a nicotine-stained thumb and index finger. "Mr. President, we're modifying the flying boom on twelve KC-135 Stratotankers. These refueling jets will give us the volume, the range, and the speed required to cover the Pacific basin. The tanks will be filled with the globular spray instead of jet fuel. Colonel Griffin had the idea, and Fort Campbell is running with the project."

The President seemed impressed. "I'm quite pleased at your resourcefulness, Boswell. But remember, we only have five days before that radioactive fallout sweeps into the ocean."

"We've already transported Exxon's current production to Guam Island. I've named the project Hot Stuff," LaCroix said.

The chief executive smiled again and winked. "Keep me posted, Boswell."

Chapter 42

THE PACIFIC FLEET had gone on emergency alert at 0100 hours on the first day of a six-day countdown. Orders from the Admiralty were sent to three fleet-carrier groups on maneuvers in the Pacific: the U.S.S. Independence, the U.S.S. Theodore Roosevelt, and the U.S.S. Carl Vinson. All three flattops had set courses for Guam where they would take positions defined in sealed orders. Patriot missiles were being installed on the carrier deck of the U.S.S Theodore Roosevelt as she steered to her destination expected to be the first carrier to arrive.

Twelve KC-135 Stratotankers were moored on the field somewhere in Kansas where they waited for orders to transfer to Fort Campbell, Kentucky. But engineering specified the modifications were late, therefore departure time was uncertain. Seven C-17A Globemaster transports sat on the tarmac with lethal cargos of Patriot missiles being loaded, complete with launching batteries.

"Tower, Patriot I ready for takeoff."

"Roger, Patriot I."

"Next stop Guam, over-and-out."

Throttles rammed forward and turbine fans screamed. The C-17A transports taxied to the runway like little chicks following the mother hen.

One-by-one the pregnant jets lifted into a brilliant sky. The lead transport set its course for Guam Island; the others pulled into formation, and set courses for destinations stated in sealed orders. Sunlight shafted through the windshields in blinding flashes as they punched through scattered clouds. There was no hint of the impending danger in outer space.

The sun blazed high and steady from its lofty perch and belched tons of charged particles that distorted the planet's protective magnetic field. Traveling at the speed of light, ultraviolet and X rays reached the earth in eight minutes, and disrupted radio signals.

Fifteen minutes later the heavier solar masses slammed into earth satellites. After forty-eight hours, massive solar particles invaded earth's magnetic field. Yet there was no sound to be heard on earth, at least not audible sound waves. However radio telescopes around the world intercepted noisy radio signals that jammed their antennas.

The warming planet soaked up the radiant energy like a sponge: the altitudes, the plains, and the oceans steamed and baked in the blazing sun. And news came down that the northern tundra had early signs of snowmelt from receding glaciers. The Atlantic temperature had elevated 0.2 degree since the solar maximum began. The sun grew torrid, the earth, and its inhabitants baked.

Somewhere in northern Florida, a military Nerve Center had recently started operations that directed Operation Lunar Storm. Landline links were coupled with microwave towers, and were established directly to the Joint Chiefs and staff located in the Pentagon. The center's interlinks finally hooked up with NORAD after the Air Force had re-established links with the GPS and military satellites. Later reports described the possible loss of several GPS satellites.

"General LaCroix, sir. Lunar Storm is underway," a voice said over a satellite link, "ETA to target is 1042 hours tomorrow."

"I'm proud of those guys," LaCroix replied, seated in the Pentagon. He lifted his eyes from the console and looked around the table at his project chiefs. "If we don't knock out those lunaroids, it won't be because we didn't give it our best shot."

"It's the fastest time on record, sir."

LaCroix peeled the label from a new cigar, "It's the time left that worries me, Colonel."

"NASA still thinks we have time, sir."

"Killing those lunaroids won't be like shooting clay pigeons. We'll have to do better than we did bringing down those Scuds in Desert Storm."

A Lieutenant's eyes narrowed. He had misunderstood the General's nomenclature and was about to end his military career. Fortunate for him the Joint Chief was a congenial leader. "Sir," he reluctantly asked. "Aren't these lunaroids technically asteroids?"

LaCroix removed his unlit cigar, his face blank. "Lighten up, son. Leave the acronyms to the boys at HQ."

"Ah-huh. Yes sir. Uh-ah, recent modifications to the Patriot missile makes her the best candidate to pulverize those lunaroids, sir."

"That's the stuff, Lieutenant," he replied. He twirled his cigar and puffed smoke above his head. "It's the first time Patriots have been launched from a carrier deck, that's for sure."

The Lieutenant deeply sighed. "Don't worry about scoffers, sir. The same naysayers objected to launching jets off carrier decks after World War II."

LaCroix stuffed the cigar in his mouth. "Yeah, but if those lunaroids come down in one cluster the naysayers will win, Lieutenant."

Bands of lunar debris raced ahead of lunaroids aimed toward earth. The radioactive armada silently sailed through the black void of space headed directly toward the earth's delicate atmosphere, gripped by the relentless tug of gravity.

A soldier sat in front of a computer console down in the Pentagon headquarters and waited for an urgent message. Words staggered across the screen as the message formed.

"General! NORAD reports meteors in the western sector."

LaCroix rocked forward in his chair, looking at the big board spread across the front of the room.

"The western sector?" he puzzled. "Those NASA boys couldn't have been that wrong."

"Looks like isolated breakup, sir, nothing large enough to escape atmospheric burn out."

The troubled Joint Chief returned to his desk and lifted his secure phone. "It's started. We've picked up a few fringe meteors in the western sector," he said to Andrew Evans.

"All right General. The President is watching this show. Let's pulverize a few lunaroids. Give the people some hope, General."

"We'll be in place to intercept incoming lunaroids by midmorning tomorrow."

"Thank you, General. I'll tell the President."

Chapter 43

NASA-GODDARD AT Greenbelt shifted to DEFCON 1 at half past midnight. Mountains of incoming data jammed the direct line to ground-based computers. The Hubble space telescope locked on a second wave of lunar objects hurtling toward the earth. Shutter frequency was set at maximum to track the lunaroids. Precise numbers on speed and direction were needed to program the Patriot missiles now stationed around the Pacific basin. Mobile Patriots mounted on three carrier decks were primed and ready for action. The computers feverously labored.

At the southern end of the eastern seaboard, the nerve center in Florida had accessed the information and planned its action. Technicians scurried to their consoles. The red horn on the wall blared with alternating blasts: DEFCON 1, not a war between opposing military forces, but a battle for survival of the planet.

A catalogue lay open on the Lieutenant's desk containing a list of asteroids. About thirty thousand pieces of rock debris, known collectively as the asteroid belt, were strewn between the orbits of Mars and Jupiter. The largest recorded asteroid, dubbed Ceres, measured thirty-three miles in diameter. Other names included Eros, Albert, Adonis, Apollo, Amar, and Icarus, ranging from ten to thirty miles in diameter. Their orbital planes did not cross and there was little danger of collision, although some scientists speculated that several asteroids would one day pass dangerously close to earth. These mysterious objects took on oblique configurations, egg-shaped or potato-shaped, even dumbbell-shaped. Their surfaces were crater-battered and carbon-rich, the darkest objects in the solar system. They reflected only about three percent of sunlight that made them twice as dark as an earthbound chunk of charcoal.

The Pentagon, at the Joint Chief's directive, established a numerical lunaroid classification from 1 to 20 which corresponded to a range of one-to-twenty miles in diameter in the "A" category: A-1, one mile; A-2, two miles, and following. Smaller lunaroids measured less than a mile in diameter were labeled as "B" category lunaroids. Thus, B-1 equaled 500 feet in diameter, B-2 at one thousand feet, *et cetera.*

An announcement suddenly blared from the big board speakers arched across the front of the Pentagon War Room.

"We have three—no make those four Class B-5 lunaroids. There is one big monster, maybe a mile in diameter. Let's call it a Class A-2. That's three Class B-5s and one Class A-2. Two of these babies will hit the troposphere in exactly thirty-two minutes."

"Roger, Control. This is Rover I, about two hundred miles east of the Philippines. I have your coordinates locked on radar. One's a mountain!" the flight controller exclaimed seated in the battle room of the U.S.S. Theodore Roosevelt.

The Captain ordered the flattop turned into the wind. Four F16 fighters launched from her decks. They provided the eyes when the lunaroids flamed into the upper atmosphere. Patriot missiles, newly installed on the flattop, launched with precise coordinates signaled from Goddard. The F16s refined the target designations when the lunaroids entered the stratosphere. If the Patriots were unsuccessful, the fighters had orders to hit the meteors with Sidewinder missiles.

"This is Rambo 1. I have two—repeat two, that's two meteors on my scanners."

"Copy, Rambo 1," the speaker blared. "We're locked on your coordinates."

"Steady as she goes. We get the second shot."

"Roger, Rambo—Control, got one meteor burning through."

"Copy: coordinates plotting now."

At somewhere near fifty miles downrange, two Patriot missiles blazed from the deck of the cruising flattop. They soared away at lightning speed toward the gigantic chunk of lunar real estate.

"Patriot I tracking."

"Roger. Altitude approximately forty five thousand feet—it's a hit! "Debris particles are nominal size, just harmless meteorites."

"Copy, Rambo, one down, one to go."

"Roger, tracking second lunaroid now. Holy Toledo, she's a monster! This baby will need four Patriots, at least."

Five Patriot missiles screamed from the flight deck of the U.S.S. Theodore Roosevelt.

The distorted potato-shaped meteor streamed like the tail of a blazing comet, now visible to the naked eye. Sailors watched through binoculars from the flight deck. Scuttlebutt spread through the ship like a virus. Sailors rushed to any vantage point available. The explosive sounds of impact followed a brilliant flash. A tremendous starburst lit up the pale, blue sky like a 4th of July celebration. But the gigantic meteor showed no visible signs of damage, as it hurtled on through the upper atmosphere like an avalanche from hell.

"Fighters, take your shots!"

Eight AIM-9X Sidewinder missiles soared from the wing hangers like blazing arrows. They all struck the meteor dead center but the monster never even flinched, as if a mosquito had attacked a rusty cannon ball.

"She's coming through, Control. The monster has lost some weight, but she's still a giant, the size of a small town."

"Roger, we're plotting her course, now."

The runaway meteor soared through the atmosphere with a flaming contrail. Her trajectory aimed her toward the Pacific basin, somewhere east of Japan. Two more Patriot missiles blazed from a coastline battery and intercepted the mastodon meteor. Impact cracked the surface. But the gargantuan monster hurtled on, cloaked beneath the Patriot screen.

F16 jets from two other carriers swarmed around the lunar rock and blasted the target with Sidewinder missiles. But to no avail. The fighters broke off the attack after all the missiles had left the wing racks. The message went out to Brisbane and Tokyo.

General LaCroix slumped in his seat at the Pentagon War Room as he stared at the live pictures on the big board. Two lunaroids plunged through atmosphere like fiery balls from Hades, and he had witnessed the historic event. One had been pulverized, however, the larger one slipped through the Patriot net with hardly a scratch. Goddard's computer models predicted the point of splashdown. The General lifted the red phone on his desk connecting a direct line to the President.

"Sir, one giant lunaroid got through the screen. It's blazing toward the Pacific near the Sea of Japan. Looks like a tsunami may develop."

Silence.

The President finally replied. "Thank you, Boswell. Thank you for this advance notice, we are notifying our embassies in Japan and Australia as we speak. Listen, Boswell we've got to do better than fifty percent. Goddard is tracking eight more goliaths."

"Hold on, sir. Something's coming in now—Holy Cow!"

"Speak up man, what is it?"

"That monster is cleaving into two pieces! We've got two gigantic lunaroids soaring toward the Pacific!"

All indicators predicted a massive tsunami if a large object plunged into the Pacific basin. But this runaway monster had a cleavage crack inflicted by Patriot and Sidewinder missiles; the cleavage split the larger A-2 meteor into a Gemini configuration. Two Class A-1 lunar rocks, each about one mile in diameter, now hurtled toward the ocean in separate trajectories.

Detailed tracking data from the airborne AWACS predicted one of the twins would crash into the outcroppings of the Volcano Island chain a thousand nautical miles southeast of Guam. The other twin would splashdown in the Pacific about eight hundred miles due east of Tokyo.

Somewhere deep under a massive northwestern mountain the NORAD facility warning horns blared and bellowed like sick cows. Highly trained military officers rushed to their consoles and answered the call of DEFCON 1. The delicate shield around the earth had suffered mighty solar storms before, but now the outermost defenses were under attack by a deadly intruder. Radioactive particles had penetrated the magnetosphere, the region in space occupied by the earth's magnetic field. The nebulous field extended about 40,000 miles on the sunward side. Fierce solar storms compressed the field to only 26,000 miles that exposed high-orbiting satellites to the solar wind.

An Air Force General pressed his pencil against his lips, "Put up those drift-maps, Lieutenant. Let's see where this stuff is going."

An engineer punched several keys on his console. The huge interactive screen lit up across the front of the amphitheater. Four sections of the globe flashed on the wide screen in the familiar shape of a pealed orange. The magnetopause, a magnetic boundary between the earth and the solar wind, was the last stronghold against radiation. The drift maps showed that it, too, was penetrated.

The science officer whirled around in his chair at the far end of the curved dais. "Sir, if we overlay the magnetic charts over the drift charts maybe we can see the polar effects."

The General nodded at the engineer. He punched several keys on the keyboard and the Polar Regions superimposed on the screen like the crosshatches of fence wire. Swirling magnetic lines formed a boundary around a bullet-shaped plasmoid, a bulge of hot plasma. It seemed to grow with the pressure of the solar wind. Outward sheets of plasma streamed away from the earth and vanished. Magnetic lines glowed red on the drift maps. Green lines represented radioactive particles as they burst into the troposphere and flowed into the Polar Regions. It was too soon to determine if the scatter-effect of the troposphere would reflect the magnetic waves. Since it was the division of the atmosphere extending from ground levels up to five to ten miles, convection winds were prevalent in the troposphere, and it contained most of the moisture in the atmosphere that formed the clouds.

"Sir, traces of green lines are beginning to form. We've got radioactive penetration in the northern troposphere."

"Notify NOAA," the General barked. His face wrinkled with signs of lost sleep and fatigue. Creeping hints of a war that he must win had caused his left eye to flinch.

Chapter 44

"SIR, THE RADAR shows an unusually large blip headed on course one-seven-six," the seaman said to his Lieutenant, standing on the bridge of the Mermaid.

The Mermaid was an oceanography vessel working near the Mariana Trench, the deepest point on the Pacific floor. The news of the tsunami first came in from NOAA Space Environment Center on the Lieutenant's second watch. Coupled with the data from an AWACS, the refitted ship was destined for a jarring blast into her bow.

The officer of the deck carefully studied the blips on the monitor. "It's that tsunami we've been expecting." he said and flipped a switch: "Battle stations! Battle stations! This is not a drill."

The Captain heard the horn from his cabin, and roused from his bunk. He rushed to the bridge and crammed his shirt into his pants before he reached the ladder.

"Captain, sir, we're tracking that tsunami now. It's about two thousand kilometers due west," the officer reported.

The Captain stood steady on his sea legs even after thirty-six hours without good sleep. He peered through night binoculars at a rising wall of water in the distance. "Get the Mermaid turned around, helmsman. We're gonna weather this storm."

"Radar has a flat wave at fifteen hundred kilometers and closing fast, sir," the deck officer replied.

"Get every reading we can during this blast, Lieutenant. And pull down those weather balloons or kiss'em good-bye."

"Sir, the AWACS data puts the tidal surge at a height of 50-meters and rising," the seaman gulped.

"Button all hatches. Close the bulkhead doors. Get this boat ready to swim," the Captain barked.

For some reason, the night sky began to wave and churn in ghostly swirls of eerie lights. It looked as though the sea boiled on the horizon.

"Those lights, Captain, can't make that out."

The Captain thought for a moment as he stared at the swirling sky. "We had reports that the auroras might be screwed up. You're looking at an overlap of the *aurora borealis* from the North Pole and the *aurora australis* from the South Pole. Protons spiraling down both magnetic poles caused those lights. That's what produced those purplish lights, son."

"Never saw anything like this, sir."

"There's never been anything to match this far as I know. You're witnessing solar history."

"I guess this'll stop the foolish talks in Congress about shooting nuclear waste into the sun. They should be putting people to work on a way to neutralize the stuff. Don't tell me it can't be done. That's what critics said about going to the moon," the Lieutenant said in nervous chatter, white knuckles squeezing his binoculars.

"Don't count on it, Lieutenant. People have short memories and politicians are spin-masters.

There's still a group of people who believe the landing on the moon was all a Hollywood movie."

He adjusted the focus of the binoculars. "The swells are increasing, sir, and whitecaps in the distance. Looks like about fifteen minutes to impact."

The Captain nodded. "Recheck all your instruments—breakout the life jackets."

A white foamy turbulence pushed ahead of the giant wall like watery teeth chewing up the surf. The surging wall slammed the bridge of the Mermaid with uncanny force, tore away her canvas covers and deck equipment, but the windshields on the bridge miraculously held.

The sturdy ship rolled and tumbled like a matchbox in a bathtub. The bow rose and dipped, lifting the props out of the water. The keel crashed on its belly deep into a trough of a gigantic wave. Tons of water drowned the Mermaid; thrust her into the briny depths of the churning Pacific. Bilge pumps screamed under crushing pressure beyond design limits.

Creaking sounds of welded metal echoed within the bowels of the submerged vessel lift a ghost ship adrift. Terrified men helplessly watched through the leaking portholes at the eerily churning waters outside the rivet-creaking hull.

The ship finally popped to the surface like a humpback whale. Swirling wash poured from her battered decks. Seaweed twisted around the forward capstan like a giant spool of green thread. The deck-mounted crane had slipped its mooring, it lay mangled, and bent as if it were wet spaghetti sprinkled with seaweed. The Lieutenant gulped and straightened his cap.

"We're through it, sir. The Mermaid held the surge. What a gal!"

"Captain," the helmsman screamed, "you won't believe the anemometer readings. The darn thing's pegged."

The Captain lay on the deck, his mouth smeared in dried blood. "Stow the chatter," he coughed, "that tsunami will push us toward the shore like a surfboard."

A roaring wall of towering and surging water rolled toward the island of Japan like an unrolling scroll. The Mermaid sat on the foamy surface like a toy boat. Unless the momentum of the surge somehow lost its strength, the Mermaid was sure to be landlocked.

Australia reported winds up to eighty knots with inland flooding. The continent would take most of the backwash. But Japan was in for a nautical thrashing by a tsunami with immense energy. The Japanese were seafaring people who understood the precautions necessary to weather a tidal surge. But the smaller islands and hamlets in the coastal regions had always suffered the greatest devastation in massive storms, yet the magnitude of this watery monster was not on the charts.

The surge moved inland about ten miles and left thousands of bodies in its wake. The Mermaid laid in the mud on her starboard side, truly a duck out of water. The crew was miraculously unhurt; the Captain had died with his ship. In his valiant attempt to save his crew, the Captain and the first mate perished in the sea.

The cost of salvaging the Mermaid exceeded her value. But the loss of lives and property and a million broken homes, lost children and dead parents could not be counted. Would they ever survive?

Could they ever survive? Would history record this tragedy or would time end for thousands of people?

Chapter 45

"WOFF NEWS REPORTS tonight that a battle rages for mankind's right to exist somewhere in the Pacific Ocean. Units of the Naval Air Force today shot down several lunaroids with Patriot missiles in a valiant attempt to save this planet from annihilation. This is Kim Marshall and you're tuned to Washington Drumbeat. Our guest tonight is General LaCroix, chairman of the Joint Chiefs and director of the President's taskforce. We will return after these messages."

A setup piece filled the monitors with spectacular footage of Patriot missiles exploding lunaroids, including NASA photos of the asteroid belt. Kim Marshall watched the light on the facing camera.

"With us tonight is General LaCroix, chairman of the Joint Chiefs. General, the world is anxiously hoping for good news. What can you offer them?"

The General rustled in his chair, fidgety fingers searching for a cigar. "Right now, we're having considerable success in bringing down the larger lunaroids, and as reported, only one giant boulder got by the Patriot screen."

"Didn't the President report that more lunaroids are out there somewhere?"

"We're tracking several Classes-A lunaroids that missed the earth. We fully expect them to reach the asteroid belt. NASA is planning a flyby Shuttle to inspect the dark side of the moon. The Hubble will concentrate on the visible side of the lunar surface," he said, with nicotine tension pulsating in his veins.

"What size is a Class-A lunaroid, sir?"

"An A-1 classification designates approximately one mile in diameter, ranging up to A-20 at twenty miles in diameter."

"And the B-classification, General, what's that about?"

"It designates lunaroids smaller than one mile in diameter. The B-1 classification designates about 500 feet in diameter."

"General LaCroix. How did this massive effort come together so quickly?"

"Our military men and women are professionals, Kim. Never in the annals of military history has an operation of such technical complexity come together with such spectacular success. Although this operation involved fewer personnel, it was a faster logistics operation than even Desert Storm."

"And how does this operation compare with the Armada that landed on Normandy beaches during WWII?"

"The invasion of Normandy sought to rid the world of a tyrant. Lunar Storm seeks to save the planet from total annihilation."

"Let's shift gears, General. What about the radioactive fallout question?"

"The Caltech spray is our best hope, Kim."

"It's a big ocean out there. Are we ready, General?"

"Specialized personnel at Guam Island and at Fort Campbell literally hold the planet in their hands, Kim. About all we can do now is to pray."

"Thank you, General LaCroix. We'll return with more on Lunar Storm after these messages. Stay tuned to WOFF NEWS where we report, you decide."

Kim relaxed as the camera light blinked off. They chatted while the program soundtrack rolled. A light on the camera blinked red.

"Welcome back. We are continuing our discussion with General LaCroix chairman of the President's taskforce. General, about this assault on the earth, when will it end?"

"The answer is at Fort Campbell, Kim."

"Can those transports really get out to Guam in time?"

"It's a tight envelope but they'll make it. They've got to make it. We must survive. We simple must keep our freedom in this war against nature."

"I'm told this victory goes to many brave Americans."

"Not just Americans. Japan and Australia fought a surging tsunami of unprecedented strength. But there is one French lady who deserves mention. She had the courage to come to America and expose her own grandfather's unthinkable deed. It was he who put those two rockets into space twenty years ago."

"You're speaking of Monique Chevet?"

"Yes, Kim. There's your uncommon courage. Most of us did what we were trained to do. She did what she had to do, disregarding the cost to herself."

"Thank you, General LaCroix, chairman of the President's taskforce. Stay tuned for the evening news."

Overhead lights blinked dim, cameras tilted on their mobile bases. Kim gathered her papers and faced her guest. Somehow she seemed despondent. She was a reporter and all the action was in the

Pacific basin. "The biggest story of the millennium, and here I am stuck in the Capital."

LaCroix sensed her desire and thought how he might remedy the situation. The girl had worked hard to inform the people, the least he could do was to help her.

"You were an embedded reporter in Iraq, right?"

Her head curiously bobbed. "Yes," she replied and watched the General pull a card from his portfolio.

"Here, this will get you out to sea. You be at Fort Campbell by eighteen hundred hours tomorrow night."

She winked and touched his hand, "Thanks General—thanks a bunch."

LaCroix smiled and wished he had a cigar to fire up. And, of course, if he were younger he might have gone with Kim. He sighed deeply. Poppycock! The President needed him more than ever, even if he was the only man who called him Boswell and got away with it.

Chapter 46

FORT CAMPBELL SPRAWLED over vast areas of both Kentucky and Tennessee real estate. The runways were laid out to maximize the advantage of prevailing winds. Most of the airfield spread over into Tennessee. But the U.S. Post Office sat just off the state borderline on the Kentucky side which gave the fort its Kentucky address. This 'land of tomorrow' derived its name from an Iroquian word, 'Ken-tah-ten.' Backwoods rumors claimed that Daniel Boone once hunted bear in this neck of woods, probably in the same place where logistic materiel laid up-and-down the plateau behind a tall, razor-wire fence.

Fort Campbell was home of the 101st Airborne Division. The military men and women in this facility literally held the world in a precarious balance. Their formidable task was somehow to protect the planet from deadly fallout. A wave of radioactive lunar dust now threatened the troposphere. Time was their enemy. But here and now, this fort was a Godsend.

Over in Hanger-B three engineering technicians had fitted a curious gadget onto a KC-135 drogue, a buoy at the end of the flying boom. A sergeant tightened the bolt circle that sealed the Neoprene gasket. Ladder platforms quickly rolled away.

"Are you sure this thing will work, Lieutenant?" the pilot wondered as he inspected the strange, U-shaped snorkel assembly.

"It's the only way to flight test it, sir."

"Yeah, that's why I'm here. My mother always said I was stupid," the pilot squawked and wagged his head.

"Okay, sir. Keep an eye on that tank pressure. She's all yours, Captain," the sergeant said while he watched him climb aboard the tanker.

The pilot waved from the cockpit, while a tow pulled the jet out of the hangar. As the copilot read aloud the preflight checklist, busy fingers flipped switches. The heavy jet taxied from the tarmac out to a runway.

A viscous liquid filled its refueling tanks to simulate the density of a globular spray he would test on this early morning flight. No need to waste the precious product for this prototype test. Both pilots knew the density of the globular substance was four times denser than jet fuel, meaning the aircraft would take longer to liftoff. Was the airstrip long enough, the pilot was to discover.

As the heavy tanker gained in speed, the copilot called off the distance to the end of the runway: '3, 2, 1,' the copilot counted in thousand feet clicks. The aircraft turbines strained under the load. But she was still earthbound with less than one thousand feet before impact with bushy trees at the runway's end. A sudden sensation gripped their seats. The aircraft went airborne not a second to spare, catching tree branches in its landing gear. The pilot grinned at the copilot.

"Whoops!"

Fleecy clouds floated high above the Gulf of Mexico like soft, feathery pillows. The KC-135 tanker disappeared into the nebulous mist. Somewhere two hundred miles south of Mobile Bay, the test pilot leveled the aircraft. The crew went through the checkout procedures and prepared for the spraying operation.

An F16 fighter lifted off with the Stratotanker and chased behind with rolling cameras. Its mission was to monitor the flying boom from the rear of the tanker.

"Okay, Control. I'm at the target."

"Copy, Hot Stuff. Check your pressure on the tanks."

"Pressure reading is nominal."

"Energize pumps at will."

"Roger, Control, energizing, now. Tanks are pumping—HOLY MOSES!" A crashing sound pierced the cone in the earphone of the ground-based operator, who sat with hands clasped over painfully ringing ears.

"Mayday, Mayday!! Losing altitude, controls spongy, cabin pressure dropping—"

An officer furiously tweaked the radio controls in a desperate attempt to locate the tanker on another frequency, "Talk to me, Hot Stuff. What's your condition?"

Static.

Finally the pilot answered. "Sir, we lost the F16," he gasped. "The pod ripped off the drogue and slammed into the jet. The pilot never had a chance to eject."

"What's your condition, Captain?"

"We've got a cracked windshield and lost some hydraulics. That's the best of it."

"Do you want to ditch?"

Pause.

"Repeat. Do you want to ditch?"

The radio hummed mute.

Finally an answer came. "Negative! Negative! I've gotta secure that screwed-up flying boom before it shakes the rivets out of this bird."

"Copy, Captain, we're with you. Do your stuff pilot, bring her home."

"She's leveling now. Giving her more throttle, airspeed increasing. Steady baby. Steady," crackled the earthbound speaker.

"We gotcha on the scope now, Hot Stuff, your flight pattern looks okay!"

"Tell me the way home, Control. I've got enough airspeed now."

"Roger, Hot Stuff. Come to course One, Seven, Niner. Make your turn when you're ready."

"Roger, turning now."

"You're good on that course. Bring her in, Captain."

Engineers anxiously waited for the damaged KC-135 to land. The chief engineer seemed angrily perplexed viewing the engineering drawing of the flying boom modification. It looked to him like a drafting student had designed the thing. He wondered how it had even passed inspection. These officers never ask engineering till it's too late, he thought.

The chief engineer had already redesigned the module while the ill-fated KC-135 was still airborne. The new design 'Y-d' from the drogue in a balanced pod. Two spray nozzles bent outboard at a forty-five degree angle supported by flying fins. A new regulation valve replaced the existing valve which could maintain a constant pressure on the pumps to prevent cavitation. The drawings went to the machine shop under emergency orders even before the KC-135 had landed. Six machinists were busy building a prototype.

Hot Stuff landed safely at the base and a jeep met the jet as it taxied onto the tarmac. The pilot and copilot were driven directly to the CO's office. The despondent pilot went to the hangar after a lengthy debriefing session, and the technicians were already installing a newly designed module on another KC-135 flying boom when he entered the hangar. He found the design engineer at a desk reviewing the installation procedure. The new design piqued his interest and even lifted his morale.

The engineer gripped a grimy valve assembly shaking his head. "This regulation valve was the problem, sir. The viscous flow pushed the pumps to redline. Building pressure blew the securing ring," the engineer explained and picked up a new module. "This new design has two spray heads to lower system pressure and give twice the spraying area. We've installed a new regulator to control the pumps."

The pilot listened, carefully absorbed the details on the drawing as he sipped on a cup of hot coffee. "Certainly appears more logical; it just might work," he said.

The project engineer stood, placed a hand on the Captain's shoulder. "I know you're a bit rattled by the accident, sir. But we've got to test this new design."

The pilot deeply sighed. All he thought about was the dead pilot in the chase plane and this engineer who had sat for hours to make the valve work properly. "Put it on. I'll test the thing, for the widow of that F16 pilot, if for no other reason."

Chapter 47

GENERAL LA CROIX FLIPPED a switch on the satellite console in his office at the Pentagon and reviewed the computer update on the Guam base as he waited for the circuits to clear. Colonel Griffin had done well in taking the lead to establish the base and he needed to know of his decision. The phone circuit buzzed, and a technician handed the General a microphone.

"Colonel, twelve KC-135 Stratotankers took off from Fort Campbell at dawn today. These babies are refitted with that new spray pod. Dr. Randall is aboard a C-17A Globemaster loaded with instruments and equipment. He'll help you in the control tower to interpret those new maps."

LaCroix paused and removed his cigar.

"I've authorized Kim Marshall to ride along, too. She's been in combat before, knows her stuff."

Colonel Griffin sat in a metal prefab building on the island of Guam, six thousand miles from the Pentagon, and wiped his perspiring forehead. "That's good to know, General. Thanks for the help. We've got two lousy days before radiation starts pouring into the atmosphere, sir. The stratosphere is slowly nearing saturation, could burst through at any time. If those new nozzles don't work, the planet is screwed."

LaCroix bit down on his cigar. "The chief engineer who redesigned that thing is on the transport, too, plus several extra sprayer units."

"He could be helpful, sir. Exxon has done a fabulous job out here, too. The Air Force flew out Hobart's spray in fifty-five gallon drums. Exxon sent a workforce along and set up a small tank farm. We've got plenty of that gel spray on hand."

The General choked on his cigar. "Ah-hum, blah! Dr. Hobart has named his product GLOB," he said then coughed, "stands for Globular Liquid Olefin Base—bah-ha! Ah hum. Fits right into our military alphabet soup," he chuffed. He tried to clear his throat without much success, and the General's secretary handed him a glass of water. LaCroix swallowed two gulps as he noticed the secretary's gaze. "Hairball," he said, "too many cats around the house."

"You okay, General?" the phone voiced.

"Yeah, sorry—you were saying."

"If Hobart's GLOB works, he can write his own ticket. The Energy Department is sure to authorize research dollars with tens-of-thousands of those nuclear waste drums looking for a place to hide."

"And many idle nuclear plants rusting away because of the environmental lobbyists," LaCroix added. "Well, I'll let you get to your instruments— bah-ha!"

"Thanks again, and take care of that cough, sir."

"Bah-ha," he coughed and dryly swallowed. "Yeah."

Griffin switched off his radio, his mind rethought what the General had said about idle nuclear plants. It was time for a breakthrough in America's dependence on oil-rich countries for the nation's energy supply. Fanatical terrorism and lunatic dictators kept oil prices up, then down like a seesaw. Uncertainty complicated diplomatic issues. The current problems with nuclear waste disposal, and lobbyist, who pushed against drilling in the Alaskan preserve, had created a political stalemate. Good science had never been brought to bear a solution for the problem of nuclear waste disposal. The political answer had been to bury it, head in the sand posture. Griffin sighed and picked up his empty coffee cup. He walked to the urn on the sideboard and poured another cup of java.

Then it hit him.

"Kim Marshall! Now she's got the General on a string," he thought aloud. His face spread into an impressive smile; he was impressed with Kim's influence.

Somewhere in the midsection of an airborne Globemaster, two civilian passengers sat buckled in flight suits, complete with parachutes and flight helmets. Dr. Randall pulled off his helmet and smiled at the passenger seated beside him.

"Well, Kim. Don't know how you managed to authorize a seat on this trip, but I'm glad to have company."

Her ruby lips moved within the padded helmet. "General LaCroix is a free spirit," she said and squeezed the helmet from her head.

"Free as the press?" he chuckled.

"Oh stop it, Dr. Randall," she chided, as she raked her fingers through red hair. "You sound like my supervisor," she added, sassily smiling.

He grinned, looking for his pipe somewhere in the multi-pocket flight jacket. Kim peered into a compact mirror and touched up her lips. "There it is," she said, her fingers pointed a tube of lipstick at his upper pocket.

"Oh, thanks, just wanted to be sure I had it."

Kim settled back into her seat. "Think this snorkel device will work?" she wondered and nodded at the equipment strapped to the floor grating and wall tie-downs.

"Yes, I do. It's good engineering, nothing untried before."

Kim ran out of questions, her face blushed. "Listen I want to apologize for my outburst in your office the other day."

"Forget it, Kim. You've got a good mind for news. I'm glad you're here. The people need to know the truth. President Darcy is keen on this point."

Kim surprised Randall with a kiss on his cheek. "Thanks, Dr. Randall, that's sweet of you."

Randall grinned at her with rekindled parental feelings; now he had two women to care about. "Feels like we're descending, could be at the base in twenty minutes."

An inclement sky produced a suspension of dust and vapor particles that reduced visibility over the airstrip on Guam. A huge Globemaster whistled through the thin air as she lowered and locked wheels, and then touched down on the airstrip. Twelve Stratocruisers circled the runway and waited for landing instructions from the tower. Down on the tarmac field mechanics moved at the speed and efficiency of a racing car team at Daytona.

Dr. Randall and Kim Marshall lugged their bags toward a waiting jeep. They drove the jeep to their quarters in the hangar. Kim went to the bathroom to freshen her face. Randall collected his things and left the jeep for Kim. He went ahead to the control tower with the equipment truck.

Several technicians hurriedly unpacked two wooden crates outside the control shed. It took them an hour to install the equipment in the component hanging racks. Griffin and Randall went through checkout procedures. There were two coaxial cables that had to be remade. Other than that, the equipment ran smooth and silent. Everything was checked and rechecked. They were ready: a miracle in disguise.

"Guess that's it, Grif," Dr. Randall reported as he twisted a control knob on the console. He rotated in his swivel chair. "Where's Kim?"

"Last time I saw her, she was in the hangar. The technicians were loading the KC-135s with the globular spray. And she was talking with the pilot—what's his name . . . Jed, that's it."

Randall's nose wrinkled at the bridge between his eyes. He wagged his head and focused on the monitor. "We're sure pushing a tight envelope. We'll barely get that miracle mist into the clouds on schedule. See those green lines there. Those are dust particles shown in real time," he swiveled around in his chair and pointed. "The little devils are clinging to specks of lunar dust."

"Like gremlins, huh?"

"More like the Christmas Grinch, don't you think? They're attempting to steal life itself."

"I hope those little GLOBs work."

Twelve C-135 tankers flew in tight formation at thirty-five thousand feet as if a war had been declared. Jed Taylor, the lead pilot, turned to his copilot. "Take it for a while, Ben. My legs are asleep, exactly where I should be."

Ben took the controls, checked the gages and his airspeed. "Have you seen our stowaway, Jed?"

An eye cocked with a lustful smile. "You mean Kim Marshall, don't you?"

"Yeah, did you see that outfit?" Jed only smiled, as he retook the controls. He had authorized her trip when she flashed an official pass signed by the Joint Chief, himself. He noticed the gauges and spoke through his helmet microphone.

"Control, Hot Stuff calling. We're at the coordinates. We're ready to execute."

"Copy, Hot Stuff. Start your run. The clock says you've got ninety minutes to dump your spray."

Jed looked at Ben. "Okay, little chicks, pressurize tanks."

Nestled in a compartment near the navigator, Kim Marshall focused her video mini-cam through the window. She'd taken off the cumbersome flight suit and helmet and stood with her legs spread for balance. She wore shorts and a tight T-shirt.

An airman smiled at his partner. "Look at that, Cecil B. DeMille in glowing pink."

A technician smirked. "Scuttlebutt says that Kim was an embedded reporter in Iraq. She knows what she's doing."

"Whatever it is she does is all right with me," the airman chuckled.

"Yeah, that's what we're fighting for, all right."

Precious minutes ticked away in a nightmare of nerves. Colonel Griffin and Dr. Randall watched the monitor growing with green lines. Griffin paced the floor, hands clasped behind his back. Randall tweaked the signal on the console and puffed his pipe. What seemed to be an eternity passed in a few compressed minutes of sheer torture.

A blaring radio speaker finally broke through the eerie silence in the Guam control tower.

"Control, mission is complete, request permission to return to base."

Jubilation echoed in the control tower.

"Roger, Hot Stuff. We're picking up rain showers on radar. Turn on your radiation counters. Let's record the radioactivity as you fly through those showers."

"Roger that; activating detectors now."

The rains fell from the misty sky like an ordinary shower on a Sunday afternoon. Curious little globular balls peppered the ocean waters like falling hailstones. They sank into the blue waters and drifted along with the ocean currents.

"Control, looks like radioactivity is nil!"

Griffin's face beamed as he spun around on his stool after he checked the meters.

"Those darn globules worked!"

Randall slapped Griffin on the back. "Woods Hole will be monitoring those globules as they drift with the currents. Some sea creatures may even consume them. It'll be an interesting study."

Chapter 48

RESIDENTS OF GUAM were all too familiar with rising tides, mostly tropical storms that brewed into twisting hurricanes. Although tidal waves were infrequent, sudden storm surges often battered tropical coastlines. And somewhere out on the Pacific, a tidal wave moved like silent death toward the coast. The speaker squawked in the control tower at Guam.

"Colonel, this is Hot Stuff. Our radar has picked up a tidal wave headed toward Guam," Jed barked with guarded excitement in his voice.

"Holy Cow, it must've been that A-1 lunaroid that hit the Volcanic Ridge. What's its position now?"

"I make it five-hundred miles southeast of Guam: course one, niner, two."

"That gives us two, maybe three hours to clear out of here."

"Yeah, we'll land there in about thirty minutes. Button up the facility. I'll take you guys to Hawaii."

Randall flipped a switch on the console and turned the wavelength. "Captain, is Kim Marshall aboard. We've lost her down here."

Pause.

"This is Kim, Dr. Randall."

"Thought I'd lost you, everything okay?"

"Just fine, Jed was kind enough to take me along. I've got my camera equipment, too."

"You're too old to paddle. Guess I'll have to accept you like you are."

"That's sweet, Bruce."

Jed smiled at Kim who sat snugly in the buddy seat behind the pilot.

"This is Hot Stuff. I want that fuel truck waiting on the tarmac. Make it snappy, guys—little chicks, listen up, this is Bigbird. There won't be enough time to gas-up twelve tankers when we land. You men strap down your aircrafts, and then get all your crews onto my flight, you maintenance guys and ground crews can hightail it inland."

Randall flipped off the radio and called over Griffin as he came through the door past the crated equipment he had placed outside. "Better notify the Guam weather station, Grif."

Griffin sat down at the computer keyboard and quickly typed a message. "It's done. They've sent out bulletins to stations along the Pacific basin. The Tokyo Seismographic Station reports a massive earthquake, no magnitude numbers yet."

Randall frowned, brain churned. "Guess we better get ready to move out of here. Soon as we're aboard, I'll call Spencer at Stanford. Maybe he has an update on that quake."

A KC-135 Stratotanker broke through the cloud layer hovering over Guam, landing lights spreading a shaft of light on the wet runway. Darkness gripped the island in ghostly shadows. Winds increased to gale force. Tides were near flood stage. She taxied to the tarmac at the control tower and cut the engines.

A fuel truck raced up to the fuselage and pulled out the flexible tubes with special fittings that fit the tanker in-fill fixture. The aircraft's fuel tanks were topped off and preflight checkout was completed in record time. The bird was ready for takeoff. Two large, wooden crates containing instruments and charts were taken aboard. Dr. Randall and Colonel Griffin climbed the steps into the belly of the tanker. Eleven crews followed. The hatch closed and locked.

Turbines whined robustly.

The tanker rolled down the watery runway and lifted into the gray clouds. Jed nosed the heavy bird to higher altitude and leveled off at forty-five thousand feet, well above the storm. The navigator set her course for Hawaii. The radio report said the storm had already passed through the islands. Mt. Aloha had erupted and spewed lava.

Seated in a small cubicle in the cargo bay, Kim Marshall reached out and touched Dr. Randall's arm.

"I'm not used to having a nursemaid. Please forgive that episode back there."

Randall's hand covered her long painted fingernails, "I didn't want to lose you, Kim. Guess it's my paternal instincts."

She smiled, hazel eyes glittering with moisture, "When will we reach Hawaii?"

"Don't know for sure. But there's another story brewing."

"Oh?"

"A lunaroid has hit the Volcanic Islands."

"Yeah?"

"Tokyo reports multiple earthquakes."

"Is there any word on the damage?"

"The Rim of Fire is heavily active but, if I had to guess, California will experience a jarring jolt unlike any ever recorded."

"The San Andreas Fault?"

He nodded.

"That fault line is the rubbing point between two major tectonic plates."

"Wow! Could be big, huh?"

"Expect so. That lunaroid was a Class A-1 that crashed to the earth at terminal speed."

"A-1?"

"Yeah, that's about two kilometers, over one mile in diameter."

Kim's rosy cheeks expanded with air and released an audible puff. "Whee."

She reached into her flight bag, pulled out her laptop, and opened the screen. She pushed a button and it lit up. Nimble fingers glided over the keys like a concert pianist. From her memory she wrote a story of Hobart's miracle globular material and its effects on the radioactive particles. Her mind's eye visualized a setup piece spliced from the video canister in her flight bag.

A second story began to form: The biggest earthquake ever to hit California. According to Randall, the extent of tectonic plate movement should be apparent by the time Kim reached Hawaii and filed her story.

Chapter 49

"THIS IS KIM MARSHALL reporting from Hawaii. Mount Aloha is active here on the islands. People are being evacuated. Damage reports are trickling in from the mainland. Much of the west coast of the U.S. is completely blacked out. An unprecedented earthquake has hit California. According to my interview with the seismologists at this local seismograph station here on the islands, the great earthquake of 1906 has revisited San Francisco. A smoke cloud hovers over the Bay City like an avenging devil. Ambulances and fire trucks seem to be the only vehicles moving through the debris and broken pavement. Countless fire hydrants have ruptured and surging water has flooded buildings. Clogged storm drains are flooding highways. Basements are overflowing through daylight windows. Fallen high-voltage wires hang from broken poles, twisting on the pavement like angry snakes. Ruptured gas lines have set most of the city ablaze. Firefighters struggle to shut down the water mains and conserve supply to fight the blaze, the demise of the 1906 disaster, when the flames burned unabated because of water shortage. More after this break, and don't change that channel. This is Kim Marshall reporting from Hawaii."

Kim ran from the set to chat with her program manager in Washington, D.C. It took almost thirty minutes to connect a call, and after she closed her cellphone, only a few moments were left, but she took the time to check the film room to be sure the video she brought was ready to run. The program director caught her arm at the door and ushered her to the broadcasting cubicle.

"No time for that, Kim. Your guest is here."

Kim rushed to her seat behind the camera and the red light immediately lit.

"I'm Kim Marshall bringing you this special report from Hawaii. The largest earthquake ever recorded has struck California. Dr. Moa Aloe of the island's seismograph station is with us tonight. Dr. Aloe, could you describe this tectonic plate phenomenon?"

He crossed his legs, fidgeted with his earpiece, and pushed the spongy thing into his ear.

"The earth's crust floats on a mantle of hot magma like a jigsaw puzzle. The crust is broken into seven large segments and many other smaller segments called tectonic plates, each plate about fifty miles thick. The expanding plates normally move about an average of a few inches each year, reflecting the earth's "breathing" process. Two major plates, the Pacific Plate and the North American Plate, rub together along the San Andreas Fault in California U.S.A. Los Angeles sits on the Pacific Plate, San Francisco on the North American Plate. When stresses build up along the fault, sudden release is probable, but unpredictable. In the event of great slippage the top plate would slide on top of the underling plate producing the earthquake.

"In such a hypothetical case, Los Angeles would move northwestward and San Francisco would slip southeastward in the opposite direction producing an earthquake of enormous consequences."

"Thank you, Dr. Aloe. Tell us how you determine the epicenter of an earthquake?"

"The area of the fault where the sudden rupture takes place is called the *focus* or hypocenter of the earthquake. The point on the earth's surface directly above the focus is called the *epicenter*. Forces deep within the earth's interior are stored up in the tectonic plates as kinetic energy. An earthquake develops when shearing forces between plates are released."

"I see. Then how do you measure these phenomena?"

"The severity of earthquakes can be expressed in terms of both intensity and magnitude. Although the terms are different, they often are confused. *Intensity* describes the observed effects of ground movement, building tremor, and natural features. Intensity often varies from place to place within the disturbed region depending on the location of the epicenter. On the other hand, *magnitude* relates to the amount of seismic energy released at the hypocenter of the earthquake."

"And how do you report these measurements?"

Aloe drank a swallow of water from a bottle handed to him by an attendant and cleared his throat.

"The Richter magnitude scale was developed in 1935 by Charles F. Richter of the California Institute of Technology as a mathematical device to compare the size of earthquakes. On the Richter scale, magnitude is expressed in whole numbers and decimal fractions. Although the Richter scale has no upper limit, the largest known shocks ever recorded had magnitudes in the 8.8 to 8.9 ranges.

"Earthquake size as measured by the Richter scale may be well-known but not well understood. As years passed, the proliferation of magnitude scales and their relation to Richter's original scale became even less understood. Richter's Scale was created for measuring the size of earthquakes occurring in southern California. This magnitude scale became referred to as ML, with the L standing for local."

"I see, doctor. Then why are there so many scales?"

He took another drink from the plastic bottle and sat it by his chair.

"As more seismograph stations were installed around the world, it became apparent that the method developed by Richter was strictly valid for certain frequency and distance ranges. In order to take advantage of growing numbers of globally distributed seismograph stations, new magnitude scales were developed as an extension of Richter's idea. These include body-wave magnitude (mb) and surface-wave magnitude (MS). But there were limitations to these three magnitude scales—"

"Pardon me, doctor—what scales?"

"I'm sorry. I tend to think faster than I speak: ML, Richter scale, of course, and mb—'b' for body wave, and MS, 'S' for surface wave."

Kim rustled, "Hum, I see," but her expression disagreed.

"And of course there is a moment magnitude (MW). Ah . . . MW magnitude scale is more reliable for measuring very large earthquakes. Nowadays, the announcement of a magnitude number rarely refers to the Richter scale."

"Somehow, it doesn't seem right after all the work that Richter did," Kim surmised.

"Oh," he smiled, "we don't use the technology of the Wright Brothers today for the same reasons."

"Progress, huh?"

"I suppose."

California seismograph Station #3 had picked up a tremor registering a 10.2 on the MW Scale. The center was as busy as Macy's on the day after Thanksgiving. Technicians scurried about, phones rang, and horns blared. Papers were strewn over the floor, overturned coffee cups flooded desktops. Dr. Rush Rickles, director of the center stared at the morning charts with disbelief. The mountains of data jammed the hard drives of computers. The results were devastating along the San Andreas Fault as well as many other places along the Pacific Ring of Fire. The city of Los Angeles had moved an unbelievable twelve feet northwest of San Francisco. Even with modern flexible building codes, structures cracked and crumbled, although estimates said the damage would have been considerably worse without building code modifications. Expressways cracked and twisted, but failed to collapse. Water, gas, and electrical lines ruptured. Gas fumes spilled into the streets, igniting fires. Flames soared up stairways and elevator shafts, trapping terrified residents. Some despondent people leaped from fourth and fifth floor windows rather than be roasted alive. Many women and children perished on higher floors. Just how many could not be determined until the wreckage was cleaned out.

Preliminary estimates had placed the dead at thirty-one hundred casualties; the numbers of missing were still unknown. Monetary cost soared to 25 billion dollars. Although the Great Quake in 1906 had claimed seven hundred lives in twelve hours, this current blockbuster quake had claimed four times that number in one hour.

"The epicenter is near Volcanic Ridge in the south Pacific," Rickles calculated from the charts.

"It was a helluva rock that did this," Dave Doughty, volcanologist on special assignment, replied.

"It was a B-20 lunaroid, about two kilometers in diameter, according to NOAA."

"Yeah, and we may see another island push up in the Volcanic Ridge chain."

"I've not climbed many volcanoes, Dave. But I've seen basalt lava boil the seas with temperatures up to 2000 degrees Fahrenheit," Rickles admitted.

Doughty slumped back into his chair. "Curious thing about lava flows. The little-visited mountain of *Ol Doinyo Lengai* in Tanzania produces not basalt, but natrocarbonatite flows, which have a chemical composition akin to laundry soap. What begins as liquid lava hits the ground with the tinkling of breaking glass."

"Unbelievable. We know so much and, yet, we understand so little. This blast will break all known records. That's for sure." He shuffled, "You want to help me accumulate these data, Dave? I'll have to make a formal report to the governor."

Although *Ol Doinyo Lengai's* summit rose 7,650 feet above a parched valley floor in the corner of Tanzania, the Volcanic Ridge chain rose 10,000 feet from the floors of the Pacific Ocean. About five hundred volcanoes had erupted on earth's surface since recorded history. Nearly sixty were active each year. Fifty volcanoes had erupted in the U.S.A. alone since recorded history. And the U.S. ranked third behind Indonesia and Japan in the number of historically active volcanoes.

Far more eruptions went unobserved on the floors of the Pacific. Submarine volcanoes released pressures at the boundaries of the earth's crusted plates, such as the Ring of Fire that surrounded the Pacific Ocean tectonic plate. Shifting plates were caused by a number of factors, principal among them the formation of hot gases emitted from the molten magma. External factors could be attributed to asteroids, landslides, and underwater explosions.

Earthquake intensity in the Palo Alto area registered a 6.2 (ML). Still some older college buildings suffered minor structural damage, a few broken water pipes, shattered glass, and cracked ceilings. Wilcox Solar Observatory miraculously escaped major damage. In the absence of Dr. Randall, Spencer Jenson supervised the repairs. Monique Chevet sat in Spencer's office punishing her mind with self-incrimination.

"It would be suicide to go into San Francisco now, Monique," Spencer advised.

"I must go, Spence."

"Be reasonable, honey. What can you hope to do?"

"Apply bandages, if nothing else. These people are going to need all the help they can get."

Spence could see that no measure of logic would change her mind. This was a new Monique. He remembered her words during their flight from Paris to America: "You're a fighter, and so am I."

It was time to cast off the role of antagonist. "Okay. I'm going with you." Yes, I'm going just to protect you, darling, he thought.

"Thank you, Spence." He's going because he loves me. How sweet, she thought.

They left the observatory after Spence set the answering machine to forward calls to his cellphone. Driving through the Stanford campus, Spencer punched a code into the cellphone with his thumb. He said a few words to someone, but Monique wasn't listening. Her mind glued to the emergency at hand.

"Thanks Don, be there in five." He closed the cellphone and turned to Monique, "let's cross through here and go by the men's dorms."

"What's the plan?"

"I'm thinking we couldn't get too far by auto, the roads will be blocked or impassable."

"How else can we get there?"

"I have a friend in ROTC, Don Harris, who is licensed to fly the helicopter they keep for training purposes."

"Thank you for coming, Spencer. I couldn't sit by and do nothing."

"I know. That's one reason I love you, Monique."

Chapter 50

DON HARRIS steered a helicopter northeast headed for a burning complex as spinning rotors paddled through the thick smoke of burning debris. The streets below were cluttered with rocky debris.

Flaming fires released smoke in every direction. Emergency vehicles had not yet penetrated this area and cleanup crews were still busy digging out the entry road. Don spotted a grassy knoll and landed the copter. The turbine engine chuffed off as if choking from the smoke. The passengers rushed toward the burning complex.

Aimlessly milling on the grass were people suffering from shock. Some had been treated; others wore makeshift bandages on their heads and limbs. Someone who apparently had first-aid training had set up a small aid station. Two women were assisting by tearing bandages from sheets. Spencer decided things were reasonably in-hand, and pointed to the complex door.

The door hung dangerously on one hinge; fallen beams had jammed it open. He and Monique entered the cluttered doorway. Managing to squirm inside, they looked for injured people, anyone who needed help. They climbed over piles of debris at the end of a corridor, and found a cleared area with clean carpet, untouched by the debris. Monique entered a side corridor and Spencer went in the opposite direction, hoping to conserve time.

Monique rounded a corner in sudden realization that she was in some kind of government building. She slowed her pace, noticing a strange-looking man standing by a mangled stairway. He wore denim jeans and a long-sleeved pullover. She noticed that he had rings in both ears, tattooed arms, and a pockmarked face. An Aztec-style headband supported his unkempt hair. On closer inspection, Monique could see that his glassy eyes were dark and sinister. Unknown to her, the earthquake had collapsed his jail cell on the top floor. He was a twice-convicted murderer and rapist waiting to be moved to death row.

Monique gulped.

"Are you injured, do you need help?"

He said nothing, the unshaven face grinned with lustful desire. He grabbed Monique in a sudden move, thrusting her against the wall. Nervously trembling hands ripped open her blouse.

She screamed.

Spencer heard her call, spun around, and galloped up the hall. He rounded the corner, sailing over debris. A ghastly scene slammed into his angry face. Monique lay on the floor partially clothed, squirming and screaming. A man straddled her fragile body, holding both her hands against the floor.

Spencer dove, hitting the floor and skidding on his knees. He collided with the man like a bowling bowl crashing into the ten pin. They tumbled and tussled on the floor. Spencer erected. He cocked his arm and plunged his fist into an unshaven jaw. Broken teeth spewed from a bleeding mouth. The man collapsed unconscious.

Spencer whirled to find Monique still on the floor, comatose-like. She looked dazed and rattled. He lifted her into his arms and hugged her against his chest for a long silent moment.

"I'm okay, Spence," she whispered.

"Well, that pervert isn't, you're sure everything's okay?"

She nodded and slithered from his arms. Monique briefly fussed with her tangled hair, and then adjusted her skirt and torn blouse all to calm her while she pushed herself to reality. Spencer allowed her plenty of space to gather her thoughts.

This terrible ordeal would have put many women in disability shock. Not Monique.

"Let's see if we can find any injured people. I'm all right. Really I am," she finally responded.

"Okay, whatever you say, darling. I'm going to tie this goon to that beam, and then we can go."

Voices in the next corridor alerted Monique. She raced down the narrow hallway and pushed against a blocked door. Spencer arrived, adding his weight to the steel closure. Electrical sparks zapped Spencer's hand, throwing him back on the floor. "Get away from that door," he yelled.

Monique squatted beside him. Spencer erected his stiff body and picked up a broom from the scattered debris. He lifted several broken electrical wires with the straw-end of the broom, and leaned it against the wall.

"Watch your head."

They passed safely under the wires, and managed to clear an opening big enough to push their bodies inside.

Monique was not prepared for the scene.

Her hands suddenly covered her nose and mouth. Adrenaline tensed her muscles. She squatted and lifted an unconscious female child about six years of age. The child had a gash on her forehead; dried blood covered her cheeks and blonde hair. Her pulse was barely detectable.

A causeway adjoined the building cluttered with debris, and Spencer left Monique checking a room while he went to inspect the area. He realized that he was in a daycare center, probably for the employee in this complex. In sudden dismay he realized the roof had collapsed. Undaunted, he pushed through the wreckage. Gazing around in the dim light, he briefly saw an arm moving beneath the wreckage and stopped. Spencer lifted fallen beams and ceiling tiles that had trapped a frantic woman. As Spencer pulled her fragile body from the rubble, she pushed him away. The dazed woman faced him with vacant eyes, and then staggered to the child that cradled in Monique's arms.

The terrified mother stroked the child's blonde hair, tears rolling down her smutty cheeks. She looked into Monique's doe eyes: Thankful, frantic, but relieved. Her silent face spoke volumes. Worry wrinkles disclosed the mother's doubts that her daughter would survive.

By the time they reached the helicopter, emergency crews were entering the sector. Don was talking to a soldier but saw them and acknowledged their arrival. He conversed momentarily with Spencer, and then called over the soldier. Spencer said something, pointing to the complex. Monique crawled in the back, and took the injured child from its mother so she might rest. Spencer sat in front seat with Don. The mother settled in the back beside Monique, who placed the child back into her arms.

"There's a makeshift medical facility a mile back, according to that National Guard Lieutenant," Don explained.

"Hurry, Don. This little girl needs a doctor," Spencer barked above the piercing noise of the whirring engine. The whirlybird lifted into the smoky air, and banked toward the medical station. Monique kept her finger on the child's pulse. The mother prayed.

It was short trip by air and the helicopter circled the medical facility looking for a landing space. The ground below looked like a junkyard left by a tornado, scattered with cars, and crumbled buildings. People were leading wounded victim's hand-in-hand into what looked like a schoolhouse. Somehow, owing to Don's expert flying, they managed to land without incident. Monique climbed from the backseat and took the child from the mother.

"Come with me, honey."

They raced across a grassy area to the building entrance where two orderlies met them with a gurney.

"She has a weak pulse," Monique advised.

"We'll take it from here ladies. You can follow us to the waiting area, if you like."

Monique and the mother strode behind the gurney engaged in woman's talk. The mother seemed distraught, not only by the child's condition, but also her inability to pay for the services. Everything she owned had gone up in flames or had been smashed by falling debris.

Monique sensed her anguish, "What's troubling you honey?"

But the woman did not answer. They sat down in the waiting area, Monique patiently waiting for a reply from the traumatized woman. They were surrounded by dozens of waiting wounded, haphazardly bandaged by novices who themselves were injured. Monique stroked the woman's tangled hair gazing into her puffy eyes.

"Is there anything I can do?"

Emotions crumbled.

Her head bowed, sobbing. She began to cry, at first restrained by shame, then followed by a flood of tears pouring from her tired dark eyes, profusely, uncontrollably, and unashamedly. Monique surrounded the woman in her arms. Nothing was said.

The woman finally wiped her eyes, sniffing, "Sorry," she whispered.

Monique smiled, "No need, honey. Do you live alone with the child?"

Her head bobbed affirmatively. "My husband was killed in Iraq."

Resolve surfaced in Monique's face. "You let me worry about the expenses. I can afford it."

"But—"

Monique interrupted, wagging her head. "Believe me, honey. I owe you and countless others more than just these trivial expenses."

Her head lowered with an embarrassing frown on her face. "I don't know when I can repay you."

"Let's consider it a gift, from me to you and your little daughter."

She sighed deeply, relieved but confused, and still slightly embarrassed.

"You're a miracle worker and I've never met anyone quite like you."

Monique stared into her wet eyes for only a moment. "I have a townhouse in Palo Alto. I'll arrange to have you and your daughter move in."

Tears rolled down the woman's cheeks. She kissed Monique's hand unable to speak.

The phone rang in the Wilcox Solar Observatory on the campus of Stanford University, California. Spence left the instrument room and raced into Dr. Randall's empty office to answer the call.

"Hello," he puffed, clinging to a wrench, grease on his cheek.

"Spence?"

"Yes, Dr. Randall!"

"What about California? Is it still there?"

"Death totals are at forty-one hundred and still rising. It was a 10.2 on the MW Scale. Just imagine the destruction."

"My goodness—what a catastrophe."

"We've had our share. It was a 5.2 here on the campus, broke some glass, scattered debris, that type of stuff."

"The telescope is okay?"

"Yes sir, it threw everything out of alignment. But I managed to collimate the system. It's working just fine, but we may have to rebuild the planetarium."

"Buildings can be rebuilt. I'm proud of you Spence."

Spence sniffed, wiping his runny nose with the back of the hand holding the wrench. "Did Hobart's globules work?"

"Like a miracle. Norm deserves a medal. He really has developed something the world can use—and Monique? How is she?"

"Monique sends her best. She went into Frisco to inspect the damage. Tried to stop her, but you know Monique."

Pause.

"It's best to let her get it out of her system, Spence. I'm afraid she harbors the blame for what her grandfather did. It will take time."

"Yeah—when can we expect you back?"

"Tomorrow, and tell Monique that I'm buying dinner for you two."

"You better make that three. Monique has gathered a friend."

"A friend?"

"A single mother and her child she rescued in the earthquake rubble. She's paying the medical expenses and providing board and lodging."

"You've got a real jewel there, Spencer. Don't muff it."

"Don't I know it?"

Chapter 51

THE PLANET FINALLY relaxed. Governments counted the cost in dollars and deaths. People counted their blessings just to be alive. Tidal surges rolled back into the seas. Landmasses dried under the warming sun. The moon waxed and waned. The earth rotated.

Eiffel Tower in Paris tilted three degrees because of persistent flooding at its base. London was still flooded, shrouded in drizzle. Tokyo coastal areas looked like Hiroshima after the Enola Gay incident. Moscow streets were knee-deep in mud, much of it frozen.

America had nearly lost its largest state on the west coast. San Francisco had moved twelve miles northwest of Los Angeles. FEMA had to call in emergency staff, and the governor activated the National Guard. Commercial companies were hired to clean up the rubble. Countless volunteers from many states donated their time, finances, equipment, and sweat.

Kim Marshall sat at her TV cubicle awaiting the camera light. A montage of scenes displayed the sun, the moon, and the earth on the viewing monitors. The setup piece flashed through astronomical events in three-second blips: the solar laser cannon, Hubble space telescope, orbiting

Shuttle, flaming lunaroids, miracle globules, and the ominous two rockets.

The video that Kim had taken in the KC-135 had been spliced into the setup piece. The conclusion of the montage was all too obvious: man's stupidity had attempted to rid the planet of nuclear waste by tampering with nature. This folly would go down in history books. The world had witnessed these events firsthand, yet historians would be charged with recording the truth as it actually happened, not manipulating the accuracy of history with revisionists' opinions.

"I'm Kim Marshall and this is Washington Drumbeat. The world was created in six days, but somewhere in the Pacific basin a handful of brave Americans managed to save this planet in six harrowing hours. Our guest tonight is Dr. Bruce Randall of Wilcox Solar Observatory. And we have another very special guest. Don't miss this presentation. I'll be back after these messages."

Kim warmly smiled at her first guest, a man she'd learned to respect. She shuffled her copy, glancing at the TelePrompTer. Her cameraman raised a finger. The camera light blinked on.

"With us tonight is Dr. Bruce Randall, Director of Wilcox Solar Observatory," Kim said, smiling at her guest.

"Hello, Kim."

"Is it finally over Dr. Randall, this nightmare that began twenty years ago?"

Randall stirred in his chair beneath the bright lights.

"This nightmare began because we carelessly misjudged our data on the sun. And no one knows what the sun might do after this event."

"Surely you scientists know something."

"We know a great deal about sunspots but in time our estimates may change."

"Doesn't that knowledge you describe provide a base to understand more?"

"Much of our data on the age of the sun and the universe is based on calculated theories, some facts, some estimates."

"Well, Dr. Randall, I've not heard that admission before."

"And you won't hear it again as long as some scientists are dishonest and simply want to protect their tenure in the universities."

"Now really, Dr. Randall, do you seriously believe the advancement of science is based on greed?"

"I said nothing about scientific advancement. I'm indicting the individual for falsification of scientific data—man is naturally driven by greed."

Kim chuckled, the only expression that she was willing to express. "Dr. Randall, you sound more like a preacher than an astronomer."

Randall smiled briefly and his eyes narrowed. "Remember that Galileo was excommunicated for his belief that the earth rotated around the sun which dispelled the century-old idea that the earth was the center of the universe."

"Well, Dr. Randall, you are the man of the hour—what do you suggest?"

"We should use the knowledge we have wisely and prudently, knowledge that must stand the proof of the Scientific Method."

"Then you are suggesting that all science does not meet the scientific method?"

"That is partially correct. The database of statistics is around seventy-five percent opinion. And much of what we theorize is based on pseudoscience."

"Now that comment is going to get me a lot of e-mails, so what do you expect will follow this horrible event?"

"We must concentrate on what we know. We understand atomic energy, the force that drives the universe. Nuclear power can be safely harnessed and used for peaceful means."

"What about reports of radiation sickness, sterility, pollution, and meltdown?"

"If our nuclear Navy can stay submerged for months, and its sailors can still father children, we can safely operate nuclear plants and reduce the cost of electrical energy through surplus supplies."

"But that seems a little oversimplified."

"I'm always amazed at how simple things can be confused by inventions of the complex mind, armed with hypothetical opinions, and influenced by half truths."

"You're saying that these warnings of hazardous radiation are unfounded?"

"Ghosts of Hiroshima. That first atomic weapon is the original dirty bomb, our genesis attempt to harness nuclear power. The horror of radiated bodies, dead women and children, has set a precedent for all time. Nuclear energy was intended for peaceful use. But mankind's ignorance has wasted yet another gift of nature."

"Do you really expect the people of this planet to seriously accept your premise?"

"Indeed, that is the question. We have traversed full circle to people, mankind."

"Then you think our problem is political?"

"We walk a thin line between comedy and tragedy. Politics is a comedy of errors resulting in a tragedy of man's ignorance, not unlike the one we've just experienced."

Kim faced the camera.

"Thank you, Dr. Randall, Director of Wilcox Solar Observatory. We'll return after this hard break with another special quest."

While the ads rolled on the network, Kim touched Monique's hand as she sat nervously waiting. "It'll be fine, sweetheart," she whispered.

Programmed music blared, the camera light flashed on.

"This is Kim Marshall reporting. Our special guest tonight is Monique Chevet, CEO of Chevet Energy in Paris. It was her grandfather who launched radioactive waste into space twenty years ago. Thank you for being on our program tonight, Ms. Chevet."

"Thank you, Kim. It's a real pleasure."

"You've just heard Dr. Randall describe the harrowing events of the past few weeks as the tragedy of mankind's ignorance. Tell us what's on your mind, right now."

Monique sat fidgety, but relaxed, because Spencer stood behind the cameras smiling with encouragement.

"Dr. Randall is exactly right. My grandfather did a tragic thing precipitated by his ignorance and greed."

"Does it bother you that your grandfather did this evil thing?"

Her eyes defiantly narrowed but she kept her focus. "Beyond anything you can imagine."

"And what will you do with your life, now? Will you reside in America or return to Paris?"

"I haven't decided yet. But I have definitely decided to establish a trust fund to study the migration of those globules that fell into the ocean. And I will also establish an annual grant for further study on how to neutralize nuclear waste."

"Encapsulation is one thing, but neutralization is quite another—"

"Don't tell me that American ingenuity cannot find a way to neutralize nuclear waste. I've been in your country long enough to see your scientists and your military save this planet from annihilation. No. I won't accept that answer. Nor will I allow this quest to go without funds."

"Thank you, Monique Chevet and Dr. Bruce Randall. I'm Kim Marshall, and this is WOFF NEWS. Stay tuned for a roundtable discussion on the aftermath of lunar upheaval. Where do we go from here?"

The guests followed red exit lights out of the studio and left by the side door. Spencer and Monique waited just outside the studio for Dr. Randall. The professor had lingered behind engaged in a conversation with Kim Marshall. Randall knew the young couple wanted to be alone and he cut the discussion short. The professor finally exited the door, and found the couple waiting.

"Monique, sweetheart, Kim was very impressed by your comments. She wants to do a special program with you as her guest. It's a breath of fresh air just knowing youth of your caliber, honey. Don't give up the ship," Randall said, and hugged the damsel like a proud father, and then waved for a taxi. "Catch you two back in Palo Alto—and Spence, your doctoral thesis is due next week."

Spencer waved good-bye to Randall as the professor got into the waiting taxi and drove away. He stepped across the parking lot and found his rented Mustang.

The red convertible finally pulled alongside the curb beside Monique. He watched her slim body settle into the bucket seat and nudged the gas pedal. The Mustang eased into the beltway traffic at great risk. Spencer knew of a good restaurant in the vicinity, and steered into the change lane taking a shortcut through Rockville, Maryland. He had decided they would have dinner before catching the plane back to Stanford University later that night.

The overhead streetlights suddenly snapped on, triggered by the sun settling majestically on the western horizon. The sodium lamps flickered as electrons stabilized in its temperature range. Monique seemed captured by the pulsating beams, her bangs freely blowing in the breeze. Spencer glanced at the woman he loved, warmly smiling, reviewing a mental image of their experiences, their first meeting, and the deep love for her that he'd come to cherish.

"You did well, honey. I'm proud of you."

She didn't answer at first, only smiled, watching the highway, the yellow line vanishing under the hood, still thinking.

"What did Dr. Randall mean, 'don't give up the ship'?"

Spencer flipped the turn signal lever. "That's a nautical expression. An officer would never give up the ship under his command, no matter what happened. Lafayette would have understood."

Her chest swelled, exhaling with a deep sigh. "There's so much to do, Spence. I'm going to need your help. Somebody has to stand in the gap with viable solutions, not this shallow rhetoric. What do you call it—spin?"

"Just what did you have in mind?" he replied.

"I meant what I said back there," she responded, as a wrinkle formed over an eye. "This Dr. Hobart, does Dr. Randall know him?"

"Dr. Hobart? Why he is an old family friend, I understand."

"And you? Can you spare the time, Spence?"

He stopped at a red light and took his eyes off the traffic. "Honey, my time is your time. I'll finish my doctorate this summer."

She placed her hand on his shoulder smiling at the only man she could ever love, this kind and understanding man who had taken her from the depths of despondency and fear to a mountain high above all she had ever expected or imagined.

"Then I'm making you the director of the Chevet Trust Fund, I suppose you know about the gold."

Spence's face registered approval but an arching eyebrow revealed he was thinking about her response. It was clear that Moreau and John-Pierre had discussed the gold, and Monique had convinced them that she knew what to do with the fortune; it was her company and she had just made her first wise decision.

The Mustang swerved into a side street that led to the restaurant parking lot. Spencer parked the car, smiling at Monique.

"Ready to eat something, honey?"

She said not a word, and slowly turned in her seat and faced him. Her slender arms reached out and cradled both cheeks of his manly face. She planted a kiss on his lips. They embraced in the rhapsody of a fleeting, magical moment, a moment reserved just for them. Yet harbored in their minds was a haunting question: Was it really over?

Finally they got out of the car and walked to the restaurant entrance, clasping hands like two giddy teens. Yet, there was no youthful chatter.

A maitre'd met the pair, bowing, "Two for dinner?"

Spencer nodded. They followed the waiter to a corner table, unaware of the people around them, the chatter, or the roving eyes.

In the flickering candlelight, Spencer gazed at the beauty of this young woman: doe eyes with a disarming smile, framed by pixy bangs, embracing a warm countenance. Her tanned skin glowed with each flicker of the candle. The last few months had aged a youthful spirit into one with careful discernment and uncommon courage. This woman of twenty-four years had eons of experience squeezed into a few catastrophic weeks. She had been tempered in the crucible of conflict.

Monique unconsciously raked her fork across the tablecloth, the parallel lines appearing like a musical score, distant keys playing her rhapsody. She gazed at Spencer, a smile formed dimples on her cheeks. Monique lay her head on Spencer's shoulder while he gave the maitre'd the order. Again, she reminisced.

This kindly man had burst into her life as in a fairytale. He was her Prince Charming, protecting her in a chaotic world. She gave herself to him and him alone.

Made in the USA
Columbia, SC
21 July 2021

42170403R00170